The First House

ROBERT ALLWOOD

Typeset in P22 Basel Roman by YouWorkForThem.

Cover illustration by Mirella Santana © 2019

mirellasantana.com.br @mirellasantana3

Map illustration by Djinn Black © 2019

@djinninthebox

For my family, and everyone who believed, thank you.

"For, as you know, no master of a household

Has all of his utensils made of gold;

Some are wood, and yet they are of use."

– Chaucer

DRAMATIS PERSONAE

Characters influenced by the tarot

(in order of appearance)

The Hermit	Lady Eleanor Saville	A mother & witch
The Empress	Sarah Saville	Daughter of Eleanor Saville
The Emperor	Lord Percy Turner	A man filled with hubris
The Serpent*	Isolde	A snake in the grass
The Fool	Alex	A thief with a heart
The Hanged Man	Cyrus	A family man
The Priestess	Goldie Frost	Daughter of John Frost
The Star	Elena Stone	A naïve woman
The Magician	Hazel	A cunning-woman

*or *The Devil* in tradition.

Characters of note

(or notoriety)

Lord William Saville	Adventurer	Husband of Eleanor Saville
Lady Sophia Stone	Solvent	Formerly Saville
John Frost	Sea Captain	Father of Goldie Frost
Victoria	A jade	Wife to Cyrus
Charlotte	A sneak	Also called Ghost
Simon	A thug	Also called Red
Malachi	A hellion	Son of Meriadoc
Meriadoc	Shipmaster	Father of Malachi
Selene	High Priestess	A witch of repute

The Astrological House

The First House	Mars/ Fire	The Self, Physicality

Tarot Cards Used

(and their meaning)

The Sun	Positivity, Joy
The Emperor	Authority, Structure
Death	Change, Endings
The Fool	Beginnings, Innocence
The Empress	Femininity, Nature
The Priestess	Intuition, The Subconscious
The Hanged Man	Letting Go, New Perspectives
The Star	Hope, Purpose
The Magician	Resourcefulness, Power
The Serpent	Attachment, Caution
The Moon	Illusion, Fear
The Chariot	Action, Determination
The World	Travel, Completion
Wheel of Fortune	Destiny, A Turning Point
Strength	Courage, Persuasion

The Hermit	Introspection, Guidance
The Tower	Chaos, Revelation
Temperance	Patience, Moderation
The Lovers	Love, Choices

Part One

The Sun

– London, Winter, 1771 –

On the anniversary of her mother's death, Lady Eleanor Saville,

wife of Lord William Saville, gave birth to twins. Everyone was

bound to the mansion on that day: staff, well-wishers, Lords and

Ladies, no exceptions. However, by late morning, those bound

had grown tired of waiting, cleaning, or worrying. Written in the

house's official records, it was "...*a day of anxiety and nervous talk

among staff...*" the more senior of which simply kept themselves

busy, lips sealed, faces askance. Upstairs, in the afternoon, Lady

Eleanor Saville found herself rolled into bed, water broken, her upper body strapped under thin blankets, and her breasts covered in modesty. The boisterous midwife and her dour assistant busied themselves around her, preparing cloth, dishes, water and instruments of labour.

Hours later, when the contractions quickened, and the cramps came full force, Eleanor smoothed her matted hair back and gripped the mattress. As it built ever upwards and needles sparked under her skin, Eleanor gritted her teeth, her face condensed in agony. Under suggestion, she raised her legs further still, and wandered her gaze onto the ceiling. She screamed fiercely at nothing. The pain itself rose to a crescendo; it strangled her body with hot ropes of agony that felt as though she was being torn in two, and wished she was. With a final cry, and enormous relief, Eleanor finally gave birth. For a moment, she turned her head towards the window and noted it was a frosted yellow sky, the colour of soured milk. The first child, Sophia, came through stubborn and crying. She screamed until rubbed down with soft cotton and nestled in brushed fur. Seconds old, and yet already used to the finer things in life. The second, Sarah, came when the storm finally broke over the Darkwater. It shed sleet, blew chill wind, and bore glum thoughts. This child arrived quiet and content. The only signs of life were two curious oval eyes that absorbed the details of everything around her.

When Eleanor's daughters were together with her, the peace was greater than she had imagined. She held them, one in each arm, to her covered breast and nuzzled them before the nervous gathering present. The staff each in turn gave their blessings, and left mother and children alone to bond, to see to the needs of Lord Saville (who took dim view of these matters). That night, she slept snug with her two winter children. She dreamt of strange things: pale men in grey cloaks, a golden warrior melting, a ship of fog, a tower cracked by sun. She saw a coast dominated by a single oak crowned by bright coloured pennants. If she couldn't sleep and see these portents clearly, Eleanor would sing songs which her mother had taught her in secret, old songs of a young witch, who falls in love with a thief, and carries on their bloodline of women lucky enough to escape

the witch hunts.

Women who could shape the fortunes of many, but

could not divine their own.

The Emperor

– Lamb's Wharf, London, 1777 –

Certainly, it was becoming more apparent that errant thoughts

in his mind were the bane of progress; slippery muses that eluded

his mental grip, that convinced him he was going mad in some

small way. But, every time he woke anew, he found that they

always faded into the aether, going to the same place all ideas that

were never written down go. He rubbed his worn eyes, scrubbing

the sleep from their corners. Today, as with yesterday, his mind

would not be still, it fired and sparked, greedy for action. He

found that the only remedy for such a cascade was to put plans into motion, or so his father had told him. Rest in peace, dear father.

Lord Percy Turner sat up with his dream still on repeat in his mind. It was of the city around him, and its preservation. The city was many things. It was the key of the world, a monster of stone and industry, a haven for all people; paragons and rogues, queer and plain. Parasites. He loathed, *no, hated,* seeing it bleed. The culture, the money, the politics, thrown onto the butcher's block and diced into tidy morsels. The interference of the Crown, and the foreign squeeze from west and east had cumulated into its degradation. He shuddered, and almost wept for his fair Lady London.

Percy took water from a basin placed on the night stand and drew apart the curtains. It was just after dawn, and at what thin light bled into the master bedroom, he smiled.

A soft knock at the door. 'My Lord—lady Isolde is here.'

Percy nodded at nothing. 'Succinct. Show her the study Harris – and bring a small breakfast also.'

'Will you be eating with the lady my Lord?'

'No—but, see that she is refreshed.'

'Very good my Lord.'

Percy washed, dressed himself and scented his clothes. A delicate little ritual. What silly rules and regulations he followed as a person. He smiled again. *Just a normal man in here,* he thought, *out there I'm importance. A rule to follow. Not so silly, not so small and delicate. A title, a name.* He sighed and balled his fists. *No more of this. I must stop listening to nonsense. The plan must have focus. I must rescue my city.*

He walked slow on purpose, a chance to play out greeting Isolde in his mind. Another change to his posture or speech, and another juxtaposed—on top. In his experience, it was always best to lead a conversation, rather than be second. Go on the attack. You have advantage. You direct the converse, the flow of words. Power. Rules. Regulation. Silly. Little. Words. Percy stopped before the threshold of the room and straightened his back.

Isolde sat in the study, at study, with one of his books folded open neatly in her lap. She had grown into a singular young woman. Always on the verge of being insolent from what he remembered of her; a victim of a sad and lonely childhood. However, she also brought about a fascination. The way her quick eyes noted lines and marks on your face, the way her character was apparent in every motion her body produced; a creature of natural charisma. Isolde's hood fell back further as she realised Percy. Her alabaster hair was tucked tight into a bow. She rested two fingers across her cheek, the other hand balancing the book on her belly. She did not rise.

'You truly have the most interesting works, Lord Turner,' she began.

She was first to speak then. 'You can keep it, if you like. I've no time for reading as of late, my lady.'

Percy frowned as the minx winked her flat brown eyes at him. For a second, the briefest moment, he saw exactly what she was thinking, and knew, he had lost all advantage in this conversation. She could probably spar with the best of them. He laughed at the thought as the butler brought his meal. A small

sausage, delicate toast, a little glass of coffee. Isolde, in turn,

watched Turner eat with the most neutral expression on a person

she had ever witnessed.

'Hungry?' he asked.

Isolde straddled the chair, hoisting herself up and

replaced the book back in its rightful spot. She ignored him.

'You've brought me here.'

'I did,' he said.

'Why now?'

'To save London from its detractors.'

'No. I know that; I received your letter. I want to know,

why *now*? After all this time Lord Turner – after what you've

given me.'

Percy finished eating. He chewed before washing down

the toast. 'You're an investment girl. That's what you are. You

have a magic with people. A talent of speech. When I found you

_'

'–when you *discovered* me.'

'Discovered. You were alone, destitute, hopeless.'

'I was whole. I was at peace.' Isolde scowled.

'You were delirious. Do you remember?'

Isolde shook. She wrapped her arms around herself. 'I remember sun. I remember a field. I spoke to someone; he gave me fire.'

'And that sounds like insanity Isolde. And yet here you are, years later, at my invite. You could have been locked up in Bedlam for your own safety.'

'An investment.'

'Correct. That old church you now reside in serves a larger purpose than just–' Percy waved his hand '–for you to enjoy at my expense. I've spared you from an impoverished life, a beggar's life, now you return the favour in helping me. But the premise is simple.'

'And what do you need from a thief like me?'

'To steal back my London, piece by piece.'

Isolde shook her head as Percy sold his idea to her. To her, it was akin to selling fireplaces to Spaniards during summer. They were going be partners; not a business, but something sinister—a cult? A following? He spoke of an organisation, a gang, with its own twisted religion, its own rules. It was unlike anything Isolde had heard of. It was genius desperation, a mad man's thoughts condensed with a drop of imagination to taste. London was being torn apart, or so Percy had surmised over the past decade. He was madly in love with it, a mother–city, one that gave life and meaning to the English. He reviled those that made her bleed, that cut and torn at her flesh; those that ate away at the trade, the liberties, the people. He spared no grisly metaphors from his rhetoric.

Percy wanted London pure again. Fresh. To steal it piece by piece, home by home, street by street, person by person, coin by coin. He wanted to make it his own, and shape it into whatever God required him to shape it into. A haven of the disillusioned? The centre of the world? Isolde had her own thoughts on what ulterior motive the mad Lord had, and doubted his faith in God and Heaven was as strong as he made it out to be. After everything had been said and his small breakfast table cleared, Isolde looked at her employer with a skewed expression. Percy was a thin man—with a thin blond moustache and arrogant eyes. He folded his fingers together as a spider hugs its prey.

'Do we have an agreement?'

Do I have a choice? You'll keep hounding me until I die white man, she thought. 'I'll do as you ask.'

'Wonderful! Can we just—'

Isolde extended a finger in warning. 'I'll do as you ask— until the plan is no longer viable.'

'Meaning?' asked Percy.

Isolde drew herself close, her voice flat. 'When we fail, when it all fails, you will not see me again. I'll disappear into the aether.'

'Oh, on that I can agree, *miss* Isolde. I will be in touch,' smiled Percy, his lips taught.

When Isolde had left, sweeping up her dress, her eyes fixed on the exit, Percy relaxed his shoulders. The meeting had almost gone as well as he had imagined it, that is to say, it was neither the very best result, nor the worst. Still, he could not trust her. *Too many thoughts inside that woman. Too much independence.* He did not need independent minds for the short term, only a sense of his plan in motion, the wheels set in traction. He noticed her expression changed when money was involved.

He had his tower to spread this false religion of his, a base of operations, and, on the other side of the Darkwater, Isolde had her dilapidated church as her own. She was to recruit, indoctrinate and train thieves, and he was to see the wealth that accumulated secured away, or invested, to be used later as capital to buy up London. A treasurer of sorts. He scoffed, and retired from the study.

Percy donned a jacket and hat, nodded to his butler and walked outside. In the low mist that lined the roads and streets, he pulled his collar up from the chill and flagged a coach. The driver, rough shaven and sullen around the eyes, doffed his cap.

'Saville mansion.'

'Yes, my Lord,' replied the driver, and goaded the horses immediately.

Saville mansion, on approach, lay squat and awkward among wet leaves, crumbling stone walls, and spools of ivy left to choke the path. As the carriage rounded the entrance–Percy took stock of the view from the hill past a copse of ash. The fog had cleared, and now London peeked out, towers and steeples first, then chimney stacks, and finally tall houses made from bright red brick. Rooftops were glazed and darkened, like the bark from a tree after rainfall. He asked the driver pause, got out before the mansion proper, and bid the driver collect payment from his house. Percy breathed the morning air in deep. Cinnamon clouds sprawled above, as the sun crowned the sky and licked the firmament; birdsong and the crunch of wet pebble beneath stirred some long-lost memory in him, but of what, he couldn't tell.

Inside, the mansion was sparse, humble, and spotless. It reeked of age and whispered of austerity. *Much like William in fact,* he thought. Lord Saville appeared at the top of the grand staircase, footman in tow, deep in converse. Percy coughed ever so gentle.

'Ah Percy.' William waved the footman away, duties to attend.

'William,' they shook. 'Faring well? No doorman?'

'Let go for pastures brighter. I need the funds for a new expedition you see; these jollies are never cheap.'

'Well, and two daughters, I imagine you're being careful with the pennies.'

Both smiled at each other.

'How goes it Percy?' William asked, his voice lowered.

Percy gestured at the reception next to them. William nodded and took a key from his pocket. 'I have to keep my books safe. Especially from Sarah, she's a trouble-maker.'

Percy simply grinned. Slowly, as if not to wake anyone, William closed the door behind him and locked it. 'Whiskey?' he asked Percy.

'Please. Just a touch.'

Two glasses were poured, and two men settled into leather armchairs. 'So, tell me. What about my legacy?'

Percy stirred the gold scotch in the glass and sipped. 'It goes well. I've taken on an old accomplice to split the work involved in half.'

'Trusted?' William asked.

Percy drank the rest of his whiskey. 'Trusted. Handpicked.'

William nodded, and rubbed down his beard. He picked a large tome off a table, that lay in front of a modest fireplace. 'This,' he held the book high, 'is my *magnum opus*. It's yours now Percy.'

Percy shook his head, brow furrowed. 'What is it sir?'

'A guide. One, that I have worked on for most of my life. I will not be around forever for advice; we both know this. It will show you how to divide those who seek to harm Her.'

'And control London from within.'

'Precisely my friend,' said William.

Percy took the book in one hand and shook William with the other. The two men held eye contact for a time longer than felt normal, but imparted more meaning between them than words could justify. This was goodbye. This was finality. *This was his legacy, and now mine to see through.*

With that, Percy walked out of the mansion, his head upright, his step confident, and errant thoughts silent.

Death

– The Isle of Rocks, Summer, 1778 –

On an overcast morning Sarah Saville woke with one of her

mother's songs stuck in her mind. The tent flap had been left

open, and now a warm breeze came through in gasps, as though

the wind had lungs and breath to use. Sarah shuffled in her

blankets and looked at her sister, who was already awake, and

being fussed over by the nanny.

'Sarah, you're next. Come on now, feet first, out of bed,' said the nanny, her mouth full of bobby pins, and hands ready to work.

As Sarah stood there, her hair knotted too tight and her cheeks scrubbed too hard, she adopted a dark scowl. Sophia giggled alongside her as they wriggled into their brown frocks and polished boots. Sophia looked as tired as she felt. From their conversation last night, neither of them had a good sleep, but neither were in the mood to close their eyes and surrender to the day. This voyage to her father's imaginary island was the highlight of their fortunate lives thus far, a rare glimpse of a world without wooden halls, chalkboards, and dour tutors. It had induced an excitement of treasure and monsters that had generated endless questions and queries mostly directed at the exasperated staff.

Yesterday, their ship, *The Lion's Tail*, had weighed anchor in a natural bay. It was a musty old thing, with creaky planks and cramped cabins that rolled unceasing in the Westland Sea. Their father had noticed a lack of sea legs in his daughters, and in his own gruff way had shown them how to steady their feet and shift their bodyweight to the rolls. On deck Sarah had overlooked the crags and beaches with wary metropolitan eyes. For one sailor it was: "*...an odd place. Compared to London, little Miss, you'll find it a miserable part of the world. More sheep than people, more rain than sun, but blessed on the days when it does shine, I suppose.*" She asked if there was a Christian mission, but all the sailors she asked crossed themselves and turned their eyes heavenward without explaining why.

Out of the tent, clean and brushed, it was not until they saw their father that the sisters straightened their spines and walked in trained step, a mask of respect on their faces. Lord Saville slouched on a stump; he had a gun in hand, his long white beard twitching in the wind. Sarah could see he was in that distant concentration of his, the one he used when something was being explained to him, but did not want to appear completely ignorant. The polished catch of the musket flipped up and down in smooth action as the sergeant beside him instructed its use.

'My daughters, good morning,' he said.

Sarah felt the thrill of blurting out his real name, William. The punishment would be severe. *Perhaps a whole week without supper*, she thought.

'Good morning father,' Sarah said in unison with Sophia. Behind them, her mother coughed for attention and was offered a chair. Footmen then served them hot tea with lemon; their polished shoes squelched and stamped in the wet sand. While she drank, Sarah felt an increase in the unease after she had taken her first steps off the jollyboat. Her mother could sense it too, but how she knew, she could not say. Their shared mental fog was spherical (she was certain); a heavy morass that floated invisible above their heads. It brought shivers and aches, but these too were hard to describe, as though the entire island was weighing down on their heads and she had stumbled upon a grand conspiracy.

The ache, and the frustration of not knowing, became unbearable on the second night at the camp. Sarah woke carefully, without disturbing her sister and left behind a warm bunk.

Outside, the clouds had cleared, revealing an orchestra of stars that played only for her. In the middle of the camp, there was one lamp that still struggled against the dark. Her mother was awake in her tent. Lady Eleanor Saville was a shrewd woman. A born sceptic who understood the world and its material temptations, and whose relationship with her father was cordial at best. Her idea of compassion was always followed by swift ecumenical discipline. She was the stick and the carrot, the judge and the jury. Sarah had felt her mother's cane rap her knuckles bloody enough to develop a tick whenever she asked a question, or set out to cause mischief. That cane was never too far away. Just outside, on bare feet, Sarah tiptoed and poked her head inside the tent. Behind a silk screen, illuminated by a single orange flicker, Eleanor jotted away with white ink onto a journal with black pages, a hymn on her lips. Her mother's clothes were soaked from the hem up, but Sarah let the question die in her mind.

'What is it?' Eleanor asked, without turning her head and no break in writing her notes.

Sarah felt her legs stiffen; her cheek twitched. It was bold for her to be here, but she needed answers, they forced her to speak.

'You have the aches too. You've felt it,' she said.

Eleanor stopped mid-scratch; the quill hovered. She looked at Sarah, at first with curiosity, then with worry. Her hands folded, and for a moment, it looked like her mother had become trapped within herself.

'Come. Sit with me child.'

Sarah climbed onto her mother's lap, poised in view of her vellum diary and scrolls. Her mother pointed to a sign scrawled on battered paper. One she had sketched in sanguine. It was a cherry red arrowhead at the tip; the body a bloody hollow circle.

'Do you know what this is?' Eleanor asked. Sarah shook her head, no. 'It signifies a planet. One of the heavenly bodies above us. It's the sign of an astrological House.'

The word astrology meant nothing to Sarah. 'The planets have houses? Do they live in them?' she asked.

'No. More like the families of old. Like the House of Saville, that's you and me.'

'Why is it making these aches?'

'The sea-folk, the people who live on this island, believe that this energy will guide them into the future. It's their religion. What you feel, what we both feel, is the energy of Mars as it spirals down from the planet itself.' Eleanor pointed to the symbol. 'It's a heavy weight we feel. A concentration of the will of a god. The god of war, in this case. *Mars* or *Aries*, depends on perspective.' Her mother bit her lip, and jotted down what she had spoken.

'What does father believe?' said Sarah.

'He's only concerned with the adventure,' she said deadpan, as though this excuse covered her father's distance in recent weeks. 'He needed fresh stories to bring back to his London club; it justifies his membership, since he has become grey around the temples, slow in his step, and cannot jaunt across the world anymore.'

'Will we meet them? The sea-folk?'

'Tomorrow I promise. Run back to bed now. I must prepare my charms.'

Sarah slid off her mother's lap, left the tent, jogged over to her own, slinked into her bunk and closed her eyes.

'Where did you go?' whispered Sophia.

'Went to see mother. She was still awake.'

There was a pause.

'What did she say?'

'That we meet the island people tomorrow.'

'Who are they? Why are they here?'

'I don't know Sophia. We'll find out, won't we?'

Inside a circle of wet branches lined around a bare hill, that overlooked a seaside village, a group of native men and women of the island sat patient. They stared at Sarah with veiled eyes, and the youngest of them, instead of a curiosity, or an invitation to play, lolled their heads with lethargy. Weathered cloaks hung around each of their necks like a noose and spread to cover their bodies. Their pale bodies were covered in patchwork clothes; as though they were shipwrecked, and had spent some years without means to repair them. Across their worn belts hung fisherman's knives and black nets, still wet from the mornings catch. Sarah winced. Her headache, *the ache*, had compounded while she had watched the welcoming ritual consisting of passing a branch from the leader of the group to her father. Sarah's own journal sat buried in her lap. Its pages muddied from bracken she had collected while in the forest path behind them; tiny, neat writing filled the blank spaces around the ephemera. Ten guards from the ship (and five left behind in the camp; her father had insisted on divisions of five) had joined them with either rifles, or pistols and swords hung around their belts. The sergeant caught her eye, and gave her a wink, to which Sarah stuck her tongue out. The rest were young men, and two women, all sharp-eyed and intent on their duty. The group in front of them were people of ancient beginnings; they spoke of moss and bark, seed and branch, of fish and tide. Each time visitors had arrived the mist had swallowed the isle up; an act of their god. When asked 'which god?' an islander scrawled an arrow into the dirt with a pristine finger, and then circled it. Sarah copied it into her notebook, and the stared wide-eyed at her mother, who did not respond. Her father had sat, on a plain cushion, inside the circle that welcomed the Saville family to the island and talked. They had conversed for so long Sarah began to feel restless, her anxiety scrawled slapdash in her journal with a thin stick of charcoal. Sophia, however, clung to Eleanor's skirt, afraid. To her, the strangeness of the place, and the odd customs and dialect they spoke (a sonorous form of English, with rolling vowels), frightened her sister. Her mother was silent throughout her sister's observations and whispers. As Sarah studied her mother's face, sometimes cracks of pain broke through, to which she drank from a canteen. A glass orb hung around her neck, which she touched with her nails, gently tapping. After a shout from the village below, a low horn resonated through the hillside. Sarah's father studied them with amazement etched on his face; William turned a spyglass

down to a squat building nestled among trees and pointed. The

islanders spoke to him of what it was, and what was inside. They

were welcome to see their temple, as long as the guards remained

close by, but did not pass the threshold. Her mother began to

protest at the invitation, but let it be and waved her words away.

She invented the need to calm Sophia and retired back to the

camp with a few of the guards in tow.

Closer Sarah, her father, and seven guards walked to the

temple, following a couple of the islanders and their leader. It was

a short hike through a shaded forest choked by thick

undergrowth; the leaves numerous and wide enough to blot the

sun. As they approached this temple, Sarah could see on top of its

oblong base was a thatched roof and pillars of whale bone as

supports. No birds settled on the building. It had odd sections

that slipped from view, walls that squeezed the ground with no

shadow. The heart of the forest around them had hushed; each

branch miserable in the quiet. From inside the temple grew an

oak that split the reception in half; it was young, supple and twisted in its trunk. The few islanders that had followed them here knelt before it and stayed. Their mouths moved in slick succession over each word of prayer. Sarah grasped her father's leg tight with both hands. There was fear here. It was an acid in the air, a diffusion that stained the moment and boiled courage.

'I'm scared father,' she said.

She looked up, a hope that William would pat her on the head or console her that the island people were doing nothing wrong. He stayed still and quiet. She could feel one of his hands on her back, the fingers shook. His jaw locked tight and the wonder had left him. William saw the hedonism of people whose minds had surrendered to nature, and had not steeled himself for it. The wind that had followed them from the hillside had stopped; they had passed a threshold into the core of the place and it stank of rot and loam. Animals pinned by wooden pegs adorned the walls, their skeletons left to hang; the meat left to deliquesce. Some islanders nodded at the trophies and boasted amongst themselves. One, a woman dressed in grey, wagged a finger at her father to follow further into the sanctum, deeper still.

From the rear of the temple was an open cave, that shrank into a tunnel; meek torches lit a path. As the group of three walked in silence down slick flagstones and through mouldy doors, eventually they came upon a natural shaft opening up to the sky. Before them lay a circular plinth, lit by what sun filtered through the shaft. In the centre was a statue of man whose skin and weapons glittered, and below, between his legs, it was a flower, stem the shade of brick, petals copper–blue. William had stopped, short of breath, as he admired the altar's size and presence. Sarah's headache had numbed to the point where she forgot she was ever in pain.

While the woman traded stories with William, Sarah ignore the statue, and reached out to the flower as though it was a long–lost toy. Even with her mother's extensive garden, she had never seen such a specimen. She felt its waxy leaves, and squeezed one in each hand testing their strength. She felt its lines and cuts, the pocks and marks that ran down the stem. Each told her a story, each an occasion of the plant's life. With a spasm, the peony shuddered. Hidden energy thrummed in each petal. It called her to pluck one; it almost begged her to do so. *It was only one petal out of so many, so why not?* As she did so, red sap bled and ran down her hand. It stained her skin pink where it touched and made Sarah pause in horror. A wiry arm flung her off the plinth with an angry rasp. The woman in the grey dress stood there, her grip tight, her voice in accusation. Sarah watched her father take action. He wrestled the woman away and onto the floor in one heavy push of his hand. There was a wet crack. The woman cried out once, and then lay motionless, her head split open against a stone on the floor. Her blood pooled beneath, red as the sap on Sarah's fingers, and snaked between the flagstones. As Sarah gasped, she could only think of the word *sacrifice*. William turned to her with a fist raised and fury in his eyes. He slapped the petal out of Sarah's hand and slung her over his shoulders. They left in a rush, each step compounding the guilt shared between them. The temple had become eerie. No bodies stirred in its halls and chambers, no islanders at worship. A sick sedation had seeped into the wood and stone and bones of the place; like the fear when they entered, it curdled the mood, bled shame, and only added to their heresy. William shuddered from the effort of carrying Sarah, his skin was milk white, his shirt ruined from the sweat that had built. When finally, they escaped, jogging outside and to the guards, who had their rifles aimed in a circle, ready to defend their Lord. There was no one there to assault them. It was the worst stillness in the forest; a heavy beat of emptiness; a remorseful nothing. Beyond the vision of the guards and William, one–by–one the islanders walked under the shade, vanished between trunks, and disappeared without looking back, their faces vengeful.

After the adrenaline had passed, William collapsed onto his knees his lips in repentance. His fingers still shook. The shine had left his eyes; his cheeks had sunk and his back stooped with effort. Each step spent more of his spirit until he conceded for a stretcher to carry him the rest of the way. Her mother glared at Sarah once they were at the camp after the fitful march back through the forest. She would not stop until Sarah had been broken and sobbed; her worry streaked across her face in raw strips. By late afternoon Lord Saville was at rest, his turn cured, his heartbeat calm. Once the news and gossip had settled, the camp was collapsed by order of the sergeant, and the guards busied themselves in ferrying people and equipment to the ship and back in tireless repetition. The Captain of the *Lion's Tail* received message to be ready for immediate departure, much to his concern. Her mother's tent was the last to be emptied of its contents, only its frame and bedding left to dismantle, and in the skeleton of poles and flapping canvas, she knelt beside Sarah, her face clear, lips pulled back.

'Tell me the truth child, from the moment you entered that damned place.'

Sarah looked down at her mother's hands. One held a glass orb, linked to her neck with a golden thread. Inside was a twist of bluebell and foxglove. The other hand held the cane. Sarah felt a compulsion to tell her mother what happened; to remember, to imbibe the truth. Her eyes locked on the cane.

'There was a temple in the forest.'

'What was in it? Were there any statues? Any worship? A god? The symbol I showed you?' Eleanor demanded.

'An oak. They sat around a tree.'

'Why did your father exhaust himself? What happened to him?'

Her mother now had dropped the cane and orb, and now had both hands wrapped around Sarah's head. Eleanor gave her a shake to ensure the answer would fall out of her daughter.

'William, *father*, killed one of the islanders, by accident.' Sarah began to cry.

Her mother's hands trembled and then froze. She brought them to her face to wipe away fatigue, her eyes set in the distance. Sarah had never seen a change of mood so mercurial over her. Rage boiled in Eleanor, replaced by quick thought. A memory danced between her eyes, where it ran down her to cheeks and twitched.

'Tell no one of this. Whatever I have seen in my dreams, whatever you have now found, whatever secret they attacked you for, is too dangerous for you to peruse. Sarah Saville, do not return to this island seeking answers even when your father is dust and I am ash scattered on the wind. Promise me child, now.'

'I won't, I won't! '

'Promise me child!' Eleanor picked up the cane, and lashed out, rapping Sarah's knuckles.

'*I promise to never return,*' Sarah winced, clutching her hands to her chest.

Pact sealed, her mother picked up the cane and broke it in two, which she dropped on the ground while spitting out a phrase in Latin. Shouts from around the camp started them both, causing mother and daughter to turn at the commotion. Guards began to fire their weapons into the trees and scrub that circled them, and from the shade, arrows returned back to them with cries of hate. Sarah felt her mother grip her arm, with fingernails dug into the skin, and drag her to the beach. The pair both ran as fast as they could, breath escaping in small gasps. Ahead, in the sea, William and Sophia were already safe and part-way to the ship when the *Lion's Tail* discharged its cannons into the forest behind them. Balls of iron sailed overhead and smashed into wood, destroying scores of foliage. The tents now empty, everyone piled into the boats remaining. Two guards screamed as arrows stuck out of them like pinned mannequins. Another guard had already passed, her body held upright by a fellow still pressing on her wound, her face ghost–white, eyes blank. Eleanor threw Sarah at the sergeant who caught her in his rough hands, and hurried herself on board. Without looking back the men pushed the boats out and then began to row in a panic, while the cannons kept on roaring and cries of pain echoed along an apathetic bay.

Sarah, when the cacophony had stopped, removed her hands from her ears and looked up at her mother, her hair sprayed by the sea, her shawl taken by the wind. She found Eleanor staring back at her, eyes wide, and full of contempt.

The Fool

– London, 1800 –

Alex had nearly taken most of his orphaned life to realise that

London thrives on money and desire as readily as his own heart

pumps blood throughout his body. Its roads and streets were as its

bones. People and traffic its meat and organs. Homes, business,

and public works its skin and hair. It was a resilient and brusque

capital. An artificial womb of history and power, culture and

want; it had changed the world to suit its own machinations and

the world had forever changed so.

In one of its proud, veiny streets, a large tower sat nestled amongst the squalid apartments of the Redbridge district. This tower was close to the first alleyways that gathered from the mouth of the Darkwater and was built like a roughshod cairn, typical brick replaced by hundreds of sandstone blocks and cut smooth as possible. From the cobblestone street was the entrance, doors always spattered with mud, always heckled by forgotten beggars and drunks. Its grounds were abandoned to grow wild, with thick thorns that scrabbled to escape from between rusted gates. The Tower had no importance that people knew of; no tax collectors or officials visited. The only signs of life were a group of around fifty shady individuals, both young and old, that common people took pains to avoid. Alex likened it to a *crooked sentinel that hid in plain sight,* and perhaps that was the point.

Inside, the master's chambers sat obtuse at the top; they overlooked his streets and denizens as lord over his realm. Below was the vault, where the spoils were kept, locked tight. Below, further from the dormitory, the council room and grand hall

squashed on top of each other. Above the hush voices and
speculation in the grand hall of the graduation of the initiates,
Alex sat on his bunk, dreaming of how to best describe London
in its entirety.

'First,' Cyrus held up a finger, 'we get those names, and,
second,' a second finger followed the first, 'we'll be shot of this
place. We'll get out of here, you and me Alex. We just need an
opportunity.'

'What? Cyrus, look, you make it sound too simple,' said
Alex.

He scratched at the plaster that surrounded his bunk and
looked at the ceiling. Alex again counted the marks chipped by
dozens before him. They were both waiting for their names; the
names that would elevate them above initiate and into adept.
While Cyrus began another plan of how to leave this life behind,
counting steps on his spindly fingers, Alex drifted in his mind.
He almost wished his world was a painting at that moment, a
choice to start over and scrub clean the canvas; he then wished to
have never grown up in such a place, to have never studied

under aged men who once played the game of shadows. There was a sharp knock at the door of the room which turned both their heads. Cyrus stood and walked out of the room, where a conversation took place beyond Alex's hearing. With a nod and smile Cyrus waved goodbye and left the door open.

The wool sheets underneath felt too warm at midday. Alex sat himself up. He rubbed his stomach where butterflies fluttered, for all of his wishing that he wasn't here, it certainly felt important to him. He paced and checked each familiar corner. There was a mismatched tile, blushed with paint, next to a drain that was never unclogged. He pulled it loose, and grasped the bag at the back of a niche. Inside flopped out a bundle of scrap paper, squeezed between two hard covers and wrapped with twine. It was everything he knew of his family, a collection of writing and sketches made by his mother. On the front cover was an embossed white rose, which he traced with a finger. It was old, he was sure, maybe a generation or two. Faint memories still spun around his mind from time to time; ones of his mother who kept him close. Although Alex remembered her as soft and kind, his father was a hard blur, a lightning-bolt of a man.

Before he had built the courage to ask about his past, his mentor died in his sleep. The only man who knew the person who had delivered him as a babe along with the journal, had taken those secrets to his grave. He spun a new reality in his mind on some of the harder nights, one where he lived with his family, and everyone was happy, and warm, and well fed. Sometimes his imagination would frighten him and provide hard truths. Sometimes, Alex would shake in his bunk, the wool wet with tears, until Cyrus would take pity and raise his spirit.

'Alex,' croaked voice behind the door. 'Alex, it's time.'

He followed the senior down a steep stairwell, the older man taking care down the steps, while he slipped down each like a child. Alex stared at the walls. Noting every patch of mortar, every mark made by a chisel as he had a dozen times. He passed one hand down a groove, twisting his fingers with the folds of the plaster as he clomped down. At the bottom Cyrus strolled forwards, his faint smile and that arrogant twitch of his head directed at Alex. They passed by each other by. 'See you outside,' Cyrus whispered.

Before Alex could reply the senior sped up his walk. The march ended before the gold-shod doors that ran parallel to the mess and training rooms. He oft wondered what was beyond. What ceremonies or hushed meetings the seniority would hold, soon he would know. He looked up at the senior who gave the briefest of winks beneath his cowl and left him alone to attend to other matters. He studied the golden doors. There were no handles, no signs of hinges or dents at the bases, they were paragons of craftsmanship. Carved symbols dotted the trim, marked with numbers and dates beside each. Two generations of thieves up there. The original ideals of the Tower were at the top: *Ignis*, *Aeris*, and *Aqua*. The names each wore crowns: one alight, one lofted by a cloud, and one sunk in a river. *Knowledge, Freedom, Opportunity.* Alex stopped gawking, swallowed hard and pushed. The polished coasters rocked the doors inwards, and the hall ahead exhaled warm air over him.

The council of the eldest thieves sat on simple wooden stools with black cloaks swaddled around them. There were twelve in total, six women and six men, each with an impassive look on their faces. He sat on the only empty stool left in the hall, the one that was in the middle of their scrutiny. He turned, facing them with hot cheeks and watery eyes. Past them, candles upon candles dotted the stills and the floor and wax upon wax melted in opaque clumps. Alex noticed the shadows of the hall had been manipulated to obscure the faces of the council, steep windows at the back of the room carefully curtained over.

'Initiate, you face our judgement today.'

Alex studied what he could of the man who spoke. He was their main benefactor, and none knew his name, his coming and goings kept secret. The man's voice echoed off the stillness; it was cold and impatient.

'Whether you are to receive a name that is unworthy, or worthy, is based on your previous tithes, and willingness to further our mission to free London from her fetters.'

He listened to the woman who spoke beside this man. She had milk-white hair, dark skin and amber eyes that belied a deep perception. He had rarely seen her before, and so nodded in respect. She raised her eyebrows in surprise, turning aside to whisper something to the Benefactor.

'I have trained and studied hard,' said Alex with truth to his words.

The Benefactor scoffed. Part of his cowl formed something of a beak and his chin jutted as he whispered something to Amber Eyes next to him. Alex now knew why the younger among referred to the Benefactor as "*the biggest bird this side of Redbridge.*" Alex caught himself before any laughter escaped.

'You have passed our tests, eaten with your brothers and sisters. You have earned your keep here at the Tower by following marks and relieving them,' said the Benefactor.

'I have,' said Alex.

'But rumour tells us that you have a desire to escape—an insult to all who live here. Are you so unhappy you wish to leave this life of opportunity—are we so repulsive?'

'No,' Alex lied.

'A lie. The boy lies. Nothing more than a child sits before us,' he continued.

'Nothing more than a child who disgraces those ideals carved on that door.'

The hoods all turned to him, expectant. Butterflies bubbled inside Alex; the anxiety spilled into his fists which he balled tight. His teeth mashed against each other until he relaxed his jaw.

'He grinds his teeth in anger,' said a new voice, slippery as wet clay.

'Why do you want to leave our family, one that has provided so much?' said Amber Eyes.

'This is all I know. All I know of the world.' Alex felt hot stings around his eyes, 'there is another waiting for me beyond these walls.'

'Answer the question,' said the clay voice.

Alex shook his head. 'Yes. I want to be free of it. The world is the tower I must climb, not here. I cannot grow anymore.'

More whispers followed. It seemed like an age as Alex waited for the verdict, an age he regretted making. *Maybe that's not the answer they were looking for. How did Cyrus finish so quickly? I just want this to end!*

The Benefactor stood and fanned his cloak about him. He looked at each of the council in turn, as if counting invisible votes.

'Then we are sure of your name, based on what you are, and what we have learned from you.'

'But you were teaching me,' said Alex.

'Knowledge flows both ways,' said Amber Eyes. 'You have a fresh perspective; the only kind that naivety and innocence can bring. Our eyes are old and stubborn—they see what they want us to see. Our organisation survives on its youngest and brightest. It must bring fresh blood to our ever-growing family.'

'Enough, Isolde. The boy is ready for his name,' the clay voice added.

The Benefactor bent low and sat back down, he pointed at Alex. 'Your previous mentor died correct?' Alex nodded.

'Then you will take on his name. I name you *Canis* in front of the council—a name which we hope will grow in renown.'

Alex sighed. He rose and bowed and shook Turner's gloved hand, who embraced him lightly in return. 'Go. You are an Initiate no longer. Spread your name and do us proud, for the sake of this fair city.'

The Benefactor indeed. Lord Percy Turner sat back onto his uncomfortable stool and examined the young man before him. He was a wiry, unkempt thief, who had a predilection to scratch at things around him, and show worry by bunching his entire face up. *If this was the quality they were expecting, standards have to be raised,* Percy thought. *But perhaps, if this young man wishes to be free, we can use that against him.*

After all his worry, the whole ceremony meant nothing, as Alex knew it would. It was all smoke and mirrors. Each of the council stared back at him, they revealed no emotion, gave away no struggle for power nor internal politics. Alex tipped his head again. He left back through the doors, struggled through the hall and paused around one of the pillars to feel his chest. His heart had calmed. His feet felt light and free as he walked down the cracked steps leading to the entrance. The cobblestone at the base was caked with muck, which he danced over. Alex spied Cyrus waiting at the market of Redbridge; his arms rested along the backs of two young women. They giggled as he pretended to nibble along their necks. One looked over at Alex, her eyes judged him in a flick before turning her attention back to the sweet nothings Cyrus spun in her ear.

'This is Helena—she's Greek, I think.' said Cyrus. He let her go, and she gave Alex a twirl, scattering the red jewels on her dress. They picked up the sun, mixing orange and burgundy into a spiral. He looked at the kohl which led straight to her eyes. 'She's ready Alex, but this one is mine.' Cyrus growled and took a playful bite at the other woman, as he shook her shoulder. 'Victoria,' he said, 'what a beauty.' Victoria gave Alex a practiced flutter of her lashes. Her painted lips squeezed together into a subtle kiss. Alex shook his head, hand scratching his brow. One night of celebration would do them both good. Alex tossed a purse at Cyrus, who hung his mouth open as he caught it.

'Then, sir, ladies, tonight we'll celebrate. Our friend Mr Benefactor is paying,' Alex said, bowing.

Outlines of smokestacks and houses melted into each other. Each shape blended into the muted river and smudged a smoked sky. It was a morning of fine benevolence; a morning where work started and finished in a cool haze; a morning where the artist felt as though he was king in a fool's paradise. People materialised from the low clouds that hung close to Alex and Helena; she purred at him as he led her back to her boudoir, made of old brick and painted wood, gaudy posters and soiled screens. She pawed at Alex, still drunk. Her mouth whispered false promises in her most convincing Greek accent before she twirled, and tripped over the front step. She lay there, just beyond the entrance, asleep. Her snores disturbed the other jades in the foyer. They began to throw pillows as Alex gawped into their hidden world.

Recollections surfaced with his appetite. He had lost Cyrus after the ninth drink last night; something he had vowed on the third not to do. Now any remaining pennies jangled sadly in his breast pocket. He knew a morning such as this could only cured with a fresh bun soaked in bacon fat and washed down with coffee. Alex followed wherever the air was fresh; he let the promise of food inspire his legs into action. He found a street baker and bought the greasy bun with half of the coins he had left and chewed it happily. After, Alex crept down ancient steps to a bank close to the Darkwater, letting his boots squelch in the filth. He threw up what breakfast he had managed to swallow. A sewage gate of iron, cut into the stone, squealed open behind him. Out of the hole there were two children, one boy and one girl.

His new students, since he was now technically a mentor in his

own right. Alex jumped up when he saw the boy with a red scarf.

The young man could not pinch pockets with a red flag hung

around neck, he would soon find a rope there instead, the other

end thrown over a gibbet. Alex walked up to them both. He

snatched the scarf away and stuffed it into one of his pockets, out

of sight.

'Like this,' he said to them, 'you either go black, or don't

bother with theatrics. The Globe is on the other side if you fancy

becoming a thespian.'

He pulled out his own black scarf, the length of a man's

arm. It wrapped his head twice, covering the lower half of face.

With his hood pulled up, he looked every bit a professional thief

spread on posters across the city.

'You're 'im' said the girl. 'I've seen you about the Tower.'

'I am 'im,' Alex mocked. 'I am *Canis*. And you two must

be my understudies.'

'We are,' came a cold voice from the boy, 'The

Benefactor sent us. You'll teach us then?'

'I will. But you'll need street names, not your real ones. Coppers will catch you before you know it. Falsehoods can be your best friend. Let that be the first lesson.'

'Are you alright? You're white as a sheet,' the girl squinted at him.

'What was your name at the Tower?' Alex asked her.

'Charlotte.'

'No, simpler than that, a nickname.'

'I like Ghost. I could sneak around easy like.'

'Ominous. And yours?' he said, pointing at the boy.

There was no reply, just a dull glare. Alex sighed. 'The boy with no scarf,' he scratched the back of his head. 'Let's call you Red to remind us all why you don't have one anymore.'

Alex removed his boots and stockings, and rolled his breeches to the knees. He played with the mud and silt beneath his toes, before stepping into the river proper. The cool water lapped up to his ankles giving small sanctuary to the boulevards that were waking above. His understudies stood behind him, waiting for him to give some clue as what to do next. He could hear Ghost cough, but he ignored it. Red had to tap him on his shoulder

before Alex sighed and removed his feet from the river.

He replaced his stockings and boots, rerolled his trousers and

then fixed the pair with a look to inspire silence.

'Come then,' Alex said, 'we'll find a mark in all this.' He

flung his arms up to frame London in its totality.

Each of them had three purses full by the afternoon.

They had scoured the Redbridge market, the canal yard and a

church. Alex chose the hardest areas to pickpocket on

purpose. He wanted to see how well the youngsters would cope.

He watched from a distance and waited for them to hoodwink

someone, and then do it himself. He showed where perhaps they

hesitated or lacked confidence. They tried it in pairs. One

distracted with a sob story or under the pretence of a street

entertainer, and one stole. Fops with ladies tucked under one arm

were easy targets; the youngest and less worldly the best of all.

You could tell from the face and hands, Alex informed them, the

less scars and stress, the more of a blessed life they had led. When

Ghost asked, Alex told them that prosperous merchants were usually not worth it.

'There,' Red said, pointing. 'That fat bastard has two guards.'

'Look at the size of his purse,' marvelled Ghost.

'It's a ruse,' added Red, 'no merchant would leave his home with that much coin.'

'Now, which of you is right?' Alex asked.

They sat sullen on their seats inside the cafe. Alex sipped his coffee while watching the merchant waddle along. A single fat hand with a collection of fat rings pointed at what he wanted to buy. A footman would saunter off and buy whatever his master wanted.

'Do you see him? That pad is the prize, not the merchant,' said Alex.

Alex stood and followed, his feet responded and put weight onto their soles. Each step he took was silent. The footman wound his way back through the market square. He made sure his master's money was tight in his hand. Down an alley, before Alex could act, Cyrus crashed into the footman, who tumbled with the master's purse onto the cobble. There was a flash of utter hatred across the footman's face before he composed himself. Cyrus apologised; with his free hand, he pointed at the purse, vulnerable and without owner. Alex roughly guessed the weight, removed it of coins and replaced pebbles inside. He tied it up and patted it down of dust. With a snatch, the footman hurried on.

'We're combing the same patch friend,' said Cyrus. Alex looked down on his friend's boots; they were slick with yellow mud.

'We don't believe in coincidences. You were late in meeting me.'

'Making new friends. By the by, there's a Lady in town, from the south.'

'Another girl caught your eye?'

'Let's be serious. There are rumours of a treasure hunt, and she's heading the expedition. The boss wants us back at the tower.'

☆

In the afternoon, clouds continued with their downpour.
It had turned Redbridge into a morass. Their Tower, Alex
noticed, was lucky to be built as it was. Several homes around
them were already waterlogged. People had gathered bushels of
straw and pails ready to fight the worst of it. Inside, after stowing
his cloak, he arrived in time for late supper, the council already sat
in a tight circle around the far end of the hall. Attention all on
them. Setters hugged the table legs; they shook from the wet, or
whimpered as food passed them by. He noticed Ghost and Red
among a crowd of youngsters huddled off to one side; he gave
them a wave, which was returned with eye rolls. Plates of
squashed potatoes and carrots mixed with loaves as black as the
table were presented. Roasted hare and duck were eaten in gusto.
The lurking dogs gobbled any scraps thrown underneath. After

everyone had emptied, or licked a plate clean, Percy rose and spoke:

'We believe there is an expedition heralded by a Lady Saville. Her ship is to uncover some hidden treasure from legend. Days before the Tower came to be,'

'What's the treasure Master?' asked a thief by entrance.

'Gold,' replied Percy.

Laughter broke out in the hall. The younger among them wiped tears from their eyes before they understood the matter was grave. Percy swiped his hand for silence. 'This gold, according to Isolde,' he wiggled a finger at the hooded woman sat to his left. 'Is important to secure our future brothers and sisters. If the Saville heiress has invested part of her fortune in this, it is worth our attention. There is a journal that survived from an expedition made over twenty years ago, when Lord Saville was still alive and Sarah just a child. We have a copy from the British Museum,' he coughed, 'thanks to Isolde here.' The woman nodded at the mention of her name. She stared at Alex, who blushed and looked down at his feet. She had been present at his initiation, same amber eyes. 'Our task is to steal this gold; in whatever form it may take. Then, sell it to the highest bidder. Business as usual.' Percy clapped his hands twice and the hall began to disperse. He walked over to Alex and Cyrus, placed one hand on Alex's shoulder, and beckoned Cyrus with the other.

As a group they walked in silence while Isolde followed behind with a cat's pace. Alex turned back to look at her, but she flicked those eyes up at him. They were two russet pips that saw straight through his soul and read his intentions before he was aware himself. They carried on up staircases. Up, past the library, past the treasury, and finally to Percy's study. He cradled a key in a palm which snapped the lock open when turned. Heavy tumblers rolled on the inside of the door, which opened further locks.

'It would take a door such as this to be here. Ironic that the secrets and valuables of thieves have to kept safe from themselves.' Percy motioned for the thieves to go in first, watching them carefully. Alex and Cyrus walked into the study. The desk at which the Benefactor worked formed a semicircle that cut the rest of the room off. Visitors, rare as they were, would have to ascend wide steps before reaching a set of worn stools, each of which looked more uncomfortable than the last. Ash bookcases lined with brass, older than Alex could have guessed at, loomed over him.

'I will be quick. Isolde is the mastermind of how we secure the gold. Please if you would.' She bowed to the men and carried from where Percy left the conversation.

'Your commitment has impressed us,' she said.

'Me too,' Cyrus replied, with a cocky smile. Alex suppressed a snigger. The Benefactor rapped his stylus on the desk. He stilled them with a look.

'Lady Saville will be looking for supplies and men for the expedition tomorrow. She'll go to Greenmarket, where the freemen gather.'

'She expects trouble then.'

'Word of my informant has mentioned she already has a ship and crew. She wants to hire guards to protect her. She expects trouble, and needs capable men.'

'This is where we are stepping in,' said Alex.

'You will need costumes and you will need history: battles, conflicts, wars. Which have you lost, and which you have won.'

'But if she doesn't buy us, the plan will fail.'

'I've bought one of her men. He will meet with me, and when the Lady Saville is seeking two guards, he will point and recommend you. The Lady will have her suspicions, no doubt, Sarah Saville is not stupid. However, coming from one of her own, she will seize the chance.'

'And then we meet this Lady, sign a contract in blood, and do a merry jig once we're away?' said Alex.

'As you say it, sir,' replied Isolde.

'Sorry, Master, but it seems an awful amount of effort for a rumour,' asked Cyrus.

The Benefactor coughed. 'As mentioned, Lady Saville is not stupid, like with her sister. Once set on a task, wealth and fortune seems to follow them. She is, of course, to be the only person who knows what this gold is, and where to find it. Her sister does not. The fact she has hired a seaworthy ship and crew is also likely it is not in England proper.'

'And if we fail to find this trove?' said Alex.

Percy folded his hands. 'Then an opportunity is lost. See that you don't return empty handed, or the Tower will be a permanent residence, for the pair of you.'

Alex and Cyrus, after no breakfast and little sleep, discussed the punishment that would await them if they failed. Cautious, they washed, dressed, and met Isolde just outside Redbridge market. She massaged deep creases on her brow and tugged her lips when she talked of her plan, and walked with them to Greenmarket, answering questions along the way. Alex noticed her hair was strange. It was as translucent as frozen smoke; it curled about her in bunches of cloud-white; it was almost as if some trauma in Isolde's past had shocked it into losing all colour. When she was out of earshot, he grumbled with Cyrus over placing both their fates in the hands of a woman, no matter how sanctioned. In the afternoon, reinventing a new past was harder than they had first thought; Isolde had helped them with the intricacies: the why, who and when. How to spot when someone (namely Lady Saville) was trying to fish the truth out of you. There was a chance of small rest before they started, and the two men dined on stale bread and thin ale.

'It was to put a mean, hungry, expression on both of you, to look the part,' Isolde chuckled.

Alex and Cyrus (dark-eyed and stomachs rumbling) arrived at Greenmarket with Isolde pacing ahead. Before seeing them, they could hear the ring of metal on metal of smithies as they toiled to complete orders for the next day. Squeezed down one alley were farriers and coopers, grasping at hoops and nails, in another slip of a street, gathered soldiers and guards waiting for their shift to be finished. Flower-girls, errand-boys, and debt-collectors rubbed shoulders as they grew closer to the heart of it all. As they followed Isolde deeper into the streets, the urgency and people in Greenmarket grew. It was a throng of timeless effort, a chorus of energy never satisfied. In the bustle Alex spotted Isolde ahead, an unfamiliar man stood next to her in converse.

'Over here,' she cried and waved to them. Isolde's bought man jogged over. He looked over Isolde's hands with as he whispered in her ear. His eyes darting from the crowd behind, and to Alex and Cyrus, who patiently waited.

'So, what now?' asked Cyrus.

'Now,' Isolde said, clearing her throat, 'we wait for our Lady.'

Alex studied Isolde, but she gave nothing away. It came to late afternoon; the sun swelled more confident, parting more heat into the air. Soon traders and their associates were out with fans and shade. The savvier of which had carts filled with cool pitchers of water or pressed juice; and if exceptionally entrepreneurial, brought out blocks of ice and began to shave them into small cups much to everyone's joy. Alex watched, on the edge of his vision, as stacks of coins disappeared into small

bags or sagging pockets. Some were tucked behind make–shift

desks, some straight into lock–boxes and carried away once full.

Isolde raised an eyebrow at him; one shared between mother and

naughty child.

'Wait. Be patient,' scolded Isolde.

'Business is good,' Alex said. His eyes never shying from

the money.

'Ours will be the sweeter.'

Lady Saville had an immediate hold on the men in the

market. She swam through the crowds with two sailors as

entourage. Men offered her drinks and shade as she came to rest

in front of the bought man, who waved and bowed before her.

They conversed openly for a time, until Isolde's man whispered

in the Lady's ear. Lady Saville moved to Alex, Cyrus and Isolde

out of curiosity.

'Lady Saville, my name is Isolde, and may I present my

men. The others have been purchased this very morning,' lied

Isolde.

'Remarkable coincidence my dear,' said the Lady.

'What war were you in?' one of the sailors asked Alex.

'Frankish.'

The sailors both nodded in unison; they whispered into Lady Saville's ear each in turn. She sent the sailors on with a wave after a discussion.

'I would give you a demonstration of their ability to fight. But London as a rule, does not allow violence,' said Isolde.

'Shame.' Lady Saville had a mongrel accent Alex noticed. English, with a twist of Southerner. 'Have they ever sailed?'

'Yes, of course.'

Alex had an aversion to open water, and couldn't bear more than dipping his toes. Cyrus, he remembered, rarely had seen the coast; he had been born amongst the slums and rooftops. A true city-man. Alex cursed to himself if the journey was to cross any great span of ocean; it was the one question he had failed to ask. Lady Saville summed them up with a twist of her hand, and paused to take in the market. She levelled her eyes at Isolde, Alex and then Cyrus in turn. With an intake of breath, she retrieved a purse, and paid with a promissory, to which Isolde

accepted with a courtesy and gave it to the bought man, who

waited as eagerly as a dog waits for his dinner. Alex noticed the

Lady Saville's demeanour had changed; she now had a curt

disinterest in everything around her. The bought man gave them

both a thin waif of a contract, which, once signed, was then

bound in parcel and twine and sealed with wax. Isolde, task

complete, left them behind, her cowl pulled tight across her head,

her white hair hidden except for a few errant curls. She gave

Cyrus a glance and Alex a wink, before she blended into the

crowd and disappeared with a skip of her feet.

Cyrus, nonchalant, spilled his charisma over Sarah

Saville immediately. He made sure he treated her as a Lady should

be. Alex suspected she could handle herself just fine. Although

Sarah Saville's sloop was the smallest at the dock just beyond

Greenmarket, it had enough room for twice their number. Two

sailors, and the bought man, the same entourage from before,

looked at Alex and Cyrus with unease. Once aboard, they threw sails, retrieved the moorings, and took the sloop out of Darkwater and towards the coast.

'Is she sea worthy?' shouted Alex from the stern. He kept a close view on the streets above as they left, trying not to look at the murky water below him.

'Wouldn't be sailing her if she wasn't,' mocked the younger of the sailors.

Alex cursed their profession, loud enough for them to hear. Below, his bunk fell down a crack of a space; a heavy throw and soft blanket waited for him on top of a hard mattress. Alex sat, and rested his feet. His wish had come true in a roundabout fashion; he had gotten his new start away from the Tower. A diluted freedom, but freedom nonetheless. He curled up onto the pillow, and before he knew it, tiredness emptied his mind and softened the world in oblivion.

☆

It was sharp metal stuck into his skin that woke him. It turned and curved along his neck, around his cheek and down his jaw. Alex's eyes shot wide as the sailor he had insulted earlier pressed a hand down hard on his mouth.

'Think you're a funny man?' the man said, eyes aglow.

Alex stared; answering yes or no was pointless. It would give him something to use. The small shank nicked on his stubble as it brushed up and down. The man on top of him was a Westlander. Alex could smell his breath and taste the sweat that dripped from the palm squeezed over his face.

'Say something funny, something funny that'll make me laugh dead man.'

The sailor twisted his torso enough for Alex to see Cyrus's dagger behind. It was gripped in one gloved hand. Cyrus pushed the blade into the man's neck. It popped through with a snap, the silver tip sparkling as it let blood. A spray of red streaked across Alex's mouth. The sailor gave a strangled cry and fell limp.

There was a moment's turn before Cyrus spoke. 'You've never killed a man before, have you?'

'No, I steal Cyrus, that's enough.' Alex said, through short breath.

'I just stole his life Alex, there's no difference. It's all currency. A man's life is no more than coin to spend. Once it's gone, you never get it back.'

Alex shook his head. He turned his hands over and rubbed the palms into his sockets to rid them of sleep that still lingered. Cyrus offered him the dagger. Something real about it worried him; a bloodied weapon, a tool that stole lives, not to cut purse strings. Alex took the dagger into his hands. He cradled it; the pommel cold, lifeless.

'Get rid of the other one now, don't be a fool.' Cyrus nodded, pointing above deck.

'I'm a thief, not a murderer. And as a thief you have a choice to return whatever you take,' rasped Alex. Ethics turned in his mind. A man's life was worth more than coin, he knew this.

Cyrus snatched back the dagger and walked away. Leaving Alex alone in the dawn's light. The dead Westlander had curled up as an infant, the body growing stiller by the second. He gave it consideration. The only course was to either wax murder with murder or shed the truth of the matter. Alex wanted truth. He may not always be faithful to truth, or be at its side, but in this moment, it comforted him. He walked down a tight passage, ignoring the lanterns that hung low, passing over cargo and stringed foodstuffs. He raised his hand, hesitating before Lady Saville's cabin. He rapped three times, unsure if she would wake at this hour.

'Enter,' came a woman's voice.

Alex entered. From the small porthole to the cracked boards underneath, everything was washed in orange. Lady Saville was sat, at rest, a book opened on her lap, angled to make the most of the candlelight. Her shoulders were bare to her cleavage. A corset and well-travelled leggings the only clothes she wore. Alex blushed. He forced his eyes to wander to the ceiling and back to the lone candle.

'You made the right choice not to kill. That tells me there's something of merit about you. It means you're a thinking man; one who understands right and wrong clear as day inside them.' Sarah Saville threw him a look, eyebrows peaked. 'He was a thug that Westlander you know. He did some terrible things in his life, terrible.'

'How could you have known?'

'I am a witch, like my mother. And you, Alex, a thief, like yours.'

'I never told you my name.'

'It didn't stop me from knowing it, has it? You've led a life of a blackguard in service to that dreadful tower and its dreadful master. But we both know that's not the whole truth to the matter.'

'I owe the Tower my servitude.'

'No, you steal to survive, and the Tower takes its alms. There is nothing else to it. There's no honour or prestige amongst your kind. No matter how much deception you use.' She gave him a comely smile before slipping a nearby fur over her skin. 'You steal to live, and it feeds you. You give yourself a false appellation and that protects you. Blankets wrapped over blankets. That Tower of thieves has poisoned young minds for years now, and yours is no exception.'

'You seem to know much of my life.'

There was a twitch that ran across her cheek, ending on her brow. Alex ignored it as a trick of the light. 'I do. I also know about that woman at the market. The one with the dark skin and white hair.'

'Isolde.'

'Isolde. Thank you. Her ruse was easy to see through. She was the one who had bought one of my men, a clever woman.' Alex felt compelled to remain quiet. *She knows it all.* He could feel his stomach sink. 'It does not matter. I will carry on and secure my prize.'

'The gold?'

'Perhaps, perhaps not; what hearsay have you been fed I wonder?' She fixed him as a spider towards a fly.

Alex swallowed. He bade her a good night, the words hollow, and left. A raw fear came over him as he left her cabin and refined into anxiety as he made his way topside. The Westlander's mate was there; sat calm on the tiller. A single mast shivered. Its canvas caught the moonlight in shades of pewter. The old sailor looked around with lazy eyes and noticed his mate wasn't there.

'It's done then. Your friend killed mine.'

'He attacked me.'

'Yes, he did—you did well not to give in. I didn't fancy my throat cut also.'

Alex nodded. Cyrus stood just before the threshold to the top; his eyes searched in the dark. They looked up, and for a second held something close to sorrow. The sailor smacked his lips and scratched.

'I'm glad he's gone.'

'Why?' asked Alex.

'He had a hunger in him. A fire that was burning him away, leaving only an animal behind. He had lost his sense of reason. He wasn' a man no more.'

'Was he sick?'

'If he were, it were of the soul. There's a story to tell. When he was young and brave, I knew little of him. Beard of red, big brawny ham fists, and he would eat and drink himself into a state. This was before we joined the *Tail*–and the Ladyship below. Connor was as good a mate as any I've had. But the violence started recent–he kept punching and swearing, sometimes in his sleep. It was always there, just below his skin, where you couldn't see it. I'm glad he's gone–that's no way to live young man, in constant rage with the world.'

☆

The sloop sailed along the coast. Layers of pearl foam that had crusted on the hull signalled the end of London's bay. Boulders, pink and blue, dominated the beachheads and cliffs topped with stubborn sod. After two days of skirting the Channel they passed Land's End. Close enough for Alex and Cyrus to see *The Lion's Tail* in her small glory. She sat there with a rogue pride in her matted sails and flaking hull; she was alone, separate from fishing boats and other trade ships that weaved about. Port's Mouth, as he knew it from gossip, had grown large enough to occupy a man for the entirety of his life. Alex couldn't see the town before him match the callous monster that was London. From the sunken piers and floating homes, he spied shallow and long faces. Cliques of priests from exotic lands gathered with shore—men and fishermen, navvies and marines. Most, if not all, flocked around brothels, whose tall tar basted planks struck Alex as twisted churches. A terracotta sky broke over the boardwalks and chaos, blending the shadows into one tone. Lady Saville walked with confidence onto the top deck. She cradled an orb in one hand, held by a golden chain suspended around her neck. Her other hand tugged over the sequins on a billowed dress lined with bronze studs up and along a high collar. What was in her hand took Alex a moment to recognise. A glass ball, filled with shellflower and a dandelion. It was a curio that winked at him as the Lady swayed down to the gangway, her snaked fingers beckoning the men to listen.

'Come, we'll meet the Captain this afternoon. We set sail in one day. Everything is ready.' Said Sarah

'Time enough,' said Cyrus, and helped the old sailor secure the mooring.

At a tavern, despite little sleep and wandering thoughts, cognizance gripped Alex. Between the food and drink, conversation stalled in his mind after the killing. Cyrus, the man he thought he knew, the childhood friend he once laughed with at the tower, had become bitter. He was a man who had been set loose; his moral leash had slipped. They talked low of murder. They talked of its semantics as much as Alex could bear, which led nowhere; both of their minds too stubborn to settle the question of how far a man should go in violence and justice. He broached the subject of Lady Saville, head bowed to the table, speech all hushed.

'She's a witch or mad, or both, must be! She had everything set against us. Knew of us, my name, knew of the Tower, and knew of what we planned to do. She knew that Westlander had died before the blood became cold in him.'

'A witch? Well, if she does know everything, we have to leave, we can't trust her. We have to head back to London. There's nothing to gain from this.'

'Cyrus, we've gone this far.'

'If we steal whatever it is that she covets from this journey, she'll know it and stop it. We're two strangers on a bought ship bound for open sea. One slip between us will be the last,' Cyrus wringed his neck.

'She can know how and why. She can cast every spell under the sun. But Lady Saville cannot protect against every outcome,' said Alex.

'What, wait until we're back in London? When everything is closer to home?'

'Exactly so,' Alex folded his arms. 'And then we'll steal this treasure for ourselves, and become rich men.'

When Cyrus and Alex finally met the captain of *The Lion's Tail* later that day, he proudly displayed a greasy black beard, above which swivelled two musket ball eyes that surveyed his domain with authority and fire. The captain took Lady Saville and her hire as guests. He afforded a generous amount of space between them and the crew, even after the sea-funeral of the Westlander, to which the crew, much to Alex's surprise, took well. Some of the sailors Lady Saville already knew by name, others the Lady took avoidance to, or they to her. Magicians did exist within London. He'd met some who could spin fire or some who could beguile ghosts. However, none of them were as powerful as Lady Saville; as she could cast spells upon men without doing anything at all. Her presence could

silence a crowd. Her gaze gave out a sailor's heart. He imagined

her reputation was fiercer by the stories built of her, and the crew

was as pious as it was superstitious Alex gathered. They believed

in devils and monsters, witchcraft and God, as men had any right

to. But there was fervour about them, a malevolent way they

twisted the fables of good and evil. Their true deity was the sea,

and she kept a dim view on dabblers of sorcery. Alex cupped his

fingers around the handles of a heavy chest, the only luggage the

Lady was taking with her. It was unceremoniously dumped on the

deck. There were no more preparations to be had; only the

voyage lay ahead. The gang was raised, the anchor scooped up,

and the ties lowered. Above a man called out, and a bell sounded.

    The *Tail* was underway, and she suffered naught but

calm water.

The Empress

— The Isle of Rocks —

As the waves churned, a chill was herald to a storm that was

spreading across the length of the Westland Sea. It began

with rain that whipped the unwary and climaxed in a tempest

that squeezed the hearts of those on board. The groans from the

wood of the *Lion's Tail* made its crew anxious as they sat cramped

in the forecastle. They shook together as the carrack listed and

spun, desperate to keep her course. In her cabin Sarah had

slouched as she tried to read in the sweat and gloom; her vision

aided by a single dancing lamp. The storm simmered in time, and died to a whimper after a turn of the hourglass. It made the sailors fall to their knees in prayer. They offered up hardtack and rum as thanks to whatever divinity had saved them. She slapped her book closed when the fracas from the celebration grew too much. She was here to relive her childhood. If she had wanted divine intervention, she would have found it at church and on her own terms.

'Alex,' she shouted.

'Yes Lady, you called.'

'What's the damage?'

There was a pause, until a heavy thud from above broke it and sent streams of dust into her eyes. Alex popped his shaven head through the soaked companionway. He gave her a wink and the sailors a nod in the haze.

'The *Tail's* good, the sails caught too much wind, tore some of them. She's a tough one.'

'That's fine. Get Cyrus and secure my trunk. We'll go see the captain.'

Sarah glanced at her vanity mirror. She was, after two days at sea, bedraggled and sleep—deprived. She tousled her hair, pulled a tie from her salt—crusted jacket, and fixed it into a bun. Her hands fitted themselves into worn gloves and she then placed a leather peak on her head. She felt she was ready for anything this haunted isle could throw at them. She braced herself against the wind and could taste the salt before leaving the hold. The captain greeted her from the stern with a hearty wave. She enjoyed Captain Frost's company. He was a businessman at heart. She paid him half now with expenses and half later.

The murk—shimmer of the island caught her breath. It was vast and green and black to the core. An expanse of rock so crowded with evergreens and heather she did not believe it was the same place. Thin clouds threw themselves at distant hills obscuring their summits.

'It's quite a sight Lady.'

'Asleep or drunk?' She employed a wicked eyebrow at Cyrus. He scratched his stubble and squinted with half—closed eyes.

'Both. Won some cards and dice, drank until I slept.'

She squeezed her eyes tight. Alex and Cyrus were untrustworthy. The educated guesses she had told Alex on the sloop had had the desired effect. They believed she was a witch with the ability to glimpse into a man's head. This was half true, she was born a cunning–woman; but as far as she knew, it was impossible to see the future or read minds. The coincidence in London was too obvious not to arouse suspicion. Her paid spies had staked the market out before any opportunists from Redbridge Tower had woken up. A spy had seen Isolde with one of her men, bribe in hand. That was all the information she needed. Now they could betray her, rob her blind, but doubt festered in them. Doubt she could use.

'Captain what news?' Her mouth spat away drizzle that had collected around her lips.

'She won't be rolling here, needs the tide Lady. Then we'll point her around; which means you will have all the time in the world to get back to shore. Boson, see a boat is ready for the Lady's jaunt.'

Sarah noted there was mirth in his voice. She didn't approve of that tone, but could not care less; it had begun. She tried to reimagine the island from her childhood. They were perhaps on the opposite shoreline; the trek should take them less than a half a day. Her mind cleared as she cast a spell of clairvoyance. The strings before her bent and twisted as clay in her hands. The ones that glowed showed her the way to the flower through memory. Her skin felt hot as her blood thundered with the strain. *I must relax the strings gently, and let them go the same.* The way was now certain, clearer than any map.

'Cyrus, make sure the Boson has everything we need. We are climbing up that.' Sarah gestured at the forests that clogged up the distant hills. She turned to Alex with her battered trunk.

'Was that a spell Lady? It won't go down well with this crew. I want to return back to London without meeting Davy Jones,' said Alex.

'The crew's opinions be damned. I will have my prize after suffering pithy bread and sea-water.'

'They think you've cursed them, that you're everything they say you are and worse. They won't show mercy.'

Sarah made a gesture of cessation. 'I'll concede—no more then.'

'We both know you're not a foolish type.'

'No. Well spotted.'

Sarah wrestled with her hat while crew scrambled to prepare the ship when the tide returned. A rope ladder cast over the gunwale led down to a jollyboat with greased ropes. Sarah found her chest dumped on the deck by Alex; and wondered if it was the thud she had heard earlier. She only needed one book from it, a battered velum diary with slick cover and worn spine. After the climb down, they soon stood on the island, the rocks beneath them broken and wet. To them it was a foreign land of little hope and stark imagination. An island which gave little adventure, and offered no respite: from the cold nooks and caves of sea—stone, to the mermaid's purses and brown kelp that tangled up beneath their boots. At the peak of the beach they could hear muffled cries of gulls carry in the wind. For a moment

Sarah looked across the small bay and to the *Tail*, where it sat in the water as if it was a favourite pet on guard.

'Enough gawping–we have progress to make,' she said.

'My Lady!' cried Cyrus.

'What?'

'Reckon there's anything to make a meal of here?'

'Just hurry, if there is something to eat, you find it and eat it yourself in your own time.'

'Careful Cyrus, she's got a knife–edge on her mind. She'd turn you into pudding and feed you to the crew,' Alex said as he hoisted a bag of tools over his shoulder.

'Nonsense, she can't do that. Can she?'

Sarah left Cyrus's question unanswered. She felt dread as they climbed further inland. Her eyes scanned the valley for the temple she remembered. The diary in her hands told her the island folk prayed to both a god and goddess. Mars and Juno; a deity of the spring and the may–flower. She studied the old book and ran her fingers over its familiar corners. She wished William could have seen her now, back again. Her mother would be furious. The rotten endplates had pictures of the flower she had touched and the golden man. They staggered up a steep path and walked along broken twigs and cracked stone to the temple from her past. What was once proud walls, were now choked with ivy. Graffiti of spears and shields had been carved into the entrance. From the roof poked a pale oak, its roots pushed past the doorway. Birds scattered as Alex and Cyrus began to clear away roots and branches that impeded them.

'Watch for anyone else. There might be eyes in the forest.'

'You've been here before?'

'Once before. We should move on inside.' Sarah reached up with a spell and tugged on the aged door with a thought. She felt the strings pull loose and unravel. 'Stand clear–the thing's coming free.'

The oak crumpled as it freed itself from the roof. Stale air escaped and vented straight into the lungs of Alex who racked his lungs. Inside the temple a strained beam shone down upon a bare sanctum; the cloister was devoid of art. It had been neglected with time, sheltered from the elements. An anti–climax. Sarah paced in anxiety. Steps led to the back, it was deep and dark, and her torch could illuminate only so much.

Sarah relaxed herself and roamed the temple. She saw Alex and Cyrus chip away at the walls in a fever, their eyes full of lust. She came to a halt before a collapsed passage and panicked in the gloom. She stumbled over stone and roots before she came to the chamber where the flower was before. It was impossible it had not changed since she had seen it last, but there it was, static and immortal. The flower's leaves were still waxy and rich, the petals still that off–blue and ochre red stem; exactly as her memory preserved it. The statue still stood behind the flower. It was the gold man proud and erect, with dour face and muscular arms outstretched in salute. Sarah ran to the peony; a glimmer from the surface of its petals mirrored the room in teal. She felt like a child again when the idea to touch and hold those petals came to her; to take one as she did before. There was nobody to stop her now. She held a petal with her thumb and finger and plucked it. It wept clear sap. She held it to the light. It was delicate as gossamer on the inside, full of fluid and motes. It spoke to her, with words that only she knew or could hear. Sarah held it against her chest, ran the petal down her breasts and to her stomach. As she made the connection, Sarah sensed a change in her body. Her breathing became tighter, her stomach tense and fragile; she shivered and grew nauseous. To scream was the first thing she did. A primordial scream born from pain and fear with no will to stifle it. The agony inside was hot and it was merciless. It grew straight from her legs, up and through the bones in her spine and sent daggers into her heart. Her pulse raced and forgot to beat. She gritted her teeth as she felt Alex and Cyrus pick her up and move back through the valley. She could only see the canopy, hear only the crack of sticks underfoot.

'Faster Cyrus, she needs to see the quack.'

Sarah heard Cyrus grunt as they quickened the pace. Before long she could smell seaweed and feel the sun scorch her clammy skin. She was rotten, dizzy, and wan all at once. Sweat stung her eyes; she felt too frail to turn her neck to be rid of it. Little by little, a sliver at a time, Sarah lost the grip she had on her mind and faded into oblivion, her arms limp and eyes still as the men rushed to the infirmary.

In Sarah's oblivion, a blood–moon outshone opaque stars on a cracked firmament. There was a city ahead of her, glorious and terrible. Aqueducts that once sparkled greeted her as she walked up a slate street. It led to an eroded temple made of alabaster and soil. From here, she could see only the splendour of the city, long before its enemies had claimed it. She heard shouts, distant screams that caused her to shrink in fear. She could sense them, she could almost see them too, but they were too fast to track; the smallest of the phantoms too agile and feint. There was a shriek, a bang of voices that shouted all at once. Sarah ran as fast as her legs could commit. Closer it came, her doom, her death, her destruction. Then silence. The howls and noise from the ghosts had stopped. She was back in her father's study.

'I–I'm not afraid,' her words came out thick and tangled.

Through the miasma Sarah could see her father stand patient. He became animated with an awareness that grew as the seconds passed.

'Then, pray, what are you?' he asked her.

Laughter rippled about. The study dimmed as Sarah grew feint; her father's statue seemed to spin as she dropped to her knees. He spoke again, his voice growling and deep. 'There are three of you now.' The spirits that had stalked her through the city had found her. They paused; claws and teeth bared, their forms indistinct, and pounced.

Sarah woke as the afternoon trickled in through a porthole, untouched by the horror. Sweat ran down a blanket she did not recognise. Sarah wiped the grime away with one hand and organised her thoughts. She wanted to stand and peek through the window, but her legs gave way and she thudded onto the deck.

The noise disturbed Alex; he rose from his position and pushed aside the curtain.

'Lady, rest now,' he helped her up. She judged by the sluggishness in his voice he'd been asleep also. She swatted at him.

'You've taken the flower, haven't you?'

Alex shook his head. He placed her back on the bed as easy as a doll

'We didn't. Better for everyone to say you found nothing.'

'Then it has been a wasted trip for the both of you. What will you do now?'

'Can't go back empty handed, not after this. Cyrus is asking the captain for any work. Better than going back to London, we're free men here.'

Sarah reached out with one hand and touched Alex on his cheek. She sighed and flopped onto the stained pillows. She felt all thirty-two years compound into a single ache that ran through her body and sapped her energy.

'Thank you. As a thought, I am in the need of hiring two groundkeepers before the winter comes.'

'Well, if you promise we're away from Redbridge proper, we'll work for you.' They shook hands.

'Excellent. You're hired on one condition: if you can leave your dishonest life behind you. Help me get some wine for tonight with the honourable Captain. I need him to see eye-to-eye with what I've found. You need to keep the crew distracted.'

'Some dice and songs and we'll give them a merry night.' Alex stopped just as he was to give her privacy. 'What else did you find in there?'

Sarah pursed her lips, they widened into a large smile. 'The find of the century.'

Night came as the ship meandered to a safer distance from the coast. Sarah had found a stuffy dress amongst her luggage, and struggled herself into it. She applied blush, and was now entertaining Captain Frost in his pokey cabin. Her impression of John was that he wasn't the rambunctious sea–dog from tales she had heard. Sarah expected pompous and preposterous tales with knee–slaps and snorting nostrils. Instead, (from his manner) she assumed he was a family man with the aspirations of a comfortable life. Their dinner of dried fish and boiled rice was over. Now she was in her element. Her voice took on a smooth appeal and she showed more cleavage than his eyes knew what to do with. She could see a red face underneath his beard.

'I need to ask a question, but I believe that you're not ready to tell me the answer sir,' she asked.

'Oh, why not ask away and let me mull it over Lady.'

'It's very risky to ask a captain something that would jeopardise his crew.'

She watched him light his pipe and puff a few times as he regarded her. She sensed his curiosity after such a bland dinner.

'There's a statue back at the temple. It was gold. If we could take a look tomorrow...' She wondered whether he had heard her.

'There's a certain issue,' he said. Sarah rolled her eyes. 'I'm keeping a tight schedule for other clients. I'd need extra pay up front, or similar rebate.'

His hand slapped her thigh and stayed there. It crept up her inner leg without resistance. She pushed her hand down to meet his, lifting his chin up with her other; her assumptions were incorrect.

'You'll get paid and more. I'm not one to cross privateers, even legal ones with writs and fancy papers to their name. I'm sure that after landing at Greenmarket, you can explain to my current lover why I was groped. He'd seek your ruin.'

John snorted and emptied his pipe. 'Who would that be?' he slurred.

'Lord Turner.'

She felt just a nudge to who steered the conversation was necessary. She could see him laugh and grin, but her stare didn't falter. Perhaps he didn't realise that a Lord paid for his marque out of his own pocket? The penny dropped as the smirk faltered on his face. *Idiot, why do think you've escaped attention from the law for so long?*

'He doesn't need to know about anything—you can always flee to France if he does. I hear they pay well.'

'What exactly do you need?'

'One day, some tools and a group of men strong enough to handle that thing and roll it back to shore.'

'Would it be worth it? Is a rusty statue that everyone's forgotten about that important?'

She prodded him with a finger and drew closer. Her mind now swayed between thoughts.

'It's a statue taller than a man; solid. Even if was just leaf it'd fetch a fair price. It must be bound by rope and dragged, but this old ship, with that crane, could take it up. Get everyone behind it and you can retire John. You can have everything you've dreamt of, and your crew can drink themselves to death in Lamb's Wharf.'

He considered her. 'Are you lying?'

'Ah! See for yourself tomorrow.'

He stumbled, placing one hand onto the table to steady himself. He wiped the other hand on his formal shirt and raised his glass of merlot. Sarah stood. It was a toast, and he knocked his glass with hers.

'To gold and greed,' John said, as he drained his glass.

'To gold and greed.'

John shook his head at her. He raised his eyebrows and folded his arms. 'Good evening Lady.'

Sarah stepped outside into the night and felt eyes upon her. Alex and Cyrus had expectant faces and mischief in their manner. She placed her hands on her hips and swayed from the wine.

'Well Lady? Get what you were after?' Alex said.

'He's agreed to lots of things. Tomorrow we'll be back on that island.'

'To what end?' asked Cyrus.

'There's a statue down there,' she said. The two men looked at her, sceptical.

'Have some faith, it's valuable. Where do you think the rumours of gold came from? If anything, they'll smelt it and everyone gets paid.'

As Cyrus thanked her, their conversation was cut short by a sea-song. It echoed across the bay with fiddle, drum and concertina. Three sailors stood, and took turns to shout the lyrics.

'She had hair the colour of the sky, stole every man's eye and made them sigh.'

'Drown those sorrows and drink your cup dry,' sang the rest of the crew.

'Tested your faith and gave you the wink, calm to waspy, in a blink.'

'Drown those sorrows and drink your cup dry.'

'Raised ev'ry mans' blood, made them curse as much as they could.'

'Drown those sorrows and drink your cup dry.'

'Fair blessed is he who lays wit' her, he's gone forever, one less to slur.'

'Drown those sorrows and drink for that man.'

'Frightful waves as heave her breast, careful your step or it'll be your rest.'

'Oh, oh, oh, fill those cups up!'

The crew cheered and cracked open another cask. It was a wake, of sorts. Several tables had been set with lanterns and dry foodstuffs giving the deck a welcome feel, a coffin lay in the middle to represent the Westlander killed on her sloop. Sarah covered herself with her arms as best as she could, she felt awkward amongst these men. Before the contract and terms were signed, there was a strict policy of her own cabin to herself, and none approached her unless it was business. The privateers in turn did not venture near her, not because she was a woman, but because of the rumours she was a witch. As per the rumours would say, she could stop a man's heart or drive him to madness. Here and now, it was becoming too familiar for her, too friendly.

Cyrus gave in to his hunger and started to eat with plenty of watered rum and wine to wash it down.

Sarah paced until she heard footsteps behind her. John stood with his door open, his shirt with spilled red wine on it and a leer in his eyes.

'Quite the performance my boys can do.'

'They're talented. Do they take requests?'

John chuckled and coughed before he raised his voice. 'Lads,' there was fresh laughter, 'the Lady would like to sing you a song, what do you say to that?'

They gave another cheer and Sarah scrunched her face in embarrassment. Before she could retort, John had stumbled back into his cabin. There was a click as the door locked shut. She swore and faced her audience with a half–smile.

'I don't know any rough songs you boys might enjoy–'

'Sing us to sleep with a lovely lullaby then,' heckled one of them. They all laughed in her direction.

'All right, something different, something for the soft boy over there.' She knew that nickname would stick.

Sarah cleared her throat and began to sing. She sang a tale taught to her long ago by her mother, a tale of a witch and a thief in love. The witch gave birth, lost her daughters and found them again, resurrected in sunlight. It was a plain song, but a joy to sing. Sarah finished and looked straight ahead. To her surprise there was no sound from the crew, they sat, still enchanted, still enthralled. She gave them a sly smile, walked back down to her cabin, climbed into her hammock, and fell into a dreamless sleep.

By first light, after breakfast, all saw the bloody blue bruises of the horizon lighten. Sarah took stock of the sea, and imagined the ship rested on sapphire, unrolled like a sheet and smoothed into place during the night by some celestial giant. The group of men sent to ransack the temple were ready to come back. She felt the carrack with quarter-sail lurch towards the bay again.

A hand thrust itself into the air with a red handkerchief alerted the Tail that it was ashore. Sarah took a brass spyglass from her jacket and held it up. Alex and Cyrus led the group back to the valley. She swivelled on the spot and spied the larger boat that was ready to take the weight of the statue. 'Fancy a look?' she asked John.

John grasped the scope and turned it to the group and back to each boat, satisfied he collapsed it and handed it back.

'Now we wait.'

Sarah tensed her legs as *The Tail* weighed anchor. Later in the day she likened she could see the statue from the aft; but it was just fantasy that played on her mind. She lurched and felt her throat spasm; she threw up the fish from last night's dinner over the gunwale. *Then it was a sickness I've caught. The quicker back home the better.*

She motioned one hand to the crew on the beach to ready themselves for the statue. They piled sand and logs to form a ramp into boat that waited. Along the crest of a dune, she could see the heaviest set sailors at the back, the strong wiry types at the front. They tugged as the ropes strained and squeezed themselves around the statue. The wooden crane next to her took the weight as the statue was secured. The deck of the carrack groaned as the statue was clear of its bondage. The rest of the crew along with Alex and Cyrus climbed aboard to help move it onto sheets of tarp. It landed with a singular thump and settled. When the toil was over, the crew studied and poked at the statue; few had seen gold, even fewer had seen a statue made of gold. John drew a knife and scored the statue across its arm, it gleamed underneath.

'I had doubts Lady–but there it is. My God. It'll bring fortune to many of us I'm sure. You'll have a share of it, perhaps a couple of ingots for your own.'

Sarah kept a healthy distance throughout the affair. Now seeing it proper, and ripped out of context, the statue was eerie. No sense of history surrounded it, as though it occupied a space all to itself, defying time and scrutiny. Now in the sun, she could see it was a figure of a proud warrior: a round shield in one arm, and spear in the other; his arms in salute to the heavens.

'I'll take none thank you. Consider my share as a bonus,' said Sarah, her cheek twitching.

For the travel back to London Sarah took a chance to recover. She warmed to the crew, shared food and drink, taught them to sing, and none heckled her again. Boson Perry took her likeness onto paper and carved a figurehead with a trunk felled from the island. She admired it as it grew in shape and form. Her nights were lonely and the days filled with chores and sun. Travel by sea was a novelty that soon wore thin. It was replaced with melancholy that stuck in her mind from breakfast to supper. She craved home and country, to be in a cooler climate, with familiar food and pace of life. She made efforts with John to join him for dinner at night, and kept to herself during the day. Without animosity between them, they discussed his plans for the gold and future business. The last day of voyage was unremarkable as they ventured into the waters of London. Frost set course for Sea Breach, a small fishing village that teetered on cliffs. There they departed onto dry land and spent a week to smelt the statue and divided the gold with a trusted smithy.

The crew each had three ingots of gold stamped with their names, each the size of a tinderbox. Sarah advised the crew to invest or hide them. The majority of the crew left immediately towards Lamb's Wharf to gamble and cavort. Others that remained looked towards their families and their future. After farewells, Sarah, Alex and Cyrus were the only three left. Sarah (as promised) hired both men. In return, she expected them to guard her estate and body. They settled at a dreary inn, and sequestered fresh horses for the next day. They were old mares, but speed was not important; they had no urgent schedule. They rode into Wood Farm one morning and passed through the glassy countryside. Frayed trees littered the road towards London, burnt outhouses smoked the skies. Gibbets swung in the chill wind filled with the remains of Westmen. Sarah gagged as she knotted a cloth square around her nose and mouth. As she looked at Cyrus and Alex, they both stared at her and breathed the air in deep; the smell was familiar to them.

'Nothing worse than the silence,' mused Cyrus.

'I'm not sure if the silence or the din when it starts is worse,' said Alex.

'I hope to never have to suffer the latter,' replied Sarah.

They hugged their clothes and pulled hoods tight as they rode in silence. The deeper they travelled inland the colder it seemed to become. Poor–folk and homeless gathered in small cliques. They stood close to fire–pits dug in the hard ground for warmth. Shacks and brittle huts had sprung up around outposts. Mercers had moved in to take advantage, and sold food and whatever fuel needed. Sarah realised the fighting had stopped here on these grasslands. The Westlanders had gone no further to threaten London. Her heart lightened to see alabaster domes shining ahead on the horizon. The city had not broken; her walls left unsullied. Ships with dull blue and square sails busied up and down narrow inlets and rounded the bay on their right. Barges

with spotted livery came to and from inland waterways.

Galleons, cogs, galleys and carracks dotted the

Darkwater, displaying a spectrum of pennants. Between two

sloops she spied *The Lion's Tail*; it was at rest, with tired sails and

scuffed hull. Sarah wondered if John had squandered his share,

or had done the sensible thing and bought fresh men. She had

never imagined a seaman to be so far from the cliché. The group

paused to see the shanty district. A hobbled collection of pubs and

brothels, set upon a rickety pier that made a crescent as it

followed the bay. Lord Turner was there. She just *knew* he was;

she just knew he expected her as soon as he saw The *Tail* dock.

They rode down small earthworks until they reached a gate for

inspection. Sarah's papers passed them without question and they

surrendered their horses to a knacker. They climbed down

steps until they reached the lowest tier where ferries made

business. The noise and rush of motion was intoxicating, she

finally felt as though she had come home.

Sarah walked towards Boxwood's customs house. It stood, as a trophy on a plinth, dead centre of it all. It was a utilitarian block of white marble and stone, with guards at every entrance. Foreign–folk would stand to gawp; locals would tip their hats to the marines on duty. Its many floors stretched far upwards. She passed with Alex and Cyrus until inside the lobby. Georgian architecture clashed with fine trim. The ensorcelled ceiling, marble busts that filled niches in the walls; London's cryptic coat–of–arms imbued into the floor visible to all who stepped inside. Sarah looked up too fast and felt dizzy at the enormous stair that wormed itself all the way up to the top flight. She looked back down at the pattern on the floor. Two rampant dragons on a fetch of silver with a gold shield that hovered above the words: DOMINE DIRIGE NOS. A congregation formed at the far end of the reception.

The steward of the house and administrators gathered around a tall man dressed in fine sable. Sarah stomped forwards, her heels clicking on the floor and swept her riding cloak up to distract. She coughed, enough for the clerks hidden behind their desks to take notice.

'Lord above, my Lady Saville!'

Lord Turner strode towards her and took her hand with a kiss. Sarah could feel herself heat at the attention and took note of any changes to Turner.

'You haven't changed my Lord. I expected a pretty creature to be hanging off your arm as you toured around the city.'

'My Lady Saville—you have more substance and grace about you than any other woman can offer. Besides I would miss your sharp mind.'

He took her with a serious look, and then laughed. He waved at the officials behind him to move on and invited her to follow alone. Sarah granted Alex and Cyrus the afternoon off—to rendezvous at her estate for the evening. Giddy, she ran after the lord through the busyness. She chased him back to his pristine office where they settled in chairs and looked out towards the docks.

'A drink? You must be exhausted,' he asked.

'Please.'

He poured two half-glasses of lemon liquor corked in a spiral glass. They both drank in one short gulp. The bite of the alcohol was overpowered by a zip of lemon; Sarah couldn't decide whether it was pleasant or a gimmick. She bent her elbows on the hard wood desk and stared at Turner. She waited for him to ask the first question.

'So, here you are,' he began, with a delicate smile. 'My people tell me there's a gang of pirates out there with gold ingots the size of a man's thumb. Frost's pirates, gladly spending it here, and I gather, spending it on more exotic pleasures in Lamb's Wharf.'

'Gold,' Sarah started. 'A gold statue just waiting out there—can you imagine it? It was pure fantasy to find it again. In fact, I'm uncertain the past week has not been some strange dream. And, and' Sarah gestured more than she would have liked, 'that flower was real. I hadn't imagined it. I was shaking with joy—I was utterly jubilant Percy.

Percy poured another set of liqueurs. 'From the start–if you please.'

It was a memory that started from Sarah's own study one summer's morning. Her conception of an expedition to reality took several months' worth of research. From what she bequeathed with her father's Will; she began to convert the Saville estate into a museum of antiquities. Any curiosities or artefacts at markets she snapped up and began a small enterprise. She repeated what Turner already knew; it took one month to ready supplies, crew, and ship. A further month spent on permissions, legal matters and writs of passage. They had formed an informal relationship from regular meetings. Lord Percy Turner enjoyed her passionate arguments for the preservation of English heritage. She admired his ambition and pursuit to place London as the centre of the world. She explained the first leg of the voyage. Smooth through the waters around London and into The Channel's current. From there it was west to the Cape of Strangers and Port's Mouth. Miles they had travelled until *The Tail* reached an island in the mist. Several pages in her mother's diary were devoted to sketches of its silhouette. Further still were dedicated to fauna and flora.

'And the flower, the peony, what is it?' he said, before she could continue.

'Something unique Percy, it was strong enough to knock me unconscious.'

'Knocked you out? Was it poisonous?'

'It survived a long time alone, untended. It seemed innocuous. I was probably taking an ill turn from the ship's food.'

He sat in silence. With a motion he shuffled towards the balcony windows and opened a small hatch that refreshed the air. He looked across the bay with an expression of worry–to Sarah she recognised it as one of concentration. Lord Turner took pride in his machinations. She sat quiet. Her mind drifted between when she returned to her home and the more recent memories on board *The Tail*.

'The plant does not interest me, but the gold changes things.' He walked towards the office doors and bolted them shut. 'How many know of the island?'

'John Frost, he's loyal to you, and the crew of thirty–odd.'

'And the statue was completely smelted? Nothing remained?'

'No, none–everyone was present at the smithy.'

'And the smith?'

'He wasn't present–we followed his instructions and rented his workshop.'

'There's no point in asking anymore questions, the news will have reached France by now.'

'I've been as discreet as possible Percy.'

He sighed. 'You're not to blame.' Percy rubbed his chin in thought. 'Did you hire help Sarah? From Greenmarket?'

Sarah smoothed her fringe and sat back, her legs almost crossing.

'I did, but did not trust them fully. The gold was to pay the ship and crew. Why do you ask?'

Percy's face dropped. If it was only in a second that his mood soured, it was only in a second that he recovered and gave a practiced smile. His fists were balled tight. Sarah cocked her head, and then rose from her seat to comfort him. Percy drank a measure of the liquor and continued.

'My next plan is to get there with as many men as possible as quickly as possible, ahead of any other competition, and scour that damn island clean.' He rolled out a map across the desk.

'A risk,'

'Then, God willing, I'll find some more gold, or similar.'

'To what end?' she teased.

He smiled at her, wrapped his arms across her back, and brought her in close. 'Enough to make this city whole again.'

Sarah took her leave from Percy's office. She hadn't been with a man in months, and it showed. She bit her lip and smoothed her riding dress as she strolled back through the embassy and out onto the docks. She breathed the air: salt, fish, guano, sweat, smoke from hot tar–to her, at this moment, it was all the same, it was London, it was home. She waved down a palanquin and it took off through the slipshod streets and through the black–stone courtyards. She would have walked, but her body was too worn to even broach of it. Just as Sarah became used to the motion of the box as it swayed in tandem, it came to a stop and settled outside a familiar gate.

'Lady Saville welcome home.'

'Hello Alex.'

The young flagman of the palanquin accepted a clutch of coins; he took her hand and led her off the box. Autumn leaves around them flashed iron and topaz; dogged spools of ivy smothered the path that led to the Saville estate. The house had always been modest and sparse in its time; Sarah saw no reason to change a traditional look. Although she had sacrificed some furniture to cover the expedition, the place had had kept its

charm; the guest rooms were famous in London for their friezes.

Its conversion into a museum was taking longer than expected for

the contractors, but there no mishaps, nothing out of

budget. Things were still on schedule. Cyrus was already inside

the hall; a cloth in one hand to wipe away the dust of one week.

'Good God,' she said.

'You need to hire some housekeepers Lady; I'm amazed

it wasn't burgled.'

'Well I won't bother with asking a thief how he managed

to get past the lock.'

Alex rolled himself around the doorway. 'We used to

clean the tower as initiates; this will be simple compared to that,'

Alex broached.

'If we all chipped in tomorrow it will be done sooner.

Did you have trouble getting here?'

'None, we walked,' said Cyrus.

'Has anyone been? Any letters left for me?'

'There wasn't,' answered Alex.

'Fine. Your rooms are just ahead of this corridor on the left. We will need food for the pantry and an inspection of the grounds. Rooms need to be aired also, but that can wait until tomorrow. There's a gun in the dining room, not loaded. See yourselves to bed. Good night gentlemen.'

The two men nodded at her; they both looked as exhausted as she felt, relieved to be set free. Sarah marched down a thin corridor which double–backed onto itself. To the right lay her private study and bedroom, on the far end of the corridor, which dominated the single space in the middle, was the library. Upstairs was left unused. She entered her bedroom; socketed and lit candles, perfumed her mattress and pillows for the night and settled into a musty nightgown. Her heart fluttered whenever Alex's or Cyrus's footsteps stomped past her door. She was not used to the company. Locked under an imagined anxiety, deep inside a part of her soul, was a simple truth that she once again enjoyed having guests. Any further isolation from society and she feared she would have gone mad. It took time when the tears started to fall, and when they did, she was ashamed of each one.

The evening dragged as Sarah read at her desk to keep her mind occupied. The candles extinguished in her room, except one. Revels started in the city as soon as the sun set and the moon waxed. Homes and closed their doors as dockworkers and sailors combed the streets in a search for booze and women. Shrieks, screams and ill-conceived shanties echoed throughout the bay an hour after. Sarah shut her window when she heard the first noise; she didn't care anymore for it. In her youth she would accept invites from friends to gather and be merry. Regular turned into occasional and occasional became rare. The accounts ledger in front of her had gathered an unprecedented volume of dust with her absence. She blew hard and it spiralled into the air, which made her cough and clutch her stomach. Sarah cast her pen onto the desk; she hated this dread that nagged her and kept her awake. After blowing out the last candle and wrapping a shawl around herself, she found the floor was warmer on her bare feet than she thought it would be.

Heart-burn, change of mood, phantom pains, and my river was late coming.

The library's chill nipped at Sarah's bare skin. She pulled on the strings in her hand and her skin made a spark spiral into the air which grew into a bubble of fire. It hovered above the wicks in a candelabrum and lit them. Sarah hefted a thick tome off a top shelf; she handled it roughly and brought it up to the light.

'Babe... See child... See conception... The blood is late coming. See gestation. Phantom pains... Cravings... Changes in appearance... Bloated belly... Birth–' she stopped herself on the last word of the entry.

The book was old and well-thumbed. It was a notebook her father had rescued from the aftermath of a house fire, back when he had the spirit to do so. It belonged to a surgeon who excelled in research. She read his notes with a fierce concentration. Repeating words in her mind until satisfied of their meaning and connotation. The symptoms fitted. But she had not shared her bed; she had not shared anything at all to her knowledge. She expected fear. It didn't feel like fear when it came, just more questions juxtaposed on top of each other.

Her plans with Percy would have to wait.

☆

When winter arrived in England, it arrived obtuse and malevolent, its grip absolute. Sarah asked the men to stop maintenance. The conditions were abominable, even for those used to it. Alex and Cyrus had settled into their respective rooms. They both promised to at least tackle the drifts along the entrance and keep her company in the bleak evenings with logs for the fire. Her belly had swollen, not to her surprise; it bulged out; a bump she couldn't hide even in heavy clothes. She slept more than usual and became worried that when the gossip would seep out and reach Percy's ears, he would disown her; perhaps not going as far to slander the Saville name, but never to be in contact with her again, and an end to a relationship that promised much. To be pregnant without the father known, nor present; to be with child without knowing why or how; she sobbed at the thought there was nobody who could intervene and whisk her away under pretence. No gallant gentleman to the rescue. Sarah dried her eyes and stumbled upstairs for rest. Before she had managed to climb up the grand stair, there were several sharp knocks at the trade door. It was down a dark passage next to the kitchen's pantry. She pinched up her layers and staggered to the kitchen, taking her time. Anyone in this weather could not be in rush? She wrenched the heavy door open with both arms, careful not to let it hit her. The bright sky stung her eyes; soft piles of slush slumped and deposited over her silk slippers. Percy sat, saddled on a cold blood, a look on his face that he had expected nobody to answer his knock. He removed his hat and readjusted his cloak. Sarah stood there transfixed. He had managed to get here, just to see her. She shivered. Her brow creased when she realised his gaze was fixed on her belly and not her.

'No Percy, please let me explain—don't leave!'

He turned with a sneer and rode away. His shape smudged by a flurry until he disappeared into the white. She fell hard onto the rough tiles below and let out a howl that tore out of her throat as a half–laugh. Sarah cradled her belly tight while a steady stream of snow gathered around her. She scrunched her dress up to soak the tears that fell and slammed the trade door. She walked towards the dining room and lit candles with a long taper. She slumped onto a chair next to the mahogany table, head lolling. Her arms spread out and she retracted them. The lines and cuts, the pocks and marks that ran down the table, each told a story, each marked an occasion. Some familiarity would go a long way, it shored up the wound in her–if only for a brief moment.

She heard Alex and Cyrus enter the dining room before she woke. They were dirty and sweaty; they had done a hard day's chore and now sought cheer and reprieve. She stood and wiped the sleep from her eyes and the film left by her tears. Sarah ran fingers through her cold hair and smoothed it as best as possible given her mood. The two men paused at the threshold of the room, unsure if they needed permission. They both wore childish expressions with scruffy beards obscuring their half–smiles. Sarah rolled her eyes and gave them a curt wave to proceed. She noticed, with horror, their boots trampled muck into an antique rug.

'Stop! Boots!' she signalled at them with a furious stare.

Cyrus mouthed pardon, while Alex blushed. They both helped each other remove their boots. With a cork in his mouth and a brown bottle of almost frozen ale in his hand, Alex sat and poured into three cups. Cyrus took one of the cups with his little finger extended, and drank without making a slurp. He had the etiquette perfected and had shown off what she had taught him at the local inn. Sarah studied them both with her head in her arms. The only visible parts were her two oval eyes and a forehead fixed in calm irritation.

'How you feeling my Lady?' said Alex.

He drank straight from the bottle and pushed a cup over to her side. She shook her head, and pointed to the bottle. Alex gave it to her. She snatched it out of his hand and drank the rest of the ale in three gulps. She sat it back down onto the table with a burp.

'We saw him ride past us. The way he bolted—villainous,' said Cyrus.

'It's over,' she said in a broken voice with none of her usual inflection. 'No more expeditions. No more connections. No more soirées. No more future.'

'You still have us,' Alex ventured. His smile reversed as she scowled at him.

Sarah again traced the table with its bumps and notches. Cyrus started the fireplace. Every other evening, they would share anecdotes gathered from their years. Other nights they would sit, watch the flames and enjoy a small feast gleaned from the pantry.

'Maybe something different tonight Lady?' said Alex.

Alex removed a sitar from a beaten sack that hung around his neck, and strummed. It responded with a bright note.

'Where did you get that?' she asked.

'Carpenter in Huntersford. It still smells of smoke from that workshop. Cyrus bought it for me.'

He started to play a simple song and it rose in complexity. It turned from sadness to joy between indefatigable hands. Sarah noted he was happy. She hadn't seen joy written on his face before. To give into a simple pleasure, one that divided creativity and intuition. He stopped half-way through a song.

'Sorry, I'm losing myself.'

'Lose away—it was marvellous.'

Alex grinned with his cracked teeth; a cap shone from the back of his mouth

'Thank you. I'm glad there's someone here who appreciates my music.'

'Have you got any hidden talents Cyrus?'

'Locks and purses,' he smiled.

'Ones we didn't already know about,' she gave him a wry look.

Cyrus retreated and brought back a script of paper with scrawls and scribbles. She took it with all the delicacy of a head teacher who found a note passed between rowdy pupils. It was a play judging from the front page. She read it over, planting herself onto a soft stool by the fire and bent over to gather as much light as possible. It was a satire on the warmongers between countries during a time of unrest and strife. Most of the history had faded into obscurity and legend. Cyrus had added political issues told from the bold array of characters; some, the vulgarities of real people. She laughed and frowned as she skimmed the writing.

'This is brave Cyrus.'

'It's a small passion Lady,' he beamed. 'The blurred boundaries between the elite and the soldiers who defend their way of life.'

'And here I thought I had two wine-sacks to keep me company this sorry evening. What about acting tonight?'

The two men looked at each other with impassive eyes.

'What are you saying Lady? *Act* Cyrus's play?'

'Come—let's raise the impoverished working class above all.'

They shuffled together with looks of disdain.

'Aren't you one of them?'

She winked at Cyrus and wrapped a shawl around her neck with a flourish.

'Since that brute of a man has left me with my love smashed to pieces, my position amongst the elite has finished.'

'And what are you now?' said Cyrus as Sarah clambered onto a footstool and struck a pose.

'A job I was born to do–to be an actor,' she laughed.

They read the lines of the play deliberate and in turn, while Sarah paced between the men and corrected their pronunciation. Alex struggled to read but she pushed him all the same. They stirred imaginations as the room became a mezzanine filled with amoral warriors and then a castle with a king admonished over a pyrrhic victory. Shawls and coats were armour of old, and broomsticks turned into swords. At the end of it they had passed another evening in winter, happy in company. As the fire died, they conceded to retire for the day.

☆

Inside her private journal Sarah made a log of her pregnancy. She filled it with her ailments and diet. Every ache and pain, every emotion she could single out from the maelstrom inside her. She woke one misty morning to slap her swollen belly in front of her bedroom mirror that she kept clean for this purpose. She wondered whether she should use a spell to peek inside and determine both sex and health of the unborn. She felt two heartbeats within when she tugged on the strings, but didn't probe further, satisfied they were well. She found comfort in the knowledge there would be two heiresses (or heirs) on the way. Other mornings she could wake in a filthy, corruptible mood: one that either stole whole days in bed or she would eat unceasing, while snapping at Alex and Cyrus.

At the start of summer, in the new year, Sarah neared the end of her term. After her water broke under thin blankets, a midwife and doctor doted over her. Sarah suffered the twists of pain during birth: the hot snaps of agony that felt like she was being torn in two. After seven hours of torment, she gave birth under a relentless sky: a heat wave London had not experienced for a generation. The sun boiled away stamina; it created a fugue that taxed everyday motions. The first child came through stubborn. She screamed until rubbed down with soft cotton and nestled in brushed fur. The second, also a girl, came quickly, during a storm that erupted over the bay. It sent warm rain and shattered the peace with peals of thunder. This babe arrived silent, only two curious eyes that absorbed every detail. When her daughters were finally together, one on each arm, the serenity was overwhelming. She held them to her covered breast and nuzzled them before the nervous staff present. The staff, in turn, gave their blessings, and left them alone to bond. She slept sound that night with her two summer children. She dreamt of portents and myths. Twisted monsters: half-men and half-ash; people with cracked smiles and fear in their eyes; a cross of fire; a tower bleached by the sun. She saw a coast dominated by a single oak, on its branches fluttered bright coloured pennants; *her* oak, *her* pennants. If she couldn't sleep in the stifling room at night, Sarah would sing to them: songs which her mother had taught her, old songs of witches, thieves, and cunning-women.

Her new-born grew to become babies proper: time moving along swifter than she expected. A year flew past in the old house; life ever expanding from itself; it changed everything she saw and knew, in ways and forms she could not anticipate. Sarah couldn't abide to grow old, but became smitten by her daughters and paid age no more heed. If she grew older on the outside, she would endeavour to become younger on the inside. Her wisdom grew in bounds, and with advice from contacts she still had left, learned all that a mother could be. Before, in a solitary life, she had never experienced a full range of emotions on her own, but now, she embraced every twinge of guilt, every protective sensation, every bit of joy her beautiful daughters brought her. Soon, as with all mothers, Sarah conceded to herself that she was their only future, their only way into the world: teacher, guardian, and anchor. It was a hard truth that drove her to seek betterment, material and otherwise.

She needed a new start, a new home, and a father.

The Priestess

– The Frost Household –

W hen her father said he was expecting guests, Gold stayed to

greet them and observed several things she did not like about

Lady Sarah Saville. She was a short woman with an expressive

face and coquettish eyes who openly flirted with her father. Her

voice was reedy and demanding, her actions premeditated. After

introductions, Gold heard two cries in the hallway. Two thuggish

men, who, with flushed faces, surrendered two babies to her

without question. She had not cared for girls as young as these, but felt motherly all the same, and swaddled them in fresh linen. They cooed in return as she fed them from a bottle and tickled their bellies. Both babies rested in her arms content and full, as the Lady and her two men settled in her father's study to talk of boring things as adults are wont to do.

'Lady Sarah Saville. Now what brings you back here?' asked John Frost, her father.

'I need passage south, back to my homeland.'

John considered her in his own slow manner.

'Sounds like you've given up on London. What do you think Gold, should we take the *Tail* up the Storm Coast?'

Gold fawned over the children and nodded in agreement. She'd always wanted to travel far south, her curiosity piqued.

'You're a natural with them my dear, I might call on your services more often,' said Sarah. Her father smiled and ruffled Gold's lax hair, which irritated her to no end. She put distance away from the adults and scowled behind her fringe.

'Gold's mother was a firecracker. She has her temper and brains–and my black hair and lazy peepers.' Gold put on a thin smile. She imagined her petulant act wouldn't pass mustard with her father any longer. She broke the silence in the conversation.

'Are they adopted Miss Saville?' Gold held up the bundled children in accusation.

Sarah looked Gold over. 'No–my daughters are mine. John, we need to discuss this properly, payment and schedule.'

'Goldie, leave us please,' her father only adopted this tone for business he didn't want her to hear.

She handed back the babies to the rough men, who began to cry immediately, and with a venomous flick of her hair made her way up to her room. The Frost household was a stone–hewn farm turned into a home by her father's father. The walls were thick in stucco; stuffy during the summer and snug during the winter, where an archaic stone fire pit dominated most of the open space that made up their first floor. Gold paced about her room strewn with trinkets and drawings. It was an organised mess that she had proudly cultivated over the past year, and her interest in the exotic and curious had superseded her

maturity. She slammed her door shut, to make a point, and

removed the heavy box she'd kept underneath her bunk. It was a

foot in length, only an inch deep. Scrawled on its pewter surface

were fantastic creatures: hippocamps, octopods, mermaids. An

orb filled with waves dominated the centre of the motif. Inside the

orb was a circle, or a shield, with a cross affixed at the bottom.

Her father, although a worldly sailor, never shared her belief of

myths and monsters. His mind was on his ship, business, and her

upbringing. Gold considered herself blessed to have such a

pragmatic father.

The content of the box had cost her father a tidy sum and

was her present at twelve years old. She smoothed her fingers

over the dents and decorations on the surface and scratched at the

patina that had built on the base plate. Inside, snug in velvet, was

an opaque jewel that looked as though emerald and quartz had

melted together in fire. It smoked in her hands and glittered and

swung heavy when suspended from its chain. Sunbeams caught

the gem and spread themselves across her walls in dots and lines.

Gold laughed as she threw open her window sash and held it up to her eye. She fancied herself able to see the world through the sight of a fish, wobbled and mercurial. She sat on her bed, relaxed her mind and conjured a daydream of the deep sea and sailing ships: which, from the fictional narrative revolving in her mind, cumulated into sleep.

She woke when her father kissed her on her forehead. It was dim outside. Dawn had crept up behind solemn clouds. Heavy rain had pooled which had turned the land into a single splotch of black earth. Downstairs, breakfast was ready. She usually made it. In her father's eyes there was a twinkle that she hadn't seen in years.

'Come on sunshine, time for something to eat, big day ahead of us.'

Gold mumbled and twisted herself deeper into blanket she had brought with her; bare feet frigid and tapping on the stone floor of their small kitchen.

'You never make breakfast.' Gold said.

'I didn't mean to treat you like that yesterday–we did not have anything serious to talk about. I'm sorry.' Her father apologised.

Gold dug into her sausage and eggs.

'You mean that woman.'

'Lady. Lady Saville, yes—but I think she's a Lady no longer.'

'So, she did whore herself?'

Her father shot a dark look at her, a sign he was on the verge of anger. Gold said sorry and dropped her head. What food had landed in her stomach had started to improve her reluctant mood; she felt more ready for the day.

'Let's not forget, she was under my protection during the expedition. Nobody dared touch her either.'

'Why?'

'A witch my crew calls her. Getting her on board a vessel with God fearing men was incredibly difficult.'

Gold nodded disinterested as her father spoke once again of this woman and how wonderful she was. She pulled her blanket tight and stamped her feet. They needed a break from this life. Every day filled with the same chores to keep the old place in check. She felt that her desire for a voyage had built up in the monotony. Her last trip to London was a few years ago and it had stirred the spirit of adventure within her. Gold now sought out pewter trinkets with delicate filigree on them; black–wood animals popular amongst children; dirty maps and crinkled books filled with distant descriptions of tales from afar. The most dramatic change was the wanderlust in her legs, they would not keep still. Some mornings she said goodbye to her father with a skip out of the front door and would run down to the market on her own; most of the merchants and stall–sellers had given her the moniker *That Black Hair Girl*. They would also give a smatter of compliments on how tall she was for her age and how she could turn a young boy's head with a twist of her hips.

Perhaps her restlessness from exploring grew from the pair of legs she had? She didn't know, nor did she particularly care. She observed her father as he wiped the grease from his lips and boarded the windows of the house. Their valuables locked away into a water-tight chest.

Several sailors entered their home after the meal. They boasted on their raucous achievements from the previous night. She was familiar with them all by name and they scuffed her head in the same fashion as her father did. Gold stowed her most valuable possessions, and helped secure them onto a carriage waiting outside. She sat on top of the tarp and ropes while the old home faded from her view. Each bump and jolt in the road shrank the house until it was gone. Her father trotted beside them on a mare while the rest of his men walked. They were happy to be outside, happier still to finally be back at sea where they could be at peace with the world; and the world could leave them in peace.

The *Tail* was almost the same before she had left for Lady Saville's expedition. The crane had gone, as had some of the

rougher edges along her prow. Fresh paint adorned the
railings. New cloth for the lateen sails, and the once tattered flags
cleaned. She was a grand old lady, a stubborn and doughty ship
that had seen many ports, and taken on many men. The innuendo
had not escaped Gold, and was a test for new crew, to see if they
had a sense of humour about them. Gold stood with John as they
admired the effort her crew had put back into her. Many had not
returned from having spent their small bars of gold. The crew
that had returned wore new clean clothes cut of modern
fashion. Those with gaps in their teeth had gold caps, and their
grins were the largest. On the busy dock Gold spied Sarah and
her men as they waited for permission to board. She catcalled at
Sarah who gave a curt wave back. The infirmary accommodated
the children, with extra care taken to make sure the room was as
warm and clean as could be. Parcels, missives and wishes from
citizens sat next to the sundries in the hold. Passengers and those
who sought asylum from London's strife took shelter in the bilge.
The journey wasn't long, within two days they would be on the

Storm Coast proper. Danger came from the lawless passage that fed into The Channel.

'We have to pass by New Port,' he said in a whisper, while they both mulled over the charts.

'Pirates?' said Gold.

'Rebels. Men not controlled by the Crown. That's what Westminster calls them. They have a small fleet in that coast. Check with the Quartermaster, would you?'

'Why?'

'I want you to make sure our cannons are ready; our swords are sharp and the besses loaded.'

Gold's eyes widened. She knew her father was making her excited on purpose, but she played along all the same. She sat up with a mock salute.

'Aye captain.'

He laughed and returned the gesture.

'Check on our Lady while you're below deck. Don't want her to feel left out.'

Gold looked at him sly.

'Should I tell her to meet you in your quarters Captain?'

She had never seen her father blush before. He drained his wine and looked at her. Gold left embarrassed. She hadn't meant to say it. *Was her father that affected by that woman?* She shuddered.

Gunners below deck had stowed the cannons and were now enjoying the interlude. Musket men checked their weapons and armour with prudence. Gold noted most of them had a long stare, a distance that remained on their faces. Some had little of their face left. Cavernous scars and deep wounds plagued the few that had seen the most violent conflicts. She strode towards Sarah's cabin as the ship picked up sail and lurched out of the bay. Incense burned in a small brass cup. It filled out the cabin in a cloying smoke, which stung Gold's eyes and made her rasp. Out of her bunk Sarah was sat next to an old tome either in study or in prayer, Gold couldn't decide. Two cots with a child in each were in a corner of the cabin. They swayed in their cotton hammocks; sound asleep.

'Makes good reading does it?' said Gold.

Lady Saville did not reply. She skimmed ahead in the book before she shut it.

'Spells can be copied onto paper. I've brought my favourite with me.'

Gold trembled, but still puffed her chest out. 'Why did you leave London? It must have been hard on you. All that gossip, all those rumours.'

The Lady stood with her book in hand and removed the cup of incense. She sat back down on her stool and moved another out in front of her. She patted the empty stool, motioned for Gold to sit opposite. Gold chewed her bottom lip and considered to walk away. She could sense it was a trap. Perhaps she was to be upbraided for speaking to a Lady without proper respect. Gold sat still for a few tense seconds.

'Hold out your hand child,' Sarah commanded.

Gold did as she was told—and placed her hand out in front of her palm upwards. Lady Saville dragged a finger across a horizontal crease in Gold's palm. She traced its path with her fingernail.

'That one is the life-line; the Cauldron. Yours is quite long and thick.' She ran her finger across a vertical line that ended on Gold's wrist. 'That's the Mount of the Sun—your fortune. Looks quite shallow, but you've got a long life line judging here. I'm sure it will have time to thicken and lengthen.'

'You're from the Cape of Strangers, aren't you? It's in your voice,' Sarah stared at Gold. 'M' Lady.'

'Call me Sarah. The Cape is where I was born, and where my parents made their fortune in land, before leaving for London. My legacy gave me freedom to travel, and opportunity gave me my title. I bought land and leased it like my parents before me. I was a businesswoman a long time before moving onto history.'

'What do you learn from history?'

'It is the study of the past. Your father told me you're curious for a girl for twelve years—what do you make of this?'

As the cabin rolled Sarah reached over and produced a book wrapped in a blue cloth with uneven pages. It smelled of smoke and caramel. Gold paused before she reached for it; the book's spine creaked open when she did so.

'You can read?'

'Yes–but not fast as my father can.'

Sarah smiled and waved a hand to the book; she bid Gold to read.

'M–anna... easily dissolv–es in water, and a drop of the sol–ution is a very pretty object.'

Gold smiled as she read the words. She knew most of them, but a few were notes in a joined script, with the words all wriggled. She tried to tilt the book upside down to see if the letters would invert themselves. Nothing happened. With a turn of the page she found vignettes of plants and signs, mesmerism, wands and runes. Her head was full of marvel.

'Can I keep it?'

'Of course, I gave it you as a gift. Let's both have a fresh start together as friends. And now that we're friends, there is one thing I need from you in return.'

Gold looked puzzled. 'What would that be?'

'Tell me what your father thinks of me?'

'He likes you.'

'Oh? That's good. Do you like me? I would like to get to know you better.'

Gold caught the disingenuous edge to her voice, like an actor who strained their lines. She rose, added a mock curtsy of her skirt, and left the conversation unfinished. With the book in hand Gold retreated to her bunk to absorb its contents in quiet. Sarah scolded herself; she shouldn't have been that false with the child. She gathered from the conversation that John liked her, and Gold was protective of her father in turn. She sighed and tended to her children as they slept.

The Tail ventured out of the Darkwater at a casual pace. Against a viridian sky, the midday clouds turned pink to cream, and to a rotten yellow. Serpentine waves threw themselves against

carrack as she lurched around the coast. The Second Mate with

his gang loosened the ropes and let all sails tack full. The weather

was behind them, and for once in a long time *The Tail* reached

full speed. She carved a path parallel through the bay of East

Stream and past a fleet of merchant and navy ships. Gold had left

her book behind and strained herself over the gunwale to look at

the famous city. Houses in East Stream were always green and

dark blue. She saw a quiver of straight stone towers rise from its

centre. A ship left the man–made harbour; seven bells rang out,

some sailors next to her cheered.

'What's to celebrate?' she asked.

A Darklander loomed over her with foul breath and

wiry beard. 'Got a new ship they have–see her?'

He pointed as the cruiser in question as it gained ahead.

All on board stopped their work to admire the vessel. It sat thin

in the water. The slim white prow sliced apart the waves with

ease. Whatever class of tonnage it was, it turned as a rowing boat

on a calm lake. It sprinted past them and both crews regarded each other. The crew of the *Tail* eyed the other ship with avarice. The proud East Stream sailors regarded the *Tail* with snobbish looks. Her father had left his quarters and waved to the other captain with a flag. The captain on the cruiser tipped his bicorn.

'Hell of a ship that,' her father jogged up to her. '*The Heart of East Stream*; one hell of a ship.' The wind and sun both dropped at once; the world covered in a dull film.

'Captain on deck! Back to work! Back at it! Rain is coming lads, get those barrels refilled!' The Quartermaster screamed. Cries of a rainstorm brewing just west of them rang out. Gold smiled. She welcomed rain.

A day into their journey and the crew relaxed into a steady rhythm. Veteran sailors each took time to enthral the newer crew with supernatural tales. The older the sailor the more outlandish the tale, the younger the sailor, the more shaken they were. Gold woke to see one morning Sarah had helped with scrubbing the deck. She hadn't gotten far with her bucket and holystone but did a thorough job which pleased the Boson to no end. Much to her chagrin Gold hadn't seen much of her father, who had spent most of his time tending to passengers, especially Sarah. She dropped the issue after saw her father's eyes sparkle as they did that morning before they set off. Sarah looked resplendent in a white dress with her hair wild. She would curl up to him at the helm as they surveyed the horizon. He was happy. It was the first he had been since Gold's mother had left them. That was everything Gold could have wished for him. He was out on the open waves with a new interest in his life and a smile on his face. She noticed that Sarah didn't have any ulterior motive. She was alone and wanted an experienced father to bring up her children. for either of them to fall in love was an added bonus to the relationship.

Gold's watch for the third day was in the nest with a weathered brass scope for company. The ship's sway was more noticeable high up on the main mast. Her legs braced themselves more frequent. The responsibility wasn't lost on her. The crew respected her serious attitude when it came to the more adult work. She memorised the seascape about her. An hour later she had surveyed her realm and half–sat, sipping on water from a skin. A shape put a stop to her breath. Just there, a black speck popped on the horizon. A dirty smudge she wished she could raise one sleeve and rub out like a blot of ink. She mumbled a warning but it caught short on the wind, not loud enough for the crew below. Frustrated, Gold screamed out.

'Sail!'

She leaned over the guard and looked at the response below. Men hurried around to the prow and gaped. Her father strode among them with his own looking-glass. He barked orders at the men on the rigs to slow; the five minutes passed as she guessed who the ship belonged to. As the vessel neared it struck colours: two black flags on the main mast, and one blue with white zigzags.

'Black flags!'

Her father donned his black bicorn along with the senior members of his crew. A sergeant and his men poured from below to stand attention on the arquebus. Two lines of riflemen in jackets gathered in rough formation on starboard and port. With a rumble, she heard the gunners below ready their cannons. A whistle blew. Gold knew it was time to take her place below deck. She scrambled across a rope ladder and shook as she made her way down. Her hands slipped twice on the rope before reaching the bottom. Her father walked over, and whispered instructions in her ear as he knelt. Gold heard her heart thump loud enough to almost drown out his words. When he had finished, she nodded and left after she kissed him on the cheek for luck. In the hold all the infirm had gathered along with the children and Sarah. Gold hugged her and told everyone present that pirates had struck their colours. Amongst the gasps and cries Sarah bid Alex and Cyrus to secure the jollyboat. Should it the ship fall, it would be the only safe venture for her. Gold noticed Sarah commit one of her paper spells to memory.

'Are you going to kill them?'

'Kill? No, I don't want to kill. Nobody should ever want to kill that readily child. It's a special spell—you'll see. Will you accompany me on the deck?' she asked.

Gold could hear the chaos from above as the senior sailors barked a string of panicked orders. The drums and shouts had stopped all at once—now they could only hear the clack of ropes against sails.

'Can we change course?' said Sarah.

They turned slow eyes on her. Several shook their heads; whether through ignorance or arrogance Gold could not guess.

'Surely we have the wind—we alter course? John—speak to me.'

'You've forgotten your place Lady,' he replied. 'Besides—look aft.'

Sarah turned with a snarl on her lips. Gold climbed with her as far aft as they could go. Two ships with the same black flags sat aft. They both waited; patient for the sky to clear and the sea to calm. Lines of worry spread along her face as Gold knew they could not outfight three ships in *The Tail* for long. Her first thoughts were of John and Sarah and her babies—her second of the crew and passengers. It was an odd sight when she saw Sarah twist her fingers; then she heard the words she had memorised for her spell. Plumes of mist raised out if the sea; they blotted the sun and encased the *Tail* in a cloud–blanket. In a gap over the water Gold could see three mute flashes of orange.

'Cannon fire!' roared John.

The few that responded fast enough dove onto the deck. Gold spun around to see a dark ball, too fast for her to track, fly past with a hollow whoop. As it broke a wave in two, it sent a shower of seawater across her face. A splinter the size of a fist struck Sarah across the temple; her legs buckled and she fell silent. Two more cannonballs smashed into the prow; the timbers shook from the impact. Below, the passengers had started to panic as the hull gasped, cracked, and gave in. Sailors with fear in their eyes began to shore up the gaps with anything at hand. They shouted and cursed over each other in a frenzy of limbs. Gold saw one of Sarah's men pick her up by one arm. He dragged to the jollyboat, ready and prepared to go. Her father stood over her, with Sarah's babies in her arms–and passed her children down to Gold. She shivered with adrenaline while Cyrus positioned himself at the oars. At once, he started to pull hard on the lines. It put vertical distance between them and her father's pained face.

'The Lady could come with us!' shouted Gold.

John bowed his head–grief suffocated him; his mouth too contorted to talk. The jollyboat dropped heavy into the water; the babies immediately started to cry.

'Silence them, or it's the end of us,' Cyrus growled as he rowed.

Gold rocked the babies while her heart hammered. She knew, as the boat moved away from the ship, she wouldn't see her father or Lady Saville again. Violent cracks of gunfire spoiled the silence. Two silhouettes emerged. A white cog with triangle sails swooped alongside the *Tail*. Its oarsmen ceased, ready to board with hooks. Another ship, a crimson galleon, waited near the cog, her cannonade aimed and ready. Gold looked at Cyrus. His face was wax. The blood had drained from his skin in exertion. The man swore as he heard the battle echo around them. Through the mist the men on the galleon fired on them. Some shot struck the boat, the holes smouldered as they punched the timber. Gold curled up into a ball and hid under tarpaulin as the assault continued. The two babies, still crying for comfort, pressed to her.

'Stay down Miss Frost—stay down you hear? You hear me? Don't peek over the edge or nothing—whatever happens to me, you keep rowing—you keep going you hear? Keep them safe. They're the only thing Sarah truly holds dear in this world—she loves them with all of her soul—you hear me girl?'

Gold could hear nothing more but spray and waves. She saw nothing more but fading light. She tugged the tarp over her and prayed to God to guide her and the little lives she kept close.

Gold's legs shuffled on their own accord. The bedding underneath was unfamiliar; the smell of the room was of cinnamon and rind, not home. She opened her eyes to see the moon scratch itself among strange stars. Thick eggshell paint covered the planks. Incense burned and lanterns decorated the ceiling with silhouettes. The floor was dirty with footprints. Gold stared at a boy in the room, who stared back. He was her age, perhaps older, his skin sore and sunburnt. His eyes were limned with kohl and copper stars stencilled on his cheeks. His wore a sheet of plain indigo which ended at his ankles.

'Are you well?' the boy spoke with a Stranger's accent.

Gold stared. Her legs now shook under the cotton covers.

'What's your name?'

'Gold.'

'A Golden Star lost in The Channel? If I was an augur–I'd pronounce you as an omen. So, are you a bad omen?'

Gold sat upright against the pillows stacked behind her.

'Neither?'

The boy raised his eyebrows in mock surprise and chuckled.

'Well then Gold–I'm Malachi. My Master is on the top deck observing. Please join us when you are ready.'

Malachi slinked away with the grace of a cat. Gold
sniffed the air: she was at sea. She drank it in—it was a heady
concoction that inspired her to wander. She shifted her legs and
felt sand spread out on the white-washed floor. A small stair led
to the upper deck, where the smell of roasted meat and wood fire
teased her stomach. She paused just before the railing. The
lanterns positioned on the ceiling looked Southern in style. If it
was true, she might be on board a merchant pink from the Cape
of Strangers. From her cabin the deck above was swathed in a
thick cloth canopy shaped into a tent of sorts. A cool evening
wind chilled Gold's arms and she folded them. Sailors and
mercers ate and drank together in small circles. One cooking
trough took up most of the mid-deck. It overflowed with fillets
of beef, vegetables and pork medallions. All, as she saw,
sticky with honey. Gold watched as a fat merchant lifted a single
medallion and swallowed in one motion. Malachi waved her over
to a pile of large silk cushions. As she walked towards him, she
noticed one group of men inhale deep from a crystal hookah.

There was a pause before each breathed out prismatic smoke, their heads bobbing as they looked at her.

'How do you like our party? Isn't it just decadent?'

'What are you celebrating?'

'Saffron for the Americas–we've just returned from the journey.'

'I've never seen a ship like this.'

'Then you have not lived. My Master is very eccentric. He has a taste for the exotic.'

'Where are the children, what happened to them? Where's Cyrus?'

Malachi smiled sly, with his eyes narrowed. He lent at Gold and whispered in her ear. Gold could smell his breath: sour milk and honey.

'Talk to the Master–he will have your answers.'

He spun her head and pointed to the forecastle. Elfin steps lead to a captain's cabin; on its door was a spear and shield fixed by a chain.

'Go on up–he'll make you his guest.'

'Is he a kind man?'

'He is a clever man, but cruel. We work for him and we are his now. That's the price we pay for a lavish life.' Malachi shrugged.

The silvered steps led to a blue door enamelled with more stars. She waited outside–she could feel a nervous twitch run through her legs. There was a desire to leap off the deck and swim to shore, but which shore would she be near? Gold opened the door with a sigh. Inside the cabin was a small lens that cast moonlight onto a desk strewn with ephemera. A short, wizened man traced the luminescence onto a thick journal. He twitched the nib in his fingers, the ink smoothed out in cryptic lines. She stood there, the noise from the celebration a distant murmur. Inside this candle–lit sanctuary, everything was measured and orderly, an equilibrium of reason and logic. The nib broke, and man coughed and looked in her direction. He was squat, with quivering jowls and bronzed skin. Hard eyes judged her over spectacles.

'You're Malachi's master?'

'I am his father. You were lucky the First Mate spotted your boat, our "Star lost in the Channel." You'll have to forgive my son's passion for flowery language.'

He turned and resumed his work—he scribbled a red blob with ellipses that interweaved through it.

'My name is Gold sir.'

'Good for you.'

Gold studied the planet he jotted down. He fixed one eye on a telescope and muttered.

'Is that important?'

'Mars is the most important. The Cape of Strangers prides itself for famous Stargazers. We ourselves sail by the stars, live and eat by the rotation of the planets.'

'What is your name sir?' she asked.

'My name is Meriadoc, Shipmaster.'

'I need to know— '

'The man you were with, Cyrus, is safe. The babies are under his care—they are in Malachi's quarters. Warm, fed, and watered.'

'What will you do with us?'

'We're headed for London. You can join us if you want, but let me first ask you a question. What do you know of The First House?'

Gold blinked away tears. 'Nothing. I've never heard of it.'

'I'm a man of a new age. Lord Saville's wife had the same interests as I. We belonged to a group who realised planet Mars is near conjunction.'

'Conjunction?'

'A rare event. Mars is lining up with others. Not since Lord Saville made his expedition to an island in the Westland Sea has it made this change. Of course, that's speculation and coincidence. His daughter had left London, did you know?'

'No.'

'How could you know? Though it is strange that a man, a young girl and two infants are found adrift—there are signs in life. Patterns, if you have the knack to read them.'

'She was on the ship.' Gold bit her finger.

Meriadoc shook his head with disgust.

'Let that be a lesson, do not lie to me. Where is she now?'

'There was an attack, the Lady was injured.'

Meriadoc twisted in his chair. He lit a few more candles, turned an hourglass, and slapped fatigue from his cheeks. He breathed a quick prayer.

'And those two infants, are they hers?'

Gold nodded. She tugged on her lips and wiped her wet cheeks.

'Those two are—oh Mars forgive me!'

Meriadoc stopped short of breath while he crossed himself. He left in a fluster. Gold was left alone in the cabin amongst his research and ephemera, confused. She picked up his journal and held it at arm's length. Mars was there, under the title of First House; a House of Self. Gold shivered. The planet's outline had been repeated in several pages; the ink still wet. Meriadoc had painted Sarah Saville's face in gouache on the other side of the page. Her gaze fixed heavenward; a halo shone above her with twelve stars. She wore a blue robe, and in the robe her daughters suckled content; one with silver locks, the other with red curls.

The party had settled, the lively guests had come to rest, and the sailors replaced with a fresh shift for the day. Blankets had placed on guests unused to London's chill weather. A reed flute played by a boy in red caught Gold's attention; the melody reminded her of days forgotten. Meriadoc sat centre of the deck, his rolls of fat bunched up his cream jacket. Tufts of black cotton splayed out of gaps. He began to talk to a group assembled around him. He didn't glance in her direction, and ignored her repeated calls. Gold's rage simmered until it hit a plateau; she kicked a brazier which spilt hot coals onto the deck. Sailors scrambled to put out the coals with sacks of sand. One held a curved blade under her chin, its point tickling her neck.

'She means nothing wrong,' said Meriadoc. 'Leave her be.'

'Are you going to harm Lady Saville? Do you mean to steal her children?' Gold asked.

After some consideration he smiled, a genuine smile.
'That's what I am here to talk about with my fellows. Mars is our
God. We worship him as a bringer of peace, like our forefathers
had.' They waited for her to answer. In that pause Meriadoc
gathered more crew around them.

'How do you know of her?'

'There are signs girl. We see them in our dreams.'

'Will you help us then; help us to get to London? My
father is waiting there too, like he promised.'

'I will. May you permit us to see the children further?
Many here wish to give their blessings.'

'For safe passage I see no harm in that. I should thank
you.'

'Yes, you should.'

Gold saw to Cyrus in the crowd and laughed. He came to
shake her hand. 'You look well enough. The children are fine
Miss Frost, no harm's come to them,' he said.

'We are getting passage to London; they want to help.'

'I see. Forgive me but, you trust them?' They're a religious cult.'

'I made a promise to my father. I imagine you've made one with Lady Saville to keep her children safe.' Gold felt her cheeks heat. He winked at her with humour in his smile.

'Then it's settled; we have no choice either, the jollyboat sprung a leak. I'll be here early in the morning. Mister Meriadoc will be thanked and I'll never set foot on this floating wreck again. Then we'll go back to my house.'

'Where?'

'You'll meet my wife. I'll do the talking. There might be a wage if you pitch in with the housework.'

'My father is still out there. Do you think he—' Gold shook her head. She felt tears welt again; her mouth fettered the rest of her sentence.

'Worry makes it worse. Eat something while our hospitality is still welcome and then get some rest. Nearly dawn.'

He passed her a plate of medallions and a bun before he retired, with a wave, below deck. Gold stumbled towards a gap between two billets and folded a worn blanket over herself. After the meal she closed her eyes, squeezed into a ball, and allowed her body to rest.

The Hanged Man

– Houndbarrow, London –

In the morrow, as Meriadoc's pink sailed in flecks of amber, the

sun brought fresh vision. London had remained unchanged since

Cyrus had left. The shanties of Greenmarket, always on the verge

of tipping into the Darkwater, were in sight: inns, factories,

refineries. Stacks upon stacks of chimneys divvied the sky with

furrows of smog. Households tumbled in place around London

Bridge; a brick and iron crown upon the mottled brow of the

narrow streets below it. Cyrus sighed and steadied himself as the

pink came alongside, on the other side of the city was his home.

'Give way to the tradesmen first, girl!' screamed the Quartermaster as Gold stood on the gang. Cyrus sighed again. This girl, Miss Frost, was as stubborn as a mule. He began to speak, but nothing fruitful came to mind. He watched as Gold gave the Quartermaster a filthy look and slipped on her heels.

'Come on girl, easy up.'

He picked her up. She weighed nothing. Pole legs, spider arms and a bouffant of jet hair with eyes like smudges of boot polish. She wrenched away from his hands.

'So what happens now? You take me behind some whore-house and slit my throat?'

'I'm true to my word,' Cyrus showed her his forearm. A tattoo of a tower was incandescent on his skin. This was his citizenship; his rite of passage, proof of his loyalty to nobody but himself.

'A tower?'

'The Tower of Redbridge–you haven't heard of it?'

'Doesn't seem like something that small could vouch for you. I do know you're a thief.'

'A changed thief,' he corrected. 'I work for Lady Saville, no longer for any other.'

'We'll see.'

Cyrus rubbed his brow. The girl was irritating. He could leave her now and vanish; he could easily slip into the crowds and forget this whole affair. 'Now look, stay close, don't look at any drunks or knaves in the eye and don't buy anything. They'll usually have a partner waiting on the side to dip his hand in your pocket. And watch for the urchins, they're the most desperate.'

'You would know, *thief*. Let's find this wife you mentioned. They're both hungry,' Gold held her cradle up high for him to see the two babes awake and unsettled. Cyrus huffed. It had the makings of a difficult day.

Houndbarrow's convergence was always filled with bright tents, tax officials and toshers. Solid stone arches supported waterways choked with debris; refuse from the market was dumped into slipways that fed to the east, and out into the sea. Cyrus knew from a boy (but never dared) that you could pilot the waterways to the heart of the city with a float; its sewers and foundations linked together before the name London came to be. And as he grew older, as the other stories and myths of London were dismissed in the cynical eye of adulthood, the legend of the slipways never went away, never disproven. At times he would listen to a tosher's tale at the *White Rose*, and sit and imagine that underneath all of them lived a beating heart of London: a heart that fed blood to the streets and people, and grew in the dark in wet slick horror. Alex's ruminations had finally rubbed off onto him.

Cyrus's house was ramshackle on the outside. Its weathered façade mismatched the rest of the housing in the street. It was two floors tall, with panels the shade of burnt wheat. The paint crumbled on diamond accents and pitted iron windows. One bull's-eye window that crowned the top of the house gave it the impression of a squat cyclops. Inside, the home was cosy. Possessions stacked in groups throughout the single open-floor room beyond the hall. Cyrus noted his Victoria's quirks had not changed with the year passed. The furniture lain out just so. That sickly smell of the honey and lemon mixture she rubbed on the rafters to keep them clean, that kaleidoscopic blanket thrown over his favourite chair. A single fresh log smoked lazy in the hearth and Cyrus threw a bundle of willow onto it. The branches curled and crisped in the heat.

'Welcome,' Cyrus said, proud.

'Warm enough,' said Gold.

'Your room is at the top. You're not afraid of heights, are you?'

'No, I'm *used* to them.'

Cyrus scrunched his lips and swallowed as if digesting her attitude. Creaking steps from upstairs heralded a young woman. He nodded at her and she squealed in joy, with both of her arms thrown around his neck. She let out a whimper. They embraced deeply; ending with a kiss on his cheeks and one on both their lips. Cyrus ventured Victoria hadn't aged a day in his eyes. She was his confidant, his joy, to speak of his ills and pains, someone to grow old with. He couldn't imagine life with her absence. He had convinced himself he was in love, and knew so.

Victoria looked over at Gold, with crib in hand, both startled. Cyrus could see the inflection stir in Victoria's eyes.

'Who is this? Cyrus, where did you meet this girl? Whose children are these?'

'Miss Frost, Gold, is a friend. You did say you need help around the home, while you're out at night.'

There was a growl, followed by brisk footsteps as she ascended the staircase.

'Gold, you stay there. I'll be a moment.'

Gold folded her arms and raised one eyebrow a touch. After the argument had died, Cyrus showed Gold her room. Large chests filled with keepsakes clotted on one side of the attic, while a bed waited on the other. It smelled damp and a steady stream of air came through a cracked window. To Gold it was as if she was back at sea, which Cyrus took as a compliment. When the two babies were at rest, Cyrus and Gold both told their story in the lambence of the fire. From the treasure on the island; to the *Tail* attacked at sea and rescue at the Cape of

Strangers. Victoria sat and listened, her questions answered and fears dissolved.

'What about money for food and upkeep? Or work? How can you afford to feed all of us?' Victoria asked him.

With careful hands, Cyrus pulled out three shining ingots of gold from his breast pocket. He gave them to her, his hand squeezing hers. 'Sorry for being away for so long.'

After a night in his armchair, Cyrus gathered himself and went upstairs to his reticent love. In the conversation that followed he took note of three things he had to do to make good on their relationship: one, make sure Gold had an allowance, sustenance, and her room was draft–free; two, find supplies and space for a nursery; third, appropriate names for the children, as their mother was not present. After Cyrus clomped back downstairs, he pecked Victoria's cheek, and waved goodbye to Gold. He walked out into the street for a carriage; his journey to Lamb's Wharf quick and merciful. Vagabonds, whores and military men littered the closer he came. He saw anti—Crown graffiti splattered on walls. The Day Watch held back crowds with their batons held high as they met out violence. He thanked the driver as he disembarked. Ahead was his business; on a yellow hill stood a church with sandstone buttresses and pearl gravestones. The doorman recognised him on sight. He lifted one arm.

'Domine dirige nos,' said Cyrus.

The doorman did not smile, but nodded. Cyrus patted himself down and adjusted his cloak. Inside the reception, it was cool. Vaulted ceilings, studded with the friezes of rogues, immortalised by their greatest heists. Murals of thunderclouds, bronze—clad bandits and geldings embossed the opulence. Dogtooth tiles lead the eye up to the halls that made up the Church's dodecagon. Up ahead the lesser hall, one of twelve, crowded with hoodwinks. Alongside was the second hall, filled with highwaymen. In each hall the rank rose, but the men and women of ill repute dwindled. His hall was the tenth, reserved for spies. A rotund room with carpeted floor and trophies from parts of the empire; it was candle lit with thick curtains that blocked out the day. Contrasted with the muddy dignitaries' hall, it was white washed pristine. Pink and yellow marble highlighted the skirt and the doors beaten copper. Cyrus looked over a fireplace he had seen in this room once before. Two lions supported pillars on either side of it. Mounted above the fireplace was the symbol of their service, a great rose surrounded by halos. Each represented a year of success. Splotches of wine matted the carpet beneath in places that made the threads stand stiff. Fresh patches still had their bright red colour; older ones had grown darker with age. While he had been gone, there were new stains shed in delicate patterns on the fireplace itself. Small spirals soaked into the pink stone. It looked as though some effort to scrub or soak the wine out had taken place, but failed.

'You mix wine and men in one stuffy hall and they expect civility? It'll be crimson by the year's end.' Cyrus noticed the familiar faces of Simon and Charlotte, or Red and Ghost as Alex had christened them. They were his forced recruitment back into a world of organised crime. Red was young and radiated an incipient worry, while Ghost was prone to laugh at any given time. However more wrinkled Ghost's face had gotten from the previous years, her eyes still shined. 'Oh, doesn't matter if you spill your wine here Charlotte, it matches the carpet well,' stated Red.

Cyrus gave a cautious laugh.

'So how was the journey? How is our Ladyship and her offspring? You do look like a man with too much green on his nails,' demanded Ghost, striking a finger to Cyrus's chest.

'More to the point how are the children? Are they well? Notice anything different?' said Red. 'Isolde is aching to know.'

Cyrus put both hands up in mock surrender. 'The journey south was fine, until we were attacked and Lady Saville injured. The children are sound; nothing strange about them than you or me.'

'We did hear of the attack. Hard to ignore the rumours,' said Red.

'And the… *magic*. One of the sailors let slip about Lady Saville,' added Ghost.

'If so, then I must be able to do my job with some insurance. There are forces against us,' said Cyrus.

'We cannot spare anything; you must realise this Cyrus,' said Red.

'You have brought us vital information, and you lose your bottle at this junction?' Ghost demanded.

'No, I have not lost anything. Sarah Saville did have an immaculate birth, a miracle.'

'So, she says.'

'So I say. But her twins are normal. No witchcraft. No geese shitting golden eggs.'

'And the whereabouts of these miracles children? Do you know Cyrus?'

'Why do you care?'

'Because, you surely realise there's reward enough for you. We can make a future with Victoria a reality, for example,' said Red. Cyrus wetted his lips.

'Perhaps the opposite can come about Cyrus, and it'll all be taken away. Think on it,' Ghost intoned. 'Our Mistress is here with an offer. Will you meet with her?'

Red and Ghost both smiled with thin lips and left him alone. Cyrus allowed an aide to him shown the thoroughfare into the central twelfth chamber. It circled around the first foundations of the church. Flagstones around him had been lain before Cyrus was born. It served as memorial and tomb, each previous Master buried underneath. From a single marker, shields of citrine and marble spread out towards pews lined with red leather. Amber light reflected off bronze spears that lined the walls. Polished lions adorned rails with highlights that caught admirers off-guard. He shivered. The aide moved to close the second set of doors that led into the chamber. The stones below radiated a chill that tickled his chin. Doors leading to the tenth hall slammed shut. A woman appeared before him, one he knew well, she nodded as he approached.

'Now here's an ideal place without interruptions,' said Isolde. 'No more banal talk with thugs; just two people in converse.'

Cyrus folded his arms. His jaw tensed, teeth ground on one another.

'Our newest agent Cyrus. I haven't seen you since your little jaunt across the sea.'

'Isolde.' Cyrus sighed. 'What would you have of me?'

'Nothing so bad, cheer up.' Cyrus' face darkened. 'While Percy is wasting time on that island, you'll report to me now sir.'

'I thought you were in collusion with each other.'

'Yes. But I did warn him it would fail eventually. I'm only hastening the process. As soon as Lord Percy Turner is removed from his power, only then will London flourish. This city can never go back, it can never be what he wants it to be. Our future is diversity. Have you not embraced this philosophy yourself?' Cyrus rose to argue but his mouth stalled. 'Like most men your morals are rotting inside you. A man, child, or woman's wellbeing is a right. A price cannot be placed on it, no matter how small the world makes it. This I strive to uphold. The lowest group of people shall obtain equal power to the highest. For a building without a foundation is nothing, and a city without its people is nothing. I trust you get the point,' Isolde fanned herself with one hand.

Cyrus regarded her. 'I get the point. And what do you need me to do?'

'Good. You need to placate Sarah Saville's sister, Sophia.'

'Sophia? Why?'

'She's powerful. Half of the Saville fortune split with her. She has the most connections and breeding, an ideal person to raise Sarah Saville's daughters.'

Cyrus swayed on his feet. 'You want me to give up those children? For what?'

'Safekeeping Cyrus. They're special, and as soon as Percy hears wind of what has befallen Sarah Saville and her miracle children, he will seek them out. He is desperate and wants every advantage he can get.'

'Surely he's a rational man? How can children, babes at best, win back his London?'

'You've seen Sarah Saville cast a spell?' Cyrus mumbled yes, he had. 'Can you imagine the control Percy would wield if these children came of age, and were under his influence? There are not many children left who are born of witchcraft, and fewer still who are born from nothing. I want them safe, nothing more sir. Just as much as you want your Victoria to be.'

Cyrus paced for a short while. His hands smoothed down his face, and rubbed away the stress from his sockets. 'How on God's earth do I convince a Lady to accept two babies for her own?'

'You can try bribery, coercion, or threats Cyrus. Take your pick. But, I myself, would choose desire.'

'Desire? What do you mean?'

'Perhaps if you offered them plainly,' said Isolde.

'And why of all things does the affluent Sophia Saville

desire children?'

'She cannot have them herself.'

Cyrus sat occupied. He was drunk. Gold, beside him,

sipped a cup of watered wine that brought a flush to her

cheeks. *The Lily* was clean. It had respectable clientele, and even

doormen that strong–armed undesirables back onto the streets.

He wondered if they counted down the hours until closing when

inevitably they would hoist some fat toff off a table and stuff him

into a waiting carriage.

'So, you're keeping secrets from Victoria?' Gold

smirked.

Cyrus raised his head and smoothed his hair. 'Did you follow me today?'

'Mayhap. But if it's a job, and one you're doing now, then why don't you tell her? She must have asked about the ingots.'

'Idiot I am. That's all the money we have. And now we are with two children and an adolescent.'

'Many have suffered worse. That woman is a blessing for you, don't ever forget it.'

Cyrus closed his eyes and drank more of his pint.

The inn filled with more bodies until a thrum of conversation and laughter prevailed. Interest focussed on Sophia Saville who arrived with entourage. She was tall, taller than her sister Sarah had been, with thin doll legs. Her hair was earth-smoke from her crown, which melted down to auburn curls. Her dress was a sheet of burgundy, with silver buttons arrayed in a fleur on her chest.

'I've got an idea,' said Gold. Cyrus felt his shoulders sink and his hands fidget. 'Become a freeman like my father.'

'Become a privateer!' I shouldn't have let you come.'

Gold shrugged. She scratched her borrowed blue dress; the stitching fell in places around the arms. Sophia walked up to their table. She stepped in noble precision, a glass of white ready in her hand before she announced herself.

'Black accented with black; you must be Master Cyrus' I received your letter to do business. But you must be brief with what you want to say.'

Cyrus shuffled to his feet and clapped his heels together. He bowed; Gold stood after and curtseyed.

'Shall we get down to it?' Cyrus asked.

'We should indeed.' Sophia smoothed herself onto a chair. Her smile turned patronising.

'And shall we talk of business?'

'With the girl present?' said Sophia.

Cyrus pawed at his hands. Gold looked as innocent as he was at her age. Words ground thick as rocks on his tongue; he found useless lies and excuses fizz to the front of his mind. He knew he needed only a whisper for Sophia to accept one of the children. For her to commit to murder was only an embryo in the back of his head. It would take more than truth and bribery. He would need to trap her with honeyed words.

'You're right. Gold please move to the table behind us.'

Gold huffed, but moved. They waited until she had settled.

'Your daughter?'

'Yes, she is.'

Sophia sniffed and sipped her wine.

'Must be wonderful to have a daughter. Do you treat her well? Spoil her?'

'As my only one, she is everything to me. There isn't a daughter more doted over her than she is.'

'Really? Well, shall we talk about the younger ones? I can see from your daughter's dress there isn't much money in your life.'

'There are two. Twins—each only over a year old, nothing wrong with them.'

'Girls?'

'Yes, they are. Tragic the way they came to us.' Said Cyrus.

'Oh? Do tell. What's the story?'

Sophia's lackeys left her. She sighed; her head propped with an open palm. With darting looks she made sure their conversation was private enough. Cyrus imagined her as a cautious feline, with all the skittishness coiled under the surface.

'A disaster with a ship; it came upon rocks during a storm.'

'Ghastly.' Replied Sophia.

'There was a thunderstorm above our village. We could see the sea filling the hold, the ship had to break onto rocks or sink. Gold and I found these children in a rowboat, still alive. The day had hardly broken; the sun was still cold.'

'And you live on the coast? Are you a fisherman by trade?'

'A shipowner Lady.'

Sophia shrank back, her brow folded. 'A wife?'

'No just me and her.'

'I see. What brings you to London?'

'To see you my Lady, I know you are in want of a daughter, and I can scarcely feed the four of us.'

'A coincidence in my favour.'

Cyrus felt his shoulders tighten, his jaw bunch. 'No game my Lady. No jape. I heard from a rumour and took a chance. It you wish to keep it private I will honour it.'

Lady Saville scowled. One hand rose to cover her chin in thought. 'It is done then,' she said. 'I will look after only *one* of the orphans. She will be well fed, well-watered, with the finest education a child can receive. A boast none other can make. You take your pick of the two. The other will be in your care. I'll send a nanny to pick her up in the morning with payment. Houndbarrow was it?' She made a move to leave.

Cyrus leaned in close to her. 'Can you suffer one more favour my Lady?' he whispered.

She smiled at him. 'Ask.'

'Let me see her when she comes to term, or at the least speak to you of her, to put my mind at ease.'

Sophia waved her hand up. 'If you must. You'll meet her at my estate, when she is a woman. Make a note of it, and bring your own daughter. I'm sure both of you will find country air the better.' She swung her dress from over her legs and left. After she left, Cyrus took up one hand and wiped away the tears still falling on Gold's face.

'You heard everything?'

Gold nodded. She wrenched his hand away and left. Cyrus sat alone, his face a dichotomy of regret and relief.

Part Two

The Star

– Winter, 1822 –

Flakes of snow had worked themselves into her hood for the past

hour. The cold chilled the sweat that had built on her brow as

Elena pushed through a rough path to the inn. She paused to soak

in the quiet and stillness of the valley. Sun-kissed white hills

curled up to meet bruised clouds. It had been two weeks since she

had fled London. In those two weeks of travel on foot she had

never felt more exhausted. She trod on to the inn, through frozen

grass and glassy puddles of mud, grasped its iron knocker and

pushed the door open. She regarded the innkeeper with his

hunched back and fat cheeks. He looked harmless. Straw and sawdust were strewn on the ground which soaked up the mud and snow, and a raised platform led to a roaring fire pit where a woman and a girl perched on benches were deep in talk. Wood-smoke permeated the air and funnelled out through an open hole in the roof. Behind the counter a creaky staircase joined with private rooms.

'Anything to drink, please,' Elena croaked.

She shook and her belly grumbled. The Innkeeper gave her a worried nod and poured from a bottle into a cup. She paid and found an inviting nook with its own curtain. It was a warm booth, rank with sweat and wax, the walls a comfort after exposed travel. Carved niches were filled with gods and goddesses, each with a statue or candle placed in them. The seat beneath was worn smooth from many a traveller. She let out a sigh and the tension from her shoulders dropped. Her eyes closed, her mind recalling the worst year of her life. The only want, the only desire she had, was to get away from it all. This dread had muddied her mind, made her aware that some of her actions were not her own. A frown knitted itself across her brow; memories broke her concentration. Blank faces, half-begotten smiles, noise void of context, locations and rooms without reference. As Elena had another vision of a young woman who whispered to her in a dark room, she drifted into the sleep that her body craved.

Before long she felt a vibration run through her mind that jerked her into waking. She spilled what remained of her drink. The inn was beginning to be an increasing bad idea to stay, nowhere was safe. Peering out a window, she saw a man, tall with a thin build, his face unshaven. She could see that his narrow eyes were searching the sides of the tavern, not the front. His clothes were tight fitted. He wore leather and heavy boots, and a dagger in his belt. A black hood lined with fur covered most of his head, which looked superior at keeping the cold out than her jacket. Elena felt a bubble of panic, the two patrons and the innkeeper had vanished, she presumed, upstairs. There was no obvious cellar to hide in. In her panic her boots knocked at a plank joined at the front of the counter which revealed a priest hole.

The thin man waited with snow falling onto his furs. The Innkeeper, his wife and daughter had fled as soon as they saw him, running off in the opposite direction to get help. Surely, he didn't look that intimidating? The mountain air had now started to make his muscles tired and stiff. Alex sighed. Breath escaped his mouth and faded into ether. His hands fingered the dagger he wore at his belt. Alex's world had crumbled since *The Tail* had battled pirates on the south coast. He recalled tumbling over the gunwale after he struggled with a boarder twice his size and weight. Although the plunge into the water was warm, and the sea shallow enough, he swam like a frightened dog. Half–drowned and half–pummelled, Alex reached the shore with the South Sea still in his lungs and stomach. From that beach he spent a week travelling north until he could find a town large enough to hide and ply his trade. It was a month before his ribs healed, a further month before his ankle was strong enough to support his weight. He wasn't sure if Lady Saville was alive after he saw her collapse from the first cannonade. He wasn't sure if Cyrus was alive either. Taking the situation in his stride, Alex discovered, to no doubt, that it was easy to be a thief in Port's Mouth, the businessmen were trusting and lax. The doubt came from something new; a feeling that Alex had never experienced before in his life. The town had charmed him. It felt right. It was not London; the air off the Westland Sea was rich and fresh. People in the town were *happy*, they actually *smiled* at him without an ulterior need. They were mollified by dazzling summers and mild winters that hardly saw snow or ice. Alex slowly, and with healthy scepticism, became used to the coast. Inch—by—inch the sea accepted him and sedated his urban attitude. Bad memories of his childhood and of the Tower, quashed in acquiescence of a simple life. He felt revived, mind, body, and soul.

Years passed until Alex caught onto a rumour that shrugged a memory loose. Lady Stone, formerly Saville, had lost her daughter. He became excited at meeting her again. His mind stormed with questions about how she could have lived, how did she escape? The job offered mention of an address, and so he followed it. He did not meet Sarah, but her sister. Sophia was such a similarity at first Alex thought it was a jest aimed at him.

She told him of the time gone by. How a master mariner dressed all in black had sold her an orphan from a shipwreck, only a baby at the time. Alex asked of the ships name, and felt bile rise in his throat. He confirmed the story was true enough, and lied he had overheard such a story all those years ago. Alex accepted the job for his mistress Sarah, but not Sophia. To find Sarah's daughter and bring her back to her rightful mother, if still alive. He recalled the girl's name: *Elena*. He ruled out a naïve rich young woman fleeing an oppressive home in search of danger and romance. He guessed she wasn't that naïve, nor was she that young or oppressed enough. Alex leaned towards fear. Elena was afraid. From Port's Mouth, the easiest path to follow on foot was to Ashtree; a landlocked village. Alex followed descriptions of a red-haired girl until he deduced where she had stopped.

He called out her name and opened the inn's door; an insipid glow spread itself across the snow. He gazed behind the door, up to the ceiling and across to the fire. He judged that she would hide somewhere close by, with enough air and space to keep calm. He looked down at the floor matted with mud and straw. Foot prints were visible near the counter. Alex ripped open the boards, and inside the hole, intelligent eyes stared back up at him.

'Good evening miss.'

She was about twenty years if a day. Pale skin, bony cheeks, and a mass of curled red hair; she had lost weight from the sketches Alex had seen. Her clothes were inadequate for travel. The skin around them rubbed red from repetition. Her cloak and hood designed for summer, her under layers were too few and the boots too light. She glared daring him to make the next move. Alex shrugged and spoke first.

'You've lost your baby–fat,' he said.

Elena kept quiet. She knew there was a glaze in her eyes that she couldn't shake; it was mirrored on the man's face. Her story unfolded without a word said. The fear that had caused her to flee Port's Mouth was greater than the risk she had put her life in. Greater than the trouble she had caused. The man removed a coil of thin rope from behind a leather pouch on his belt.

'Pervert,' she rasped.

'I'm not here to hurt you. Honest.'

'What are you here for then?' She tilted her head back defiant. Alex sighed.

'So how do feel after your journey? Stupid?'

'Not as stupid as you when I tell my father you've mistreated me.'

He frowned, glanced behind the counter and grabbed a bottle. He pulled the cork and drank. Red wine spilled from his chin as he replaced the cork and left coin should the innkeeper return.

You're a disgrace.'

'Why leave?' Alex asked.

He wiped his chin clean. Alex guessed the girl was of a set immaturity overlooked through her life and was never challenged.

'There's food in my pack outside, food and warm clothes.'

'You sound sure I want to go back.'

'I would have thought the comfortable life that Lord Stone provides would smell less.'

'It–it did,' replied Elena.

'So why leave?'

Elena sobbed, just once, a bitter choke that made the man roll his eyes.

'My name is Alex,' he ignored her tears. 'Elena Stone, I'm here to return you to your mother.'

Elena tried to speak but the words grated inside her throat.

'I know. I found you because I asked the right questions to the right people. Also, I have a horse. That helps to cut down the travel. Did someone hurt you?'

'No.'

'Threatened your life?'

'No.' she closed her eyes. The hunger and thirst were unbearable. All she had to do was tell him the truth of why she left. She bunched up and breathed deep. She hated telling the truth, it had a weight to it that chewed up her words and dulled her tongue.

'I'm cursed'

Alex sat unblinking.

'It started when I was twelve, out of nowhere.'

'What started?' said Alex, full of doubt.

'The dreams I have—of an island sat alone in the sea—a girl that looks like me, and strange visions and the rest. It keeps me awake at night. I haven't had a full sleep in a year.' She tugged and smoothed her hair.

'Surely dreams cannot hurt you or your family. There's naught to be afraid of. There's real food out there, if you're hungry.'

Elena nodded. Her hands had formed white spots; there was drowsiness in the way she moved. 'How did you know?'

Alex tapped his nose. 'We have to go—my horse is used to the cold, but starts to whine if she's left alone for too long.'

Elena pulled herself onto her feet and hugged her jacket to keep the last of the warmth in. She took Alex's guiding hand onto her shoulder and followed him to the horse tied outside. The snow had stopped, but air had taken on a fierce bite. His horse was cream in colour, with thick legs and mud—stained fur covering its hooves. As soon as it spotted Alex it nuzzled him and let out a cough of relief. Elena giggled as man and horse went through a ritual of letting each know it was time for them to leave.

'What's her name?'

'Whiterun. She's borrowed.' said Alex.

In a saddle-bag Alex produced a fur coat, which was a size too large for her. She came close to Alex on the back of the saddle and wrapped herself around a screen that separated them. Into dusk they rode on, the fresh snow crunched beneath Whiterun's feet as she made light work of the path. Soon the sway of riding and the warmth from the fur lulled her back into sleep.

'I was at home again,' Elena mumbled.

'Were you?' said Alex.

Elena shifted upright and looked about. The morning sun shone down a small muddy path ahead; between them were thickets and open fields. Ice had wormed its way into corners and pockets of the greenery around them, it persisted in the shade.

'Yes. I was in my father's study.'

'We'll stop there.' Alex pointed at a copse. Leaves and pollen tumbled around them as they slowed. Elena looked at Alex for direction. His face sank, his eyes were puffy and his figure slumped. He staggered to the trunk of the tree and sat.

'Are you all right?' She asked.

'I haven't travelled a full day and night in a long time. It's not something I've done since coming here.' He pointed at her clothes and *Whiterun.* 'Move her near to the tree–she'll appreciate the shade. And take those furs off. It's much warmer down the valley.'

'Not much snow has fallen. Why is that?' Elena asked.

He shrugged. 'I don't know, but it's a nice change. I don't like the cold where I'm from'

'How do you like it then?'

'Mild,' said Alex.

'That doesn't sound better.'

'It doesn't, but we usually have no choice in London.'

'London? You didn't mention you're from the city.'

'Doesn't my accent give it away?'

'I wouldn't know. I don't meet many men.'

Elena blushed. She lacked experience. Going from her mother's wisdom, men were difficult to please and landed you into trouble. If you untangled yourself from the trouble, they proceeded to place themselves in trouble. Enough vitriol had been poured into her ears to put her off courting for life.

'Is it true?' asked Elena, a well of endless question within her. Alex got up from the rest and opened up the camping satchel.

'Is what true?'

'London men can see in the dark, because it's so gloomy there?'

'Yes, that's true. It's a gift most men from London are blessed with,' answered Alex with incredulity.

Elena sat back in marvel. 'And the womenfolk, what do they boast?'

'They have vows of silence.'

Elena considered this. 'We have the opposite in Port's Mouth. Men go quiet for long periods of time.'

'Would these be married men?'

'Yes.'

Alex smiled.

Elena grasped *Whiterun* by the neck and hugged her. The horse released a sigh and carried on with the task of filling her belly with grass and dew.

'Once you've stopped being friends perhaps you can collect some dry wood.'

Elena screwed her face up. 'Where would I find that?'

'Underneath damp wood, beside tree trunks–didn't your father teach you to make a fire?'

'We have help to do that.'

'And what? They do everything for you?'

'Of course, one man collects the wood for the fires. He buys it from the market.'

'Has your mother taught you anything?'

'She was always too busy.'

'Father?'

'Too grumpy.'

Alex sighed and folded his arms. 'Did your mother make you leave?'

'No–she wanted me to live and be happy.'

'And she's married into riches.'

Elena could feel a tug in her belly and a voice whisper in the back of her mind. It felt as though they both had arrived at an understanding. How critical she was, which was alien to her, to be valuable enough for her parents to send a stranger.

'Please don't say anything about dreams or visions to them.'

'I promise,' Alex nodded. Elena gave him a withering stare until he held up his hands in surrender. 'I swear on my life.'

They both searched for wood amongst the path with Alex inspecting what Elena had brought back. Elena noticed a change in her temperament; she was a completely different person to last night. She had colour back to her skin and her step had more energy to it. The pair sat and ate scraps of dried fish and hard fruit loaf. As soon as they finished, and the fire doused, they both mounted and set off.

'We have to pass through Doubleford and then Marketfort.'

'I recognise Marketfort.'

'It's a township—most of it belongs to your father.'

'He's mentioned it before.'

The dotted woods smoothed to high meadows after a spell. When they arrived in Marketfort Elena wondered what the attraction to the town was, until she saw a bustling market hidden by a circle of buildings. *Whiterun* jostled her reins and motioned with her hoof, while Elena giggled. The trough was outside an unnamed inn, which was more ominous than welcoming. After dismounting, Alex explored inside. Relics from the coast littered the whitewashed walls, suspended by iron nails. Graffiti marred parts of the ceiling where prayers and messages left by travellers; a rickety ladder on the opposite end of the inn hinted at how they got there. The innkeeper greeted them from behind a table covered in bottles. Alex paid for two rooms and stable for the night, a bottle of wine and two cups.

'I don't drink,' moaned Elena.

Alex poured wine until both cups were full.

'To good health,' drinking his cup in one swallow. 'What do you drink, if not this?'

'Hot tea.'

'Hm. Sounds healthy,' Alex poured himself another cup.

'That, *fellow*, is keeping an eye on us,' Elena said. 'Do you see him? What do we do?'

Alex turned with a smile on his face towards the innkeeper and nodded. 'I know. Two men have been following us since leaving Ashtree.'

Elena became aware that aside from the innkeeper, who was now starting to sweat, the place was empty. Alex had seen the two men yesterday, unsubtle in their craft. They were after Elena, that was obvious, they just wanted Alex to do the hard work for them; all they had to do was to steal her away in the night. As Alex had told the girl on the journey here, the bounty for her safety was not much. It belied her importance. It was, however, enough money to keep a down—trodden man in good spirits for a month or two.

'How did you know?' asked Elena.

'There are two tracks in the dirt outside. Both leading out of Marketfort, the hoof prints are deep and spread. So, they must have galloped straight through the town in hopes that we were just ahead. I can understand their frustration; it was why I was riding so slow yesterday.'

'Well, what can we do now? Do we run?'

'Nothing,' he said with a small gesture.

'Nothing?'

'Just drink, eat and sleep.'

'Won't they come here to look for us?'

'They might, or they might have given up,' Alex pointed to the innkeeper who stared at them and blushed, 'they've paid him off.' Alex shook his head, 'how much did they pay up front?'

'They didn't say how much,' whispered the innkeeper.

'Don't mess around,' Alex wagged a finger.

Elena chuckled as the innkeeper looked like a guilty child.

'I—meant no ill intent sir, young lady,' the man stammered.

'Too late for apologies. I'll string those boys together,' Alex pointed outside, 'and leave them out for the town to judge. Make up the story they threatened your business through extortion. Agreed?' the innkeeper reluctantly nodded.

'Thank you.' Alex winked at Elena who laughed like a girl half her age.

'We'll eat then wait for them to wander in at night with your door unlocked. Elena, I need you to do something important,' he pointed at her, 'you'll be upstairs to warn me when they come.'

After they ate, Elena bounded up to the nearest window overlooking the town square. She watched as the innkeeper hid himself in a neighbour's cottage, and yawned herself as the light grew dimmer, the meal making her sleepy. The shadows squeezed thin. Downstairs, Alex wouldn't know how strong the men were until he had tackled the first. The second would either be outside on watch or wander in with his friend. Seeing figures approach, Elena gave a low whistle to Alex back down and through the inn, and hid herself under the bed. Below, Alex reaffirmed his grip on the chair, in position to give an overhead swing. He tensed his arm as the first man came through the door and Alex landed a blow across his temple. The body went limp and collapsed; Elena looked out of the window and saw a second man glance around the town, nervous. Alex waited until the second man came through the door in concern, and landed the chair across the back of his head.

The men were young, with several days' stubble and lean figures. On their person was a note describing their task, and marked with a single I. Alex dragged the two men outside and left them at the base of the market stone. He signalled to the innkeeper who made a hurried jog back to his tavern. He thanked them, hands clasped together, and wanted to repay Alex for his efforts with no charge. Most of all, he apologised to Elena, to which she turned red. After a long conversation over a second meal (on the House) Alex stretched. He bid goodnight to Elena, and stumbled upstairs where he found their beds and collapsed

onto his, boots still tied. Elena found him soon after. She took up
her own cot and laid still, the theme of her dreams turning
between Alex, horses, bandits, and hot tea.

In the new day they followed the south road. They
admired the hills that led to quaint retreats and hidden passages in
fields of flax. Alex could see wood smoke plume and catch over
the horizon, where it added to low clouds. The air had a chill
draft to it; a reminder of the plummeting temperatures of
Ashtree. They passed by pilgrims and vagrants, who were trying
to reach the old road back to Port's Mouth. Standing up in the
saddle Elena could almost see the rooftops and spires. Every
metre taken quickened her excitement. 'Nearly home then,' said
Alex. They dismounted *Whiterun* and travelled on foot for the
final mile. Elena smiled back at Alex. Six days of awkward travel
had lengthened his facial hair into bundles of wiry tangles. She
would, at times, watch him out of the corner of her eye. His gaze
was always locked on the fields, watching for something or
someone. When it came to midday Elena looked up at the sky, at
the lumber camps, and to the river, which ran wild, bits of ice still

clinging to its banks. Her thoughts drifted to home. She could feel her cheeks hot with guilt as she imagined the argument with her enraged mother. What had possessed her to do this was now buried; it no longer plagued her.

'Alex, do you hear that? It's strange,' she asked.

Elena's vision lost focus. Trees melted in bursts of light. She squeezed her eyes; her heart thundered out from her core which left lightning pricks on her skin. Her mind felt as though it was separating in two. She could feel strong hands grasp her body as she shook and knelt forwards. Nausea erupted from inside her; vertigo bided her to be sick. Time forgot to move on.

Elena realised she couldn't hear anything of the earth any longer. She found herself borne among clouds. Soft hands fixed her under her arms: one on the left, one on the right. She was flying above Port's Mouth, above England, above the world. She rose higher, afloat on wisps. In the air she looked at her kidnappers: they were women both, dressed in black rags that left only a slit for their eyes. Her head flopped as they passed through a fogbank that emptied it of thought.

Before Elena could fathom her circumstance, she fell

unconscious.

The Magician

A thunderhead muted the valley while Gold watched puddles for

precipitation. Her days were easier when summer arrived. Its

light rain didn't cause havoc around Houndbarrow as did winter,

now. Before dawn she had fletched a quiver, restrung her bow,

ate, and caught a bundle of fowl just as the sun had rose. She

shivered and spurred herself on, slipped down to a stream and

forded it. Her mind drifted with the passing landscape; the calm

of the abundance around inspired inner peace she had not touched

upon in a long time. The days of hoping to see her father again were long past. Years had eased her pain, but not cured it. It drove

her on, motivated her, and forced her to take stock of the nature

on how people suffer, of how anguish in people is usually

invisible and rarely spoken of. Gold was now her own woman, in

life and career. Cyrus had taught her of hunting, fishing and

fighting; to never fear hunger or money. Cyrus and his wife,

Victoria, had accepted and loved her as a daughter. Which made

it the more painful when they sold on one Lady Saville's twins.

That was back when her innocence of the world was unspoilt.

Gold emptied her lungs, and drew air back in.

She turned her hand up to the sky as she felt a drop land.

As the rain increased its *pitter patter*, there was smoke visible

through the marsh. Gold frowned. It wasn't black like oil smoke,

nor grey like wood. She started to run towards it. Wet soil flicked

itself up and across her face; her arm moved up and wiped away

the grime. In a shallow dyke she saw a body motionless next to a

patch of stickyweed that smouldered unchecked.

'Alex,' Gold whispered to nothing.

She hadn't seen the man since the *Tail*. Since that awful day. Gold shivered; the scene was anodyne. A second of inflection passed through her before she acted. Her hair spilled across her jerkin as she crouched to judge the tracks on the ground. Alex had tried to crawl away, but was in too much pain, he had tried to stand, and was overcome. Something had attacked him on returning to London. She wasn't strong enough to lift him up, but she could tend to him on the side of road. The trees provided some respite from the weather. She dragged him under shelter and stamped out the smoke; there was a strange heat that sat in the air, persisting. She gasped at Alex's wound; it had burned the skin from the left half of his face, leaving a bloodied mess. His damaged eye winced at her touch. Her hands shook as she cleaned the wound, and removed dirt from it. Their tent formed part of a branch. Alex nestled at the base of the tree, two layers of cotton blanket underneath and one on top. Gold's fire was sloppy with dry sticks scrounged about her, but it only needed to last until she signalled for help. She gripped her cloak around herself tight for comfort, and stared into the fire. Its flames licked and hissed with the raindrops that fell down from the canopy. She heard a familiar horn blow and responded with three from her own in return. Gold stood. She gathered Cyrus was close, and had brought aid. She spotted Cyrus riding at speed, before he saw her. Gold checked on Alex inside the tent. He had turned pale. She gripped his arm to wake.

'Who are you?' he asked, eyes wincing.

'You know me,' she said without taking her eyes off Cyrus in the distance. There was a pause in the man. Alex cocked his head at an angle, his mouth working over his next words before they came.

'Frost's daughter? Your name was Gold wasn't it?'

'Still is, sir.'

'So, you all survived. Thank God. Good, that's good.'

She opened his good eye and glanced at his complexion. She held her cross in one palm and prayed that he would recover in good time. Cyrus, hooded and impatient, came to the camp and nodded at her, with no words exchanged between them. He manhandled and carried Alex out, back onto his feet and swung him onto his horse. Looking out across the woodlands she packed the tent and left the fire to drown. She noticed him taking firmer ground as Alex clung on, almost unconscious. Gold could only imagine what had happened. She packed everything and secured it. As she began to walk back home, she recalled Alex's wound. It had to be of a rapid heat that scorched him. It left an injury like one she had seen when lightning had struck a farmhand from the previous year. She shivered, coaxed her legs into action, and took the slow road back to Houndbarrow.

Gold preferred to enter Houndbarrow from the tunnels. Cyrus, she recalled, had shown her after she wondered how the smugglers and toshers moved around London so quickly. One night, when everyone else in the house was asleep, Cyrus placed one hand on her shoulder shaking her awake. He placed one finger up to his lips, *hush.* Gold got ready, laced on high boots and a slicker, put a pie hat on her head (to stave off drips from the ceiling of the sewer), and left the house without waking anyone. Cyrus slinked like a cat around the moonlit streets of London, his hand waved in the air when he wanted Gold to stop and be quiet.

With a length of steel, he opened a grate, turned up the flame on his lantern, and measuring every step, made his way down into London's depths. Gold's eyes, when eventually used to the gloom saw Cyrus and other men about. The toshers. They were dressed as she was, armoured in long strips of waxed leather, boots long and thick enough to wade through the sea. They waved hello to her, bowing in mock ceremony, welcoming her to a hidden kingdom. All of them were men with cracked teeth, boils, or pocked faces. The undesirables, the lost and damned, the roughest life the city had to offer. In the next second, after waving back, the smell punched Gold's nose as though it was a solid mass that clung to everything, cancerous and spreading its evil unchecked. It was the worst smell she had ever encountered, and would ever encounter in her life. Even after a bath the next day, and her clothes soaked in perfume, the smell lingered, imprinted in her memory forever. *If there was ever another thing I could not forgive Cyrus for,* Gold thought, *it was introducing me to that stench.*

It was that smell that assailed her nose now, as Gold stepped through a hidden grate on the outskirts of the city. She stepped over refuse and moulded foodstuff, over faeces and clumps of fat, bones and brick. She gagged, closing a glove over her mouth; with the other, she placed a perfumed neckerchief over her mouth and nose, and wrapped it twice around her head before tying it. Gold tensed her legs, and began to wade through the filth. She counted steps until five hundred, about quarter of a mile. She grasped the ladder in haste, her body begging for fresh air and a hot, clean, bath. Above, on a street, a cover was popped open and two dark eyes peeked about. Gold climbed out, stamped off worst of the muck from her boots, and walked home, her lungs drinking in the fresher air.

After a hot soak before supper, (her clothes left outside without comment) Cyrus thanked Gold in his own begrudging fashion. While she had grown into a young woman, Cyrus was now grey in flecks around his temples and grumbled as her father used to. Alex, laid to rest on a wood bench, was swaddled in the same blankets as he had arrived, his head supported by a feather pillow, candles circled around him in case Alex woke during the evening. To Gold, he appeared to be a shrouded saint, hallowed in death. He no longer shook; his breathing at ease. Gold removed Alex's bandage and shut out the sun as best she could. With a candle in hand for light, she washed and cleaned the injury, and applied more ointment. Cyrus inspected her work, relieved that his friend was still alive after all these years. He told her of all the adventures they had shared. The fateful day of sailing to an island that, back then, did not exist on every map, and was not well known across the country. She could see it in the way Cyrus' eyes would become blank sometimes. Inside them, at those moments, there were little fragments of time that tugged his heart in directions she could only guess at. Over the years Gold noticed Cyrus would take longer to return to reality after reminiscing. She always asked if he was happier then or now. He would always reply with now, but a sad smile would spread across his face. If it was a life full of regret that had greyed his hair, Gold had never asked.

'Cyrus, his burn needs to air and this ointment applied every day until the swelling disappears. Just keep it clean and your friend will be fine,' Gold said, folding her arms.

'Yes, seems he'll live. How did you find him?'

'Saw some odd smoke over the hills, I went to have a look. If it wasn't for that I wouldn't have seen him. He was alone and without a horse, and there were two sets of footprints in the mud.'

'He wasn't alone then. Who was the second person?'

'I don't know, their footprints were light.'

'A woman?'

'Won't he tell you all the details when he wakes up?'

'He might. He might lie. Alex might not be the same friend from those years ago.'

Gold huffed, flicked her hair, and left the old man to speculate in peace. She sought out his wife, Victoria, who sat, as usual, beside a lit stove in the kitchen. Gold had an inkling, ever since living with Cyrus and Victoria, that you could tell much of a person just by the rooms they frequented. The way objects and items were put away, the colours and decoration, and the little touches of personality. As of now, Victoria's hands busied knitting warm gloves while the stew cooked; the kitchen's surfaces immaculate, the stew colourful and heady in smell. Despite being a year older than Cyrus, Victoria's beauty still stole looks from other men in the city streets. There were few things not shared between the two women, ever since being forced to reside with each other. Gold remembered the awkward early days that ran into weeks, weeks into months, and months into years, before both women conceded that her stay was more permanent than expected. Victoria, and her open heart, was the absent mother she had never had: confidant, friend and shoulder to cry on. Even though Victoria was always available to vent problems or ease her sadness, Gold had not spoken of losing her father in a while, and no one had asked; which, she suspected, was out of consideration.

'Victoria, I used your salve on Mr Alex. He's at rest now. You may need to keep Cyrus away from that burn, he doesn't know a thing about healing.'

Victoria smiled at Gold and pinched her cheek in thanks. 'Hello love. You know, I've told Cyrus it does more than keep the beams clean. He doesn't listen.'

Gold fidgeted on her feet, bit her lip, and pulled on Victoria's hands until they stopped.

'Can I ask—how is she doing?' Gold asked, her head nodding upwards.

'She's better. Her dreams are more... tranquil. Last night she had a pleasant one. It was of you, and us.'

'She's been talking in her sleep again.'

Victoria sighed, and closed her eyes. 'I know. I can hear her from downstairs. It always starts as whispers and then it becomes a full conversation. That part has never changed.'

'But a conversation with who?' said Gold.

'With her true sister.'

☆

Hazel was, for lack of a better term, an unnatural person. She looked as a girl should at her age, but there was a wicked sapience in her eyes, an intelligence that processed the world around her with ease. It was her inherent omniscience that had frightened Gold. The twin daughter of Lady Sarah Saville had unnerved even Cyrus, who considered himself worldly and hardened to such things. Upstairs, her room was a thick indigo over plaster, although in shadows and at night, it appeared black as coal. Hazel had covered the windows in thin strips of white cloth, which bled slices of daylight in, and danced softly whenever a draught was present. Every ornament to every piece of wooden furniture in the room was broken in some way; an aesthetic that weighed the room in stories. Hazel sat poised as a marionette on her bed with a tome balanced on her lap, shoulders relaxed, gaze serene. She breathed in deep as Gold walked up to her, her fingers tracing over the writing without pause, as though she could absorb the knowledge straight off the paper.

'He's a different man Goldie,' said Hazel, without looking up from her book.

'Who?'

'The one downstairs, the one you found.'

'Alex? I never knew him well enough. Victoria mentioned... you've been talking again?'

'Yes. Is there something wrong with talking?'

'Well no, I suppose not. But who is it?'

'I don't know her name. She looks a bit like me, with red hair though.'

'And what does she say?'

'She's scared–she has dreams like me.'

'Nightmares?'

'No. People call them waking dreams–you know the sort. Look, I've been reading about them. I'm trying to help her.'

'For what reason?' asked Gold.

'I don't know–I feel close to her, like we once knew each other.'

'Do you think it's yourself in the dreams? Hazel, are you afraid of something?' Gold pursed her mouth. It was difficult to get through to Hazel once her mind was made up. She couldn't keep pretending that she was her sister forever. Gold knew, at the back of her mind, there was a conversation in the future that would be difficult to navigate no matter how wise or prepared she became.

'Please don't look sad–I'm being stubborn again,' said Hazel after a moment.

'No, I'm being pig–headed. As long as you're happy, that means everything to me.'

They hugged before Victoria asked to join them for supper from downstairs. Once seated, with a knowing smile shared between them, Gold led them in Grace; the fowl she had caught earlier praised. Cyrus sat at the head of the table, his manners loose and uncomplicated. Victoria was ever the opposite, a napkin spread down from her delicate neck, her spoon taking no more than a thimble of stew each time. After, dishes washed, they took seats and huddled for warmth by the hearth. All listened as Cyrus recounted fables. Gold did not mind the fiction that was built in each one, and when he stalled in talking, Victoria reminded him of the next sentence, her eyes aglow in admiration. There was one story that caused Cyrus's voice to crack and tears began to welt from the old man's eyes. As Victoria comforted him, Alex woke beside them; his body shifting under the blankets. It was as if they had forgotten him in their reverie. He drank a mug of water, sipped some of the stew that was left in the pot, and gave thanks to have food in his belly.

'I had dreams of the stories you were telling my friend, they became one in the same,' he told Cyrus.

Cyrus nodded and wrung his hands. He took a bottle from a cupboard and poured two cups. They drank the gin in a sombre inclination; both men conscious of the women around them. Victoria looked at Gold and Hazel, and summoned them up with a shake of her hand.

'Perhaps we'll leave the men to it. It's been a long day husband. Don't stay up long.'

Cyrus shook his head and kissed his wife goodnight.

Gold took Hazel upstairs and tucked her into bed; she doused all

the candles but one, and left her to sleep. On the landing before

the staircase, as Victoria retired, Gold listened to the men thank

each other. They conversed of what had passed in those years, and

then fell into a comfortable silence, grateful friends together

again. Her head sank against a bannister, body relaxed. With a

waking dream that she could not resist, she soon drifted off

herself.

Gold's dream was lucid and fat; ripe with colour and

imaginings. In the relative quiet of her room, Hazel focussed and

slipped her mind into her sister like a glove. She found herself on

a ship made of song and soft light that glided over the waves.

Gold, on the prow, looked safe and happy, talking with a man.

Hazel studied this man. He was indistinct, a blur; tall, imposing, in command. As the dream wavered, Hazel realised her sister was a lost soul, trapped in a world of her own making. Some unclear event had broken her heart and those wounds had faded with time. The dream repeated itself. To Hazel, it had the stickiness of *déjà vu* to it, like her mind was a stage, and Gold and others were actors reading a script. Gold had to find a part of herself that was missing, it was all she could think of. Ravens wheeled overhead and smothered the dream as her sister woke, neck stiff from leaning against a bannister.

Hazel shook her head to dispel the magic, and hugged her blanket as the house settled. The murmurs of conversation downstairs came to an end. She could hear the soft tap of her sister's feet as she went to her own room to sleep. Hazel's room overlooked the jagged silhouette of Houndbarrow. Shouts and laughter in the streets would not die until the later. It was not a place for a happy childhood. She remembered days of mud and catcalls, scrapes and bruises; crude games and strict tuition. In the dark, Hazel got out of bed and edged her fingers along her dresser, until she found a cup and drank from it, cooling her

throat. It would help her sleep easier amidst the creaks and sighs

of the old house. Her first waking dream, at the age of twelve,

was of howling tempests. Lightning, gales, and torrents of greasy

rain would assault her mind in immanence. It was her sister who

would always wake her, it was Gold who would always cradle her

in the dark and comfort her. When Cyrus or Victoria asked if

everything was well, Gold would always admit to the disturbance.

Now Hazel knew that they all knew she was a freak. She had

heard them whisper in secret through the floorboards. She had

used her gift and dreamt their dreams that revealed what

they thought of her. She glanced into a mirror suspended above

her headboard and saw herself looking back. Her silver skin

flared in the moonlight. She could not sleep any longer. Her

thoughts a maelstrom.

The stillness at night would reach out to her and show

her gossamer and iridescent tangles that went to and fro. There

was a dreamlike quality to London and its buildings; an

unbreakable equation that suspended itself above all, daring to be solved. She had been reading for most of the day on how to quash

dreams, or at least control them for her own benefit. It was an

uphill struggle, as the dreams she had were not interpreted so

easily. With her mind on sleep, she laid thinking of the other

girl: the frightened one who spoke back to her in a dream with

half–closed eyes and a well–to–do accent. She looked like her, a

doppelgänger made flesh, expect instead of silver, there was a

mass of red hair. The conversation was odd, a conversation

which filled her with wanderlust. To go, to do something of life,

as if fate had cut her loose and caution was a sin. In a way the

feeling was overpowering, a taste of a life outside of these walls

gave Hazel a hunger to be more reckless.

With every care, Hazel donned a hat and covered herself

in a coat. She slipped a penknife up one sleeve, and placed a boot

on each foot. A box was placed in a pouch and slung around her

waist. She crept down the stairs (skipping the boards which

creaked) and unfastened the bolts of the front door painstakingly

slow. Hazel noticed, once the door was closed, London, despite

the chill, was starting to brace itself for revelries. The Night

Watch with dour capes and black hats stomped in the lantern-lit streets. As Hazel slinked along keeping to as much shadow as she could, she noticed the Watch were avoiding the more notorious alleys on purpose. With a thrill inside her, Hazel ran the last few metres to *The White Rose*. It was a crooked building with crooked patronage. It was the only pub (so it boasted) in London where everyone became as equals once inside, high or low, foreign or local. It treated everyone with the same sullen indifference. At first Hazel hated sneaking from home to go to the *Rose*. In time, her curiosity had outstripped what cowardice she felt. She enjoyed a relationship with one gentleman who had treated her with respect from the first evening they met. Pipe smoke vented into the night air as she swung the entrance open with both hands. Hazel braced herself for the quiet that would always fall as all eyes shifted to see who was entering. As the din returned, she spied him seated in a nook away from others. The man looked up; a red glow in his eyes burning themselves into her.

'Hello Hazel,' he croaked as he pulled a pipe away from his mouth.

She spun both ways to observe the rest of the tavern before greeting Percy with a curtsey. He in turn, raised his smoothed eyebrows and slicked his greying hair back. A man of this importance wouldn't meet alone. She looked over his shoulder; his escorts observed her. She sat, expectant, and removed her hat. Hazel always enjoyed her talks with the old man, but preferred a polite distance. She noticed his pipe return to his blackened lips. The skin on his tobacco stained fingers seemed to crackle as he moved them.

'Hazel my dear, how are you? How have you been?'

'In good health,' said Hazel.

'Excellent, better than mine, I hope. Let me see the cards—I need your gifts in these troublesome times.'

'Of course.'

She removed the box from her pouch and set it down on the rickety table. From the box she shuffled a pack of illustrated cards. She looked up while doing so. Percy was focussed on the tarot, as per usual. His old eyes darted as she flipped them between one another and dealt seven in a horseshoe. She turned the first.

'*The Tower*,' she said. 'It signifies upheaval. A bad omen to start with. Something went awry in the past - an event beyond your control.' Hazel raised an eyebrow.

Their deal, since Mr Percy had found her drinking alone and asked what she could do for him (in jest), was money in exchange for a reading. Hazel realised not before long that her readings must have been coming true for the old man, as he kept returning to meet her, the same time, the same night, each and every week. She would turn over cards until he nodded satisfied and left her a note. Tonight, felt different. Hazel revealed the second.

'*The Fool* reversed. The wanderer. A time of risk-taking and recklessness, unwilling to accept the unexpected. This is your present situation—the status quo.'

Percy grunted. He pulled on his knuckles and stared at Hazel for the next card. If she were the old man's friend, she would judge him to be on the brink of an episode.

'*The Empress*, the hidden influence in your life–unusual it would appear for you. It's also reversed, which means ill: a lack of stability or harmony with others–doubt.'

'There's certainly doubt in my enterprise,' he relied, pipe extinguished.

'The next is the *Hanged Man*. An immediate challenge in your life, it can mean good, transformation and change. Sacrifice for something of greater value.'

'The cards are saying I should stay my course?'

Hazel ignored the question with a motion. She continued, and flipped over the fifth card. '*The Priestess*–it represents the environment around you, duality, divinity, duty.'

Percy removed the ashes in his pipe and stood. 'This has been more than enough. Fate takes too much of me, and gives too little,' he placed a banknote onto the table, to which Hazel quickly hid.

Her heart sank as Turner bid her good evening and left.

She sat alone, her reading unfinished. If Mr Percy was not

interested it was serious indeed. She decided to reveal the last two

cards to herself. Next was *The Star*, his guidance, the best path:

balance, serenity, and fulfilment. She hesitated before revealing

the last card. Her fingers shook as she held it. It was his future, the

cornerstone; an aggregate for all others. It was the card that

showed what will be.

It was *The Serpent.*

The Serpent

The next day, after a fitful night's rest, Alex took a moment to gather

his thoughts in the half-light of the morning. The conversation with

Cyrus from the night previous disturbed him. Cyrus told him of Isolde

and her machinations against Turner and his syndicate, the very Tower

he had grew up in. Alex did not show how foolish he had felt inside,

when the revelation that some Lord had controlled his life. In theory,

Isolde's crusade was the more noble endeavour. A place where the

people profited from reformed rogues and villains, to build a future for

London, rather than shackled to one man's vision. But both sounded

mad. They were flawed visions driven by power and money. Nothing

more. Cyrus had retired from his duty to Isolde, to spend the rest of his

life indebted with wife and home and surrogate daughters; his model

family. Cyrus told him: *She's not the Devil you know. Try her house,*

her ideas and philosophy. It may not appeal to every man, but her deals

are honest. Your wishes granted in full, with a price.

With a price. Alex struggled downstairs in his friend's

black suit; careful not to spoil the sanctity of the house. He ran out into

the street and flagged down a carriage; his journey to Lamb's Wharf

awkward and slow. There were waifs and beggars on the streets, each

with a solemn indifference about them. The walls were clean of

vandalism; the Day Watch tired and disinterested. He thanked the

driver as he disembarked with a tip. Ahead stood a church with yellow

buttresses and shining gravestones. The doorman lifted one arm in

warning.

'Domine dirige nos,' said Alex.

The doorman smiled and nodded. Alex entered through the

doors and paced along its salt–and–pepper floors. He viewed its devils

and heroes frozen as busts and murals, as his shoes clicked along the

dark corridors. His shirt, folded, pressed and scented by Victoria, itched in places he'd never thought could be. He fantasised of his mother telling stories about how his family descended from nobility; to have something to his name, to be more comfortable and secure in affluence. If it meant throwing the whole of London into chaos just to satisfy personal greed, Alex could make do without affluence and comfort. The hall split into one auditorium which oozed expense. Several parts of the room were under development. Architects and plasterers hurried around with diagrams and clipped conversations. In the centre, sat on a gilt chair, Isolde crossed her arms. She gave him the slightest of smiles.

'Isolde.'

'I was expecting surprise Alex. Even distrust.'

'Why, because you worked with Lord Turner? Do you remember the last time we met? You were signing me over to Lady Saville. Years have passed since.'

'Yes. I see a change in you. You've lost that innocence. What do you think?'

Alex cocked his head. Isolde cast one hand at the partially finished room. Alex studied the work. It was replete with modern furniture. Panelled walls fitted with exotic wood, antique chairs with stuffed leather seats. It dawned on him where the money had come from.

'Has the penny dropped? Lord Turner's Tower was an abomination, a tumour in this city which gave him a monopoly—so I took it from him. It was he who attacked Lady Saville and her children on that ship, did you know that?'

Alex shook his head. 'For what gain?'

'To keep the island and gold a secret—and he nearly succeeded if it wasn't for your efforts, and Cyrus of course. If he had succeeded? Well, perhaps this conversation would never have happened.'

'Is Sarah Saville dead?'

Isolde shook her head. She propped one leg on top of her other and untangled her hair. It still flowed like frothed milk from the first time Alex had met her. He judged her laughter lines were the only imprint the years had caused on her face.

'So, this is all progress? This is better than that Tower? Another den of thieves?'

'It's the only way to prevent men like Turner from gaining traction.'

'And you are what? The queen of such?'

'A facilitator, a mother, not a ruler or tyrant—I don't serve myself.'

'That throne you're sitting on says otherwise.'

Isolde paced towards him and took his hands into her own. Alex blushed.

'Join me,' she said.

They walked past grand doors where an entrance in the wall turned into a spiral stair. Ahead, cut into the thick stone was a stair almost hidden from view. Under a stone portal Alex found himself in an austere office. A desk, two chairs and a fireplace tried their best to fill the space. Isolde sat; her arms still crossed. Alex eased himself into his chair.

'Cyrus. He isn't a godly man, is he?' she asked.

'From when I knew him, no.'

'Superstitious?'

'No. Not from what I saw in his house.'

'My house in deed, his wife, Victoria, in my employ. Tell me, do you believe?' she pointed to the ceiling.

'I'm uncertain, to speak the truth.'

'I imagine it was that girl, Elena, that gave you that uncertainty. She has set your mind free without knowing it.'

Alex took to removing the fatigue from his face. His hand passed over his burn; the scabs sharp and sensitive. His thoughts drifted from the fireplace and to Elena. He missed her enough. From the hardship life had handed him, his time with her was balance, a joy he had

not experienced before. Her capture still played in his mind, over and

over, looped in eternal scrutiny. She was carried up into the sky, as

sure as he could ride a horse or hoodwink a mark. It was the speed of it

that had injured his faith in nature and science. The impossible

was conceived before him. An awkward dissonance grew from that

knowledge, which reminded him of ghosts and spirits, of Heaven and

Hell, and he could do nothing with it.

'She has changed some thoughts of late,' he lied.

'Let me tell you a tale—my interpretation of events. The truth,

even if you won't accept it.'

Alex shrugged. 'Tell me then. The truth of it all.'

Isolde cleared her throat before starting; her eyes met his.

'There's much about the world that hides itself from the

business of men, and women. Long ago Gods created all that we see,

well back in antiquity, before the days of written language. These Gods

had wives and offspring, and they all lived in the clouds, content to be.'

'The Church would say this is heresy.'

'Yes, I'm speaking of polytheism. Do you know of the

Houses?'

'Heraldic?'

'No, no. These Houses are not of this earth.'

'You're being literal?'

'Factual. You've heard of astrology?'

Alex coughed. 'Heard of it, yes.'

'There are twelve Houses in the discipline of Astrology. Each governs an aspect of our lives. The First House, the House of Self, is governed by Mars.'

'Which is?'

'A Roman god. He is the god of war and peace, of blood, summer, and harvest. But the names and origins don't matter. What matters is that each House corresponds to a planet.'

'This sounds like nonsense.'

'It's relevant.'

'And where do we all fit into this grand scheme?'

'We had it all wrong. Turner had it all wrong. Lady Saville, as a child, took part in an expedition to an island, one that you know well.'

'She mentioned it, yes.'

'I assumed that was the only time she had been. But she was there years previous, with her father, mother and sister. Her father, William Saville, was a loudmouth. He enjoyed the attention of a crowd, the stories of far—flung places, and the prestige it brought. That's why he was there. Rumours tell of his wife, Eleanor, had a book. A Roman diary that showed a colony that had never left, a cult that worshipped Mars and never went back to Rome, *Mars Romulus.* The mad idea to find this hidden island tormented William until he finally figured where and how. And do you know of what he said when he came back to London?'

'No.'

'Nothing. The man was as quiet as mouse; until he died of old age, where he became even quieter.'

'A sad end.'

'An ironic end. William Saville's silence was the loudest he had ever been. A man who had changed so dramatically like that, tells me more than if he was here telling the story himself. A man that quiet kept secrets to his grave.'

Alex nodded. 'And there's more to this?'

'Much more. What do you think of my story so far?' she teased.

'Would it matter to you?'

'Oh, it would mean something to me Alex. A fresh perspective on this grand conspiracy.'

'It sounds ridiculous. All of it. A fairy-tale concocted for some ulterior motive to further your position.'

'And this is why you are here. Cyrus was right, a cynical mind never changes. Indulge me.'

'There's truth in-between the fantasy. Every story must be based on truth. It must have some starting point. We can say that Sarah was a child at some point, and that her family exists. I was hired by her sister Sophia; I know of Elena and Hazel also. But what was on the island? What changed so many things?'

'That cult protected a statue of gold; it was their idol. But they also kept a boon hidden. Perhaps the reason Sarah went back to the island.'

'A boon?' asked Alex.

'I don't know of what, the book was vague. I had hoped you would have remembered something significant from that voyage.'

'I recall she was sick and became pregnant thereafter.'

'Well what was it? What did she touch? Eat? A rough tumble in bed with one of the sailors?'

'When she turned for worse, we picked her up, myself and Cyrus, and brought her back to the ship. It was like a fever. She rambled and muttered about a flower. She spent a day in bed while I watched.'

With puffed cheeks Isolde caught herself before speaking. Alex sat with a sentence of his own half-formed in his mouth. Isolde had caught a memory that almost came to her, and when it failed, she rolled her eyes and gritted her teeth. With a wagging finger she placed a heavy book onto the desk, adamant on finding a particular page.

'Here,' Isolde held the book up. It showed a drawing of a peony.

'I never saw this flower she mentioned.'

'It's part of a myth, a creation myth.'

'Mars?'

'The very same. Flora, a goddess of fecundity and youth, used a petal on Juno. Who gave birth to Mars himself.'

'I was there. Sarah had twin daughters—both different and alike.'

Isolde lifted her wrists in agreement. 'Would you say it's a coincidence?'

'I-I'm not sure. I'm not sure about many things at this moment.'

'And can you fault me for wanting to know? To be curious, to seek the truth?'

'I cannot. I would have done the same. So, tell me, what plans do you have of me?'

'None as such. You will be well compensated however.'

Alex bit his tongue. 'For what?'

'To bring Elena and her sister to me safe and sound.'

The Moon

— The Storm Coast —

The air tasted foul. Drops of lead ran down her face and pooled into

her lips. She opened her matted eyes and found herself kneeling before a

statue of a pregnant woman with a body of alabaster. It turned its

hideous focus on her with the rumble of grating stone. Rivulets of iron

cascaded out of the statue's mouth and splashed below into a grate. Elena

screamed, the sound echoed and reverberated. Ruby fire ensorcelled

her; the fire seared the air which smoked and stung her eyes. A dark congregation of hooded men seated on onyx pews, swivelled with blank looks to study her.

'Welcome home,' a voice ran through her.

Elena stirred from sleep into darkness. She lay on her side while her arms cradled her head, her eyes searching for light. She felt blank at first, but the dread from yesterday soon built again. Her legs rocked with fear. Elena wrapped her arms tight around herself; she dug her fingernails deep into her skin. She had never felt so much despair before. The dirt beneath scattered around her cell as she thrashed her legs and pounded her fists on the walls. She heard footsteps above her oubliette; they sounded slow and deliberate. Elena wiped the grime off her arms and looked. She could see the silhouette of a man, the sky behind him too bright to make distinctions. He looked down impassive and waved to someone beyond her sight, before moving on, maintaining the same ponderous march. She worked hard to untangle her lank hair and smoothed it out as best she could. The dreams and visions had gone for the moment, her mind felt clear enough to think. There must be reason behind all this. The floor was sand, the thin walls were a rank iron, rusted and black as tar. One wall held a mirror, grime speckled around the edges. Her travelling clothes were gone, replaced with winter clothes. Her brow creased. She wished Alex was here now, another mind to make sense of it. As she calmed and started to drift into a slumber the mirror glowed. It was enough to prevent her from falling asleep. Elena stood and stared at the refracting light. As she walked closer a face emerged from the surface: it rippled as if she was looking at a reflection in water.

'There you are,' said the apparition, its voice smooth.

Panic squeezed Elena's heart. The woman in the mirror was terrible and beautiful at the same instance. Long gold hair framed two eyes which searched like a hawk. Her lips stained red; they splintered whenever they moved.

'Why am I here!?' cried Elena.

'At my behest.'

'What are you?'

'Is a mother not allowed to see her daughter?'

'Go away monster!'

'Why are you frightened child? Don't you know me?'

'Know you?'

The woman posed. 'Do I look like her? Like my sister, like Sophia?'

'Aunt Sarah?'

The image seemed to effervesce on the mention of the name. Elena threw herself back as the smoke erupted inside the image. When she looked, the woman wore an expression of arrogance. It communicated a mind with dark intent.

'Yes, your true mother.'

'No, it's not you.'

'I thought you were lost, child. I thought you were dead. And now here you are, returned to me.'

'My mother and father brought me up–they cared for me.'

'My sister? Care for you? She never would have shown you half the love I did the day you were born.'

Elena stalled. Her memories failed as she tried to summon an example of her childhood. A happy memory, one of love Sophia had shown her, or her father. There were none. She remembered a cold room with cold emotion. Maids and nannies who gave her indifferent, mechanical care. No friends; no peers with similar interests; no unlikely bonds formed with her tutors. It was a life that had disguised itself in the succour of never needing to want for anything; a sheltered life that had never given her doubt or hardship.

'I cannot remember.'

'A lie. I can tell. I used to tell them at your age,' Sarah smiled.

'They did not care for me. No. Why are you doing this to me?'

Elena had never felt such a sensation before. It felt as though an animal was working its way up her from her stomach and through her throat. Pangs of filth and nausea made her head spin and she collapsed on her knees.

'They did not care for you. And now look. You're frail, unable to stand. You are special my daughters, you and your sister. What name did they give you? For all of my sister's foibles, she has taste.'

'Elena.'

'Elena. Don't cry. Don't be sad sweet Elena. You are home now.'

'Where are you? Or are you an eidolon within glass?'

There was a pause while Lady Saville thought on the question. Elena wiped her mouth clean.

'I am real. Like you. You do not know how long it took to find you, nor how many nights I spent searching for you. Do you know what happened? The truth of the day I lost my world?'

'No, my mother never mentioned it.'

'She wouldn't. I would have. I would have disclosed the truth to you.'

'Tell me of it then, when you lost everything.'

'You were a baby—you and your sister. Just innocence wrapped up in my arms. I fell in love with you both, you know that? I used to sing songs of joy and it gladdened my heart to see you both smile when I did. We were so happy.'

Elena saw drops fall from Sarah's eyes; her sorrow ran deep, the pain still fresh. 'What happened? What caused this?'

'W—We were attacked on a ship. They came at us with cannon and men and fought back. I was injured. When I woke, you were both gone.'

'We were in danger?' Elena rubbed her temples. 'I never knew I had a sister to call my own. Where is she?'

'Lost. She was like you. You viewed the world with hungry eyes, whereas your sister, she saw everything as a puzzle to solve. The world as a curiosity. You would have grown up together. We could have been as a family.'

'But where did we go? How did we separate?'

'Frost's daughter and Cyrus both saved you. They rowed to shore. Why I have not heard from them in years, I do not know. My sweet child soon it will be time.'

'For what?' asked Elena.

'For you to be let out of that cage so that everyone can see you. I am sorry to have kept you this way.'

'You're fading.'

'The spell is weak. I cannot hold it much longer. You'll be freed, and they'll take you to me. Courage. Don't be scared Elena.'

The image of Sarah Saville dissipated as fast as it appeared. Her cell rose up with a grinding of chains. At first her arms flung up to shield the worst of the daylight. Then she heard a seagull above the chains, its keening rising above the thunder of waves and the whisper of dry grass. She saw around her, through a squint, a low cliffside which almost tumbled into the water; her cell, one of many, poised above the waves by a single rusted link. The man who looked into her cell was absent, as was the mechanism which had elevated her prison, though his footprints were still there, and chimney smoke rose from a lonely hut in the distance. She crawled outside in the mud and ate herbs and thick bulbs of grass and sipped water from puddles and crags. Her only shelter from the wind was back inside the cell, where she stayed and waited for the sun to return and her hunger to fade.

☆

Her thoughts were a conspiracy as they flooded her mind, telling her to doubt everything she saw. She shut them out until it was hot enough to warm her skin and the wind had died. What the monster in the mirror had said, Elena couldn't fathom. She couldn't believe in a truth that pushed everything she knew aside and replaced it with a falsehood. She took a clump of grass and chewed what water remained inside its stem. She had lost a disturbing amount of weight. She felt along her protruding ribs and her hips that now rose out of her skin. Elena paused mid-chew and took stock of her new world. A bust of energy brought her up to her knees; she could smell cooking past the cliffside. The coast was as alien to her as a full stomach. She recognised a few trees and bushes, the rest unfamiliar. She walked until her feet blistered and her sandals cracked. She flopped against a rock and sank until comfortable. Her vision blurred, her stomach rumbled and she rubbed it in hope of relief. The forest conjured phantoms made from mist that clung to the tree-tops and eavesdropped. *Mother, father, please forgive me.* Elena sobbed. She scolded herself for doing so. There was no point in wasting energy over being remorseful for the past, over what choices made. At this point she wished she had her old life back before the curse. Before leaving home and to wander towards

Ashtree and beyond; she wished she had seen her mother one last time,

or be held by her father. The memories swarmed and stung her. The

few happy memories came back to her: being with her family during

parades and festivals, her mother's perfume, the grand days she would

be free to walk the garden during summer. Most of all, she remembered

Alex.

'Why so sad on a day like this?'

Elena looked up. A band had strolled through the forest to

meet her. She lifted her legs and tried to steady herself.

'We were told to meet a girl, word from the gaoler,' said a

rough shaven man.

'She looks about the right age,' said a woman next to the man.

Elena hesitated. 'Do you know the woman in the mirror?'

'We do,' said another male. He was bald, with elliptical scars

running across his face. He dropped down to eye level. 'What's your

name?'

'Elena.'

'Look at her eyes. The same as hers,' said the woman.

'What's wrong with my eyes?' said Elena.

The band was silent as they exchanged glances.

'Where is she?' Elena addressed the bald man.

'To know that, miss, you'll have to follow us to our village.'

Throughout the forest dusk had settled in. The village was on the crest of a hill, which overlooked a fast river that drained into the coast. The band of hunters told her there were seven farmers, twelve wives, five carpenters, one blacksmith, ten freemen, two teachers, four babies and five children old enough to play games with each other. It reminded Elena of the streets surrounding Ashtree. Paths trampled through mud on top of mud that ran next to slanted houses. In the thick of it a forge and workshop made a constant din and she could smell a distant tannery over the loam underfoot. From the yew and ash trees she spied a church of sorts; its foundation built on a knoll. A great oak had grown through the middle of it, arching its branches towards the sky, its bark slick with recent rain. Coloured pennants woven in the oak fluttered and danced in the breeze. The bald man and the woman pushed Elena up a shrouded path, around a middling garden and into a warmed hall. It stank of fresh wood, forcing her to sneeze. At the back of the hall stood a highbacked chair with four cloven feet and polished armrests; on it sat Sarah who glanced at her with a curious tightening of her face. An older man stood beside her, with beard dark as soot. His skin was pitted with experience, but his clothes clean and civil.

The woman who had followed her from the forest knelt before the throne and took her place beside it. Perching herself on a stool to the right of it. She removed her hood and checked her posture. She looked at Elena with mixed interest. Her skin was as grey as ghost–trails and she looked as hospitable as a winter sky. Elena noticed one of her arms was missing.

'Where do you think you are child?' asked Sarah. She rested forwards with her chin supported by one clutched hand.

Elena thought back to when her Sophia first taught her court etiquette, and ignored it.

'You tell me,' Elena replied with smirk.

'The Storm Coast,' she laughed. 'By the river Plum.'

'I want to return home. My father and mother will have sought me out?'

'You *are* home now sweet Elena,' said Sarah. Elena fell silent, her mouth glued. She could feel her stomach drop as the fire within her faded.

☆

An open pit fire heated the hall when night came. The village had huddled underneath the oak and roof to hear Sarah's tale of how her daughter had come back to her. Droplets of rain hissed as they hit the hot slate near the pit. Logs split into quarters were placed in beaten iron sconces that roared around them. Fur blankets spread amongst the sick or feeble. Hot broth, spiced with coriander, was soon served in large cups. Elena started with a sip, but was soon cupping the broth back, drinking it all. The meat melted in her mouth; the gravy as good as she had back home. After the broth came spelt loaves; broken amongst the still hungry with a nod and a thank you. It was wholesome bread, scooped from the baker's oven and still warm on the inside. The blacksmith, a man with puffed cheeks and scrabbly beard, knocked his tankard onto the stone floor. Everyone grew silent, conversations ceasing mid–sentence.

'Are we all well and warm?' began Sarah, standing above them on a stool. The hall murmured approval with taps of their cups. 'Decades ago, my daughters were stolen from me, stolen by a man twisted by greed. One of them has returned. They have named her *Elena*, a part of the infamous Stone family. They had no *right* to steal her in the first place,' she hissed.

Sarah motioned to Elena to take her side. Elena stood, aware of eyes on her, shuffling towards Sarah. She could hear the whispers and glances of the villages beneath their cowls or blankets. She could hear malcontent with sharing their food to a stranger, another stranger out of the blue. Elena recognised the characters behind a few of their faces, mostly bitter and hard. They were sailors and craftsmen, traders and rogues. Her heart trembled in her chest as she took Sarah's hand.

'There is revolution spreading through the world. The Continental States has sparked liberty in our hearts. We are the fire that will excise the fat from our country.' There was cheer amongst the crowd. A murmur of approval as they stoked the fire again. 'With our *Sisters* we will take back London, take back what was stolen from us, from me.'

As the crowd settled, a cook brought platters of roasted greens with him. Together the village ate again. For companions lost, they left seats empty. Others ate alone or with a prayer on their lips. Through it all Elena studied the villager's expressions.

'They're scared. Deep down,' she whispered to Sarah.

'They are frightened of the winter; the rain turns as bitter as the sea around these parts.' Sarah sighed with her eyes closed. She

appeared a degree more human in Elena's eyes, not the monster in the
mirror.

'How do you know I'm your daughter?'

'You must have felt it,' Sarah said as she wiped her eyes. 'You
must have felt the bond between us.' She pricked Elena with her thumb
onto on her stomach. Elena sensed a tingle that warmed from her cheeks
to her heart. 'Come child, there is something I need you to see. Selene,
get cloaks for us and some torches, we are taking the coastal path.'

'Yes Cwen,' said the woman with the lost arm.

They paced out into the open air. The world had turned
opaque with nightfall; everywhere a royal purple died on top of a failing
sun. Above, a flock of crows scattered in formation, cawing in
adulation. Elena had donned brown cloak which reeked of horse. Sarah
lit their torches with a bend of her wrist, casting a spell. She handed one
to Elena. The path took them down through muddy dykes and bogged
trees. She looked at crumpled cliffs, hedgerows filled with stumps
shrivelled by the wind; at the end of one path stood Selene who escorted
Elena from the forest. She gave a nod to them both and creased her face
into a smile when Elena got close.

'We haven't been introduced my Cwen. So, this is Elena. A
spitting image of you, but she doesn't have John's sable hair.'

'No, she doesn't, and I've explained her birth. Elena, this is Selene. She and her Sisters helped us, after we fought against privateers.'

'Fought? You didn't come here by choice?' said Elena.

'We had no choice. We had to land here or be destroyed. Our ship was almost sunk.'

'I've heard of it. From my father. The *Tale of The Lion*? It's a popular story.'

'That man is not your father,' Sarah seethed behind her cloak, 'try and be mindful of what you say around me.'

'I'm sorry my Lady for offence,' Elena tipped her head for effect.

'No harm done my child,' Sarah reached out a hand to caress but stopped halfway, her eyes hesitant.

'My Cwen, we are waiting for you,' Selene's voice broke the trance of the moment.

'Yes. Of course, come.'

'But one question my Cwen—can I ask your daughter something?'

'You may. Elena you can answer Selene's question?'

'I can certainly try,' Elena said with a frown. 'What is it?'

'You don't see anything do you?' Selene held up her false arm.

'No, just your shoulder. I am sorry.'

'She must be your daughter Sarah. She can see right through my glamour.'

Sarah smiled and nodded at Elena, who still frowned.

'Understand the confusion. You can see through a witch's glamour Elena. To ordinary folk it would appear as a normal limb, an illusion.'

They walked down to a cracked strand of beach, past long grass and clumps of samphire. There came a honeycomb cave set into a cliff, its passage lined with candles held in niches. At the end of the cave stood pillars of granite, dark as kelp. They supported a roof for the beginning of a dock that stretched back into bare earth. *The Lion's Tail* slumped in the dock, its timber and sails had seen better days. Elena did not need to be a mariner to figure it was an aged vessel, one that would be more suitable now for firewood. A relic someone was holding dear to.

'Impressed?' said Selene.

'What is this place?'

'We call it The Hollows. We've got the whole coven down here—all of the Sisterhood.'

Elena gaped as they rounded a corner and saw how extensive the channel was. At the mouth was a tall pair of sluice gates waiting to flood the dock at command. Wisps skimmed off the top of waves, coating the entrance with salt. In moments the sea turned ink and the sky unfolded. A group of women in riding habits glided from the air with torches in one hand and a bundle of twigs in the other.

'You're a coven?' Elena asked.

'The Sisterhood of the Plum has protected us Elena, our ship was almost lost to us with all souls on board. But we fought back against Turner's lapdogs. In the end, we prevailed with their help.'

'I know the story. You summoned a dragon to fight back against the pirates.'

'A dragon?' Sarah laughed. 'Oh! I wish I had. My live would have been complete.'

'You know why it's called *The Lion's Tail*?' Selene asked.

'Nobody has ever caught it,' Elena repeated from memory.

'And nobody has ever caught one of us,' said one of the incoming witches, stepping off her staff. Elena studied the witch that spoke. Her broomstick gnarled around one gloved hand with a band of twine holding a bundle of twigs at one end. She was older than Elena, with tossed hair and sun-kissed skin. There was a carefree smile on her lips and confidence in her eyes as she led her group into a set of doors set into the rock face.

'Welcome to your legacy, Elena Saville,' Sarah said, as a rare smile stretched on her face.

The Chariot

— Houndbarrow, London —

The day began with Mr Alex leaving their home before she was

awake. The sight of the man, the singular way he spoke and

moved, had stirred too much of the past in her. On her bedroom

floor she closed her eyes and prayed, fingers wrapped around her

cross. As she knelt, Gold recalled why she felt troubled as of late.

Not because of anxiety. She felt as though her mind was

reorganising itself. She could sense her eyes moving while

dreaming. Seeking out new images, new faces. She saw it all in

sharp clarity. Her worried mind comprehended the smallest

details, to the biggest vista: the sounds, the colours, and the taste

of the air on her tongue. To her, it signified change, but of what

nature she was not sure. As Cyrus woke with a sore back and a

cold attitude, she told him that Hazel was missing, much to his

appal. They searched her room with fervour; it was empty, as she

had said, with Hazel's clothes and boots gone. Together they

made the decision to not involve Victoria, as it would only serve

to stress her, and let her sleep. Cyrus could not bear the thought

of her missing. They dressed in hunting frocks, with knives and

daggers concealed in their jackboots. They stomped about as if

their noise would wake Hazel and all would be well. Out on the

street, Houndbarrow expanded as a maze in all directions.

'Why wouldn't she tell us? She promised me she was

happy.' said Gold.

'I don't know,' said Cyrus, whose mind had just started to

stir.

'Did she mention anything to you?'

'No.'

'Where would she have gone in Houndbarrow? It's a rat's nest.'

Cyrus looked at Gold with a drawn face. 'I don't know.'

Above, Gold saw the ashen pall of clouds now within striking distance of London. The nightmare she had in the early morning still harrowed her. She saw her sister snatched by black claws; twisted hags sneering at her; her legs heavy as stone. Gold whispered a prayer to bring her a sense of calm. In the dream she wielded a sword made from white roses and struck down those that would injure Hazel. She wished it was so in the real world. She ignored the fantasy, steeled herself, and walked towards the market square, one hand beckoning Cyrus. Gold clambered up an iron gate and squeezed herself into a passage. Muddy water flowed around her boots; her jerkin and mittens felt tight as she stretched them.

'Why here?' asked Cyrus. 'We're heading towards the middle of 'Barrow.'

'I've got a feeling,' replied Gold.

'I taught you not to rely on feelings. Perhaps Hazel was kidnapped and she's halfway to France by now.'

'Regardless of where we start, Hazel can't have gone far in one night. She's not the adventurous type.'

The cramped tunnel ran on ahead; Gold tensed her muscles once more and forced herself to calm. She moved towards the end of the tunnel and lit her lantern. Cyrus stood facing her; his boots pasted in muck, a neckerchief over his nose. While Gold strained her eyes in the gloom, the water around them started to flow quicker.

'It's starting to rain.' said Cyrus.

'Must be that storm we saw. Must have broken faster than I thought it would. You didn't see anything odd about it did you?' Gold asked.

'None. Except it was a clear morning.'

Gold nodded. Would they chase Hazel forever? Was this her life? The frustrations of the previous weeks brought her down. No wonder Hazel left home. No number of platitudes or burying the truth could stop it.

'Lead on then. Let's see where your feelings take us.'

'This is pointless. We'll not find her Cyrus, it's my fault she's ran off.'

'Nonsense girl. She's got Saville blood in her; God only knows what she thinks at any given time. You were the best thing in her life. She never admitted to it, but she thought the world of you.'

'Thank you,' she squeezed Cyrus. 'Let's try at least.'

'All we can do in life.'

They quickened pace until a loose grate caught Gold's eye. She peered through it with her light and came face to face with rats tumbling and spilling out through the bars. Gold called out to Cyrus. The rats were scrambling to get ahead of the torrents of water that were becoming stronger by the minute. He held her arm and took her aside. Cyrus pointed up at a ladder leading towards market and the start of their search. She gagged at the thought of the vermin; her legs wriggled by instinct whenever one came close.

'I hope you're not afraid of them,' asked Cyrus.

'No, it's more the fear of how filthy they are.'

Cyrus laughed. 'So, you do share something in common with Victoria. She shrieks like a banshee if one gets into the house.'

They clambered up the ladder, up towards the heavy door that led out onto the streets and opened it. Cyrus took stock of the situation as Gold leaned from the ladder below enjoying the wisps of fresh air. He motioned to her to follow and she took care not to make any noise. The public square looked larger in the wet and without stalls. She could feel the sky was boiling in anger. Not a single soul was out on the streets that shouldn't have been; the rest had fled the downpour. A deafening peal of thunder came in answer; the rain doubled in effort.

'Let's try the church,' she cried over the rain. Cyrus grunted. Gold ditched her lantern in an entrance and jogged across the market avoiding puddles.

'What was that?' shouted Cyrus.

A shadow hovered above. It craned its neck at the streets; its shawl flittered about in the storm.

'It's one of those things Alex described,' Cyrus whispered. 'Two of them took Elena just before he reached here.'

Gold knelt behind a cart. The witch was in a black dress, and held a gnarled branch in between her thighs. Tiny baubles and glass balls fixed to her hair jangled. Gold gasped when she looked at the witch's face: it was a woman, scarred from her lips to the top of crown, her eyes cold. She cocked her head, as if hearing a distant call. The witch smoothed her legs along the length of the stick and flew off at an alarming speed.

'God preserve. Did you see that? No wonder your friend was so shaken.'

Cyrus turned to Gold and waited for the wind to simmer down. 'We don't need daggers and knives, we need rifles and pistols.'

'What did happen to Alex?'

'Two of those things snatched a girl he was with, Elena. Before he could save her, and he tried to, fire caught on thin air, hence the burn. He was terrified Gold. I knew him as foolhardy, but never shaken like that,' Cyrus pulled on his knuckles.

'Where is he now? He left early this morning.'

'He's speaking to a mutual friend.'

Gold pulled her hood tighter and ran through the streets to the next junction. Ahead Cyrus had paused in front of a crumbling church.

'Here,' he said.

'Looks like the doors are locked and boarded.'

'Well, help me with them,' Cyrus breathed deep and started to remove the boards to church. Gold kept one eye on the clouds and one on the empty streets. She glanced at Cyrus, who met her stare.

'I had a waking dream last night,' she said.

'Can it help pull down planks and nails?'

'There's something vile in the air over London. It's like a miasma, and it's not just this storm.'

'One bad dream and you get all prophetic. When did you become so superstitious girl?'

'Since finding God that day you saved me.'

Cyrus nodded, conceding. Sounds of a skirmish echoed through the square. Shouts of men and the clashing of swords grew louder; after a moment they heard gunfire. They hurried to remove the last of the boards, and stepped inside the cloister.

'No. Nothing here,' said Cyrus as he mopped his brow.

'She's a needle in a haystack.'

'Anymore insights or feelings?' he mocked.

Gold looked around the old church. It had seen plenty of feet pass through its narrow entrance; the marble steps underneath concave with age. She grasped a pillar with one hand. Its chiselled lines pronounced in groups of three. Above in a space that attached the ceiling to a rib, was a rose carved from the same stone, washed a thin white.

'What's that?' Gold pointed.

'Seems to be a rose.'

'What's the name of that inn; the one where all those charlatans and drunks go to for attention?'

'*The White Rose.* It's a street from home. Smugglers'
tunnels run through the cellar. Plenty of shelter for the whole
district.'

Gold and Cyrus took what remained of the door and
closed it, careful not to draw further attention. They picked up a
pace, and jogged to the *Rose*.

Hazel rushed past empty barrels, her wet boots slapping
on the smooth flagstones. Her heart raced as she pushed herself
through the cramped tunnels. She watched the last of men from
the inn brave outside. She told herself to calm. *If Gold was here,
would she fight?* The smuggling den, once used to distribute of
all manner of goods was now a shelter. Pews and chairs
made barricades, with muskets positioned along the balconies
above. She saw cowering faces of the children tucked close to their

mothers. The only seniority around was now a pack of wizened men. Candles dotted about burned low; the old men placed on guard shared dark looks. Flashes of lightning broke her concentration, and the thunder stopped it altogether. Outside was quiet aside from the downpour. She hadn't heard rain this heavy since Gold took her to the sea one summer ago. The water there was freezing when she dipped a reluctant toe into it, but she adored the wind and running across the sand. They made and flew kites of all different shapes and sizes, trying to best one another. She used to cry when it rained, especially if she was flying a new kite, intent on it being the fastest. The paper would turn to mush and disappear before her eyes. Gold would shrug when this would happen and smile. Three more flashes outside convinced Hazel to take cover under a discarded blanket. She prayed her sister could not only find her, but forgive her.

☆

Gold rounded the corner with Cyrus ahead. The only other place was now the inn; she prayed out loud that her younger sister would be well and, in her arms, soon. She could see the flattened roof of the *Rose* as they drew closer; its pale, chalky tiles contrasting with the sickly pastels of the houses around it. Gold realised they were both in the eye of the storm. The wind howled outside the eye; small drops of rain periodic. The battle still raged at the gates to the district. Gold could hear it; militia in groups of twelve marched past the inn. Movement above forced her to crouch and try her best to hide in the niche of the doorway she was in. Seven witches flew only a metre away from her. She could feel fear creep up her spine and along her arms. Among them was a tall witch, clothed in white. They all let out a shrill noise. Gold likened it to a pack of feral cats. Three militiamen, brandishing rifles, charged them from the opposite end of the street. The witches fired arrows at them perched on their branches, felling two men. Once their quivers were empty, they drew curved daggers that flashed in the lightning.

Before Gold could shout, Cyrus dashed ahead, his dagger poised with the grip reversed. He stabbed the closest witch straight through her heart: the tip erupted clean from her chest. A strange choking noise carried its way out of the witch's mouth as she collapsed. The other witches ceased their attack and looked dumbfounded. The tall witch dropped her bow and quiver and lunged at Cyrus with her own blade. He twisted his heels to the left and with a single stroke lopped her right fingers off; blood pumping from the stumps. As she let out a scream, the rest took flight and carried their wounded sister off into the skies. Gold could hear them fade into the storm with whistles and hisses. The militiamen standing rushed ahead to join with their fellows.

'Poor fighters,' said Cyrus. 'All noise and posturing.'

'They seemed competent enough, and well-armed,' said Gold, wide-eyed.

'It worries me though. Why are they here?'

'They snatched Hazel's sister you said. Elena? She must be important enough for the risk.'

'Black ones that could fly–just as Alex described.'

'I remember her. She was only a baby.'

'Sarah Saville's children, yes.'

'Could Elena have told Sarah Saville where her sister was?'

'Mayhap. If Sarah Saville was still alive to be told; which I find hard to imagine.'

Gold locked her jaw. A miserable group of old men were present at the entrance of the *Rose* and nodded as they passed into the inn. Inside Gold wrung out her hair and patted down her soaked clothes. What light there was, shone on people, some stabbed, others with burns. Several children ran past carrying clean sheets and jugs of water for the worst off. An older woman coordinated them, tearing the cloth into bandages. Gold walked up to her; dabbing rainwater from her cheeks.

'Madam.'

'Yes?' the woman looked puzzled and glanced at Cyrus. Gold could see her eyes move down to their scabbards.

'We're not militia, or soldiers,' Gold held her hands up. 'My sister is missing, she's got silver hair, skittish manners. Have you seen her? She's only young.'

The woman looked down to her shoes as she talked. 'That young miss with the hair like steel? She left. She left for you. She wouldn't listen to me now, she insisted in going.'

'She's stubborn.' Gold said.

'Aye, very. Not much sense in her head. Told her I'd stay away from fighting if I was you.'

'Which direction was she headed? Which street did she take?'

The woman shrugged and waved her hand towards the district gate. Gold stopped, her mind turning.

'If she comes back, tell her I'm looking for her, and I'm taking her back home'

'No promises dear. But who are you to her anyway?'

'Family,' said Gold, and marched her way back outside.

✩

Hazel pushed past a mob of men shouting at a witch sprawled on a patch of mud. The mob had bound her mouth shut; bands kept her arms tied and unable to move. Hazel grimaced at the thought of what justice they would deliver. An arrow whistled past her head as another guard fell from his parapet clutching his throat. She could see through the smoke and fires a throng of witches pushed out of the main gate and into murder holes. Men-at-arms threw themselves into the mass and shouted over the cries of the witches. Officers on horseback isolated batches of them and shot until their prey no longer moved. The spells and curses the witches used in return caused men's skin to blister and their swords and rifles melt before their eyes. Bolts of energy erupted from sinister wands causing horrific wounds. Hazel turned from the violence and coughed up the contents of her stomach. She knew on some level how visceral fighting would be, but the smell of burnt skin had pushed the limits of her nausea. The screams of the innocent and the report of rifles were too much. She stumbled into a stack of straw as a militia man shoved her aside. She found small comfort nestled in the bale, and turned to look at corpses lying on the ground. Priests from under a shelter grasped those still alive under both arms and drag them away for aid. Hazel turned around and amongst the torches she spotted a familiar face, her sister had come.

'Gold!'

Hazel embraced her from behind and held her tight. Gold spun and held her sister in return. They didn't have need for words; the relief felt was the only thing Hazel wanted at this moment. Gold saw red streaks on the side of Hazel's face and started to clean them with fresh linen. They crumpled to the ground as Gold tended to her cut.

'I'll always be here for you, you know this. *Sisters.* We have to stick together,' Gold shouted.

Hazel nodded; her lips trembled. Gold watched her sister's face fold in pain. It was natural let go of the emotions she had pent up. Hazel grasped her mouth to stop a squeal from escaping. Gold kissed her on the head; the little shakes and sobs smothered by her cloak.

'Come on, come back home with us.'

The thunder subsided as if it mirrored her relief. Storm clouds passed with the wind–the sun shone down on men at the gate. The witches had scattered. Captains now issued orders to extinguish fires and remove the dead. She lifted her sister up and led her back home. Gold watched the crowds of people for Cyrus. He stood just beyond the gate and pointed to follow; his face ashen.

☆

The rain had begun to cease just as Simon folded his spyglass away. He placed one hand on the roof slates and one on a cornerstone and jumped. He landed onto a wooden balcony, pushed open an unlocked window, and stalked through the home. He pulled apart Hazel's drawers and bookshelves and inspected the contents. Nothing seemed out of the ordinary. Some clothes, a few trinkets, the occasional book on nonsense. Isolde did not ask him to steal money or possessions, just an answer on why Cyrus' child would meet Turner. Why would a young woman with a deck of cards be seeing him? If he found any answers here, they had further reason to suspect she was also a witch, a miracle child... and born of Sarah Saville, not Cyrus and Victoria as they thought. If it was true, they could use her gifts to make Isolde's vision a reality. He looked at Hazel's desk and paused. He drew himself eye-level; more books and journals and nothing more. He left the bedsit, passed the reception and went through the front passage. After the fighting there was no noise aside from the distant shouts of men. He strained his hearing. There was one sound he could make out from the quiet; a scrape of metal against stone. He spun. On the corner of the street Cyrus stood, his dagger nicked against a wall, his eyes locked onto him.

'How did you know?' Simon asked.

Cyrus pursed his lips. 'You're not supposed to be here, lad. And you can put whatever you've stolen, back.'

'And you assume that I've taken something that's yours? Isolde owns this house and everyone and everything in it.'

Cyrus took stock of Red. From the last he saw of the fledgling thief he was a scrawny boy all dressed in red. Now he was a young man, filled out, spry in his step and determined. 'You're feeling brave old man? You want to fight me? I think you'd lose,' Red unbelted his sword, the blade shone.

'You *think* I would lose? That doesn't sound sure. But I *know* her sister wont.'

Gold rushed behind Red with a cry and lashed her dagger out; he parried the blow. She backed off. In the glare of the sun it was difficult to focus. Red twirled his blade flashing out to strike her head. Gold felt time slow and reflected his sword back to him. The ringing noise was still in her ears as she used the opportunity to jump. She spun around his waist and knocked his feet underneath him in one movement. He lashed out at her with his pommel, smashing her nose. Screaming, Gold threw all her weight into a punch. The blow knocked Red to the side and he fell to the cobbled street, sword clattering. She positioned her dagger and drove it through his chest. His hands reached up to ward off the inevitable. There was a murmur, like a whimpering child, and he took his last breath.

On the street it was silent, aside from Gold's ragged breath as she panted, drinking in the air. She jostled her dagger out of the corpse, the heady smell of her own blood making her gag. The only thing left to do was to go home. She removed a mitt and wiped the sweat off her brow. Cyrus propped her under one arm, and Gold pushed her thoughts aside until the morning.

The World

London was still sleeping as Alex prepared for his journey.

Bakers and drunks were the only sort awake in the glower. He looked at Isolde's church one last time, steadying himself on his horse, and gestured at it. Cyrus and Ghost followed his lead out of the gates with their own provisions and weapons. He had sent word for Gold and Hazel to join them later. Alex needed Hazel, she had talents beyond his comprehension, and Isolde needed her as part of their deal. It was on faith that he hoped she could sense her sister, or Lady Saville, and guide them in some small part. Birdsong played around them as their horses struggled through churned mud and scattered stone, pausing at times to check

equipment and rest. After a full day, night came upon them

sooner than Alex appreciated. They camped far off the road,

under the shadow of an old mill. Its sails turned in the wind,

grinding away nothing. Their first meal was in a sullen quiet, as

though the journey was a false start, a non-adventure. Haunch,

rainwater and fortified bread eased their stomachs enough for

sleep beside hot embers. Later, two torches appeared by the road,

both jumped up and down, held by people on horseback. Alex

woke Cyrus.

'Two riders.'

Cyrus and Ghost drew their weapons and kept watch

over the camp. Alex stalked through the darkness, careful not to

reveal himself. He overheard the horsemen chatter; one was

younger than the other, a girl. The other was a woman with hood

pulled tight over her face. He recognised her clothes, leather

breeches for hunting. Her boots tied loose like Cyrus did. The

two figures paused. The older one shone her torch across the

field. Alex stood, with his arms held upright.

'Gold?'

Gold tilted her head as she recognised Alex's voice. She came off her horse, which spluttered and shook. They embraced at the roadside and shared accounts of how they fared against the witches, how Gold's nose was bruised purple, but not how Red had lost his life, Gold and Hazel taking turns to glare at Ghost. They rested their mounts, and forced their way inside. Rotten flour and dust had thickened the air in neglect. There was room for all, and they all crowded over the millstone. A board acted as a table top and Gold unfurled a map, lighting candles after. Between the group of five, the silence was broken as Alex spoke.

'I made my mind up while speaking with Isolde,' he looked at Cyrus, who nodded.

'And who is that?' said Gold.

Alex scratched at his stubble. 'She is, or was, in league with a fellow called Turner. Who was the master of the Redbridge Tower; where myself and Cyrus are from.'

'And me,' Ghost interrupted.

'And Charlotte. I need everyone's help to bring Elena back, safe and sound.'

Silence grew in the mill. The creak of the sails turning counted the seconds for them.

'And why *is* she here?' sneered Hazel.

'Charlotte is here because she wants to be with Cyrus. She has decided, in her own way, to leave the service of Isolde.'

Ghost smiled. She brushed her brown fringe to one side. 'Well spoken. It's true, although, you two especially,' she pointed at Gold and Hazel, 'might find this hard to believe, but I'm finished with working for either Turner or Isolde. Plain to see that their empires are crumbling around them, and I'm not one for staying on a sinking ship. After all of this is over, I'm leaving London behind me.'

'Well, what do we call you now?' asked Gold.

'Just call me Charlotte, do away with that nickname. It's stupid.'

They all nodded at her and agreed on such, except Hazel, who kept a healthy distance.

'To business then. We can gain passage from Sea Breach,' said Gold. 'Difficulty lies in finding Elena and Sarah Saville. But we have a solution.'

'I can divine their whereabouts, or at least catch their trail.'

'I knew it,' said Alex.

'Mr Alex. Pleased to meet you sir. I'm Hazel.'

'Hazel. We've met, a long time ago.'

'What's the first step?' asked Cyrus.

'I'll take a guess that you need something to catch the trail of a witch in the first place. Like an object or memory of such?' said Charlotte.

Hazel looked impressed. 'I do yes. I'd need it to be fresh, or still have a pattern about it. Everything is connected. When the strings of life become tangled,' she motioned to Alex's scar, 'or abused, they twist back to their origin, which I can follow. Like a bundle of wool, unravelling.'

'Why did you point at his scar?'

Hazel looked him over. 'There's a knot still left there. It keeps the wound from healing. If you'd permit me.'

'If you must,' said Alex.

Hazel rolled back her eyes, her breathing short and sharp. She reached out with her hands as if knitting. Alex felt his scar tingle, scratch, bite. He winced at the pain, but it was over before he could ask her to stop. He felt where his scar should have been; he could feel was only smooth skin, no marks or scabs. He caught Charlotte's expression out of the corner of his eye. A loose pride formed in her eyes as she folded her arms in thought.

'She is a witch then. The stories were true,' marvelled Charlotte.

'There's nothing evil about her. Just gifted, that's all,' Gold warned.

'What did you see Hazel?' said Cyrus.

Hazel was stood, still in a trance, her eyes sullen and puffy. She slumped forward onto her knees coughing in short breaths. Gold took hold of her, easing her up.

'Anything?'

'Nothing, there is nothing. The pattern ends up into the sky, it goes south, then nothing.'

'A dead end.'

Hazel shook her head. 'No, it ends abrupt, like a patch of night in the middle of a perfect day. It's here.' She pointed at the map, her finger tracing down from London, to the Cape of Strangers.

'The Storm Coast. Can we get passage Gold?'

'Easy. I've a captain in mind who can take us,' she pointed at a coastal town on the map.

'Any other thoughts?'

'I've a ship ready for myself and Charlotte,' smiled Cyrus. 'She doesn't fully trust me yet. Do you?'

'I don't trust any of you,' Charlotte said, laughing.

'Likewise, young miss. Gold, Hazel, I'll be with you. Cyrus and Charlotte, on the second ship. We'll meet here, right in the middle of it. Hazel, you are now our *guide* through this,' Alex gave her a smile, which made the young witch red as a strawberry.

By first light they had left the mill and saw Sea Breach peaking above fog that had pooled with the first rays of sun. The town gave golden promise on the white-bricked road that fed into it. Spires crowned with silver-slate tiles ran with a spectrum of flags. In the busyness outside, soldiers patrolled the area while harlots harangued passers-by. In time the town opened gates for the day's trade. Taverns inside Sea Breach were few. Shops dominated most of the business along a single stretch of the quayside. At midday Gold had secured a ship to the Cape, leaving in two days. A merchantman by the name of the *Crescent Harp*, which would take them as passengers; Cyrus and Charlotte would leave on the *Rancor*, a sloop.

'Nothing about both journeys is without risk,' said Cyrus, 'but we're committed. Might as well enjoy the respite while we can.'

'We'll have to give up the horses, we can't rent stables for them,' Alex spoke, setting down a drink. 'They should fetch a fair price.'

'Our horses will stay here. I couldn't face selling them Alex, we've been through too much,' said Gold. Cyrus nodded.

'I understand. Anyone else have any attachments?'

There was a shake of heads. Charlotte laughed.

'Half of you must be wondering why I am here.'

'Aside from the coin,' teased Alex.

'Just know I'm not like *Red*. I'm not a fool. Just here to help, and get my cut.'

'We know. Can we look over the map once more?' I want to be sure of where we land,' said Cyrus.

'Here.' Gold unrolled the map again, spreading it over the table. They estimated how long the journey would take. With the drinks dry, the hearth low and the Innkeeper glaring at them, they retreated to their beds. After another night, the group split into two. Alex clambered aboard the *Harp's* gangway and onto the deck. It was a thin vessel, with greasy sails and nonchalant captain, who Gold knew from her days of sailing. Their fee was exorbitant, but the Stranger crew welcomed them with an open cask of black ale and supper.

'Friendly. I thought they were all set against us,' said Hazel, once the meal was finished, and they had all settled on respective bunks.

'The majority are set against the Crown yes, but these are Stormfolk. They have very different opinions on English rule. They were once a free people, with their own lands.'

'Like the Westlanders, or the Darklands north of here.'

'Exactly so,' relied Gold.

The ship proudly flew its black and white stripes as they cut through the Channel. It mocked Alex's opinions of how seaworthy the craft was, and not before long he started to fall into a deep sleep, a part of him strangely glad to be back at sea. It was at midnight he woke without reason. The ship gently lolled from side to side as he looked across his cabin, and to the door. Hazel was standing there, dressed, her head tilted.

'Hazel. What's wrong?' Alex whispered, his eyes trying to adjust.

She traced one hand in the air, as if feeling for invisible grooves in the dark.

'You don't see them sir?'

'See what?' Alex covered himself with his sheets as best he could.

'Look, they're everywhere. There's one, there's another,' she giggled. 'It flew past your head.'

'Shh. What are you seeing? I don't understand.'

Hazel paused. In the dark Alex could only guess at her expression. His eyes adjusted, and she loomed closer to him. She removed her boots, her shift, and wriggled out of her undergarments. She slid under his covers, forcing her legs between his. He leaned towards her, one hand pulling on her neck. It started with a peck rather than a kiss, and became more as they explored each other. They tested boundaries. Alex breathed her perfume in deep: it was honey and wine, soft and sickly. He held her tight around the waist and they gave into lust together. The night fell away from them before they had finished, and the new day welcomed their guilt.

First light saw the ship anchored just before the Storm Coast. Alex looked through the captain's glass. He saw enamelled cliffs rise up ahead, topped with wild greenery. On starboard sat a warship, its cannons prominent. Two tars lay across the gunwale, flagging the *Crescent Harp* down. His heart jumped when he saw Royal Navy colours, it was in position to come alongside.

'They never do this,' said the Captain, still in his cups, sweat dripping from his brow.

'They may have been tipped off.' Alex noted. 'If they find us, they'll be questions.'

Gold turned to Alex. 'We could hide, now.'

'There's an old hatch right on the bilge,' said the Captain. 'Bit 'o a squeeze for three, but I'd imagine you wouldn't argue, eh lad?'

Alex grunted. 'I'll only be grateful once we're out of sight.'

They followed the doddering captain down into the hold. At the rear, where the ribs of the ship held the hull, was a slim hatch not noticeable until the captain lifted it.

'Had it fitted to smuggle valuables out of France once. Got a home there too. But my wife doesn't know that.' He roared with laughter. Underneath the *Harp*, Alex could only smell rotten timber and salt. In the heat, sweat soon dripped from his brow. Their collective breath soon stifled the tiny space. *Enough room for three children meant that old drunk,* thought Alex.

He waited until the clumps from the captain's boots were well away. 'Keep still and don't sneeze,' he said.

Hazel was stuck between Gold and Alex, as all three of them gasped for air in the smuggler's hole. It reeked; the smell of mould would send her lungs into fits if she tried to hold in a breath. She couldn't even consider opening the hatch a little to freshen the air. Her arms crossed over her chest, as if placed in a coffin. They heard bell tolls along with distant whistles and yelps. All was silent, until slow, cautious footsteps came from above. She squirmed. Her heart pumped quicker. The boots stopped above her head, casting dust into her eyes. Through the gaps in the planks, Hazel spied a mariner, with red and gold uniform, brandishing a rifle. He turned a lantern over one corner and then another watching for anything amiss. How long was he going to be standing there? She started to count in her head. Two minutes passed, when another soldier joined the first. They began to stomp on the planks with their heels, testing for any hollow spots. Gold nudged her and motioned to hold the planks with their hands. There was a sharp crack as one of the soldiers stomped too hard. He paused frowning, mentioning it to his companion. A third came below barking orders. Hazel's anxiety lifted as quickly as they left. She sneezed, a short escape of air that set Alex and Gold in panic. They waited until lighter feet came and opened the hatch.

'Like fish in a barrel you lot. Cramped and stewed,' the Boson rumbled, helping them out.

'The Captain?'

'Arrested. Crimes against the Crown. Shoul'n't be a problem now, we'll make sure you three are to your destination.

You kept us in enough coin to keep these boys soaked for ages come.'

'And you're not worried? With no captain?' said Hazel.

'Nah lass. They're easy enough to replace,' replied the man with a shrug.

In a jollyboat bound for the mouth of the Plum, two of the *Harp*'s sailors rowed them the short distance to shore. They gave Hazel forlorn glances, until she pointed to her sister's dagger. She gazed coy at Alex, who ignored her in return. *Is he warning me off? Is it my sister?* She thought back to last night. She had not gone mad; it was the strings that were dancing around them both. Dancing around Alex and her. Pulling her towards him. *There's a strange destiny with this man.* She fumbled inside one of her sleeves and wrapped her cloak around her, fighting off the sea-breeze and spray. In her hands she manipulated her tarot, and made a simple cross with four cards. Her past, present, future and mind; in her imagination she could see a black cloud, an ivory tree and a grey tower. The cards were vague until the last, *The Serpent*. She had pulled it just before the storm in Houndbarrow.

'Weather's changing,' Hazel said. One of the men tasted the air, and nodded. 'Good nose on her,' he said. He pulled out some skins for each of them, Alex wrapping his hood tight over his head. Rain thundered down on them; warm in taste and laced with salt. They hit the shore with a long scrape until the boat shuddered to a stop.

Hazel leaped off first, followed by Gold who gave her a small hug. Alex came off last, after giving thanks to the men who rowed them there. Sunbeams calmed most of the rain. They dispelled clouds in the sky and tickled Hazel's face with a tepid warmth. It was cold here, colder than London. She found herself wanting to see more nonetheless.

'Hazel we're in your hands,' said Alex, above the crash of the waves.

Hazel nodded. Gold drew the map out of her satchel and placed it across a stone that was drying in the sun. 'We're here Hazel,' said Gold, pointing.

Hazel traced her fingers across the map. It tingled under her touch; giving her a taste of *déjà vu*. Her eyes rolled back into her head as she tried to focus her mind on where they needed to be for the others.

'No. We're here,' she pointed. 'The sailors on the *Harp* got it wrong.'

'Or were too scared to get closer up shore,' Gold muttered.

'It doesn't matter as long as we're on *terra firma* and close to Elena. It looks like a day's walk,' said Alex.

Hazel's boots skidded on the stones, but she persevered. She kept spying on Alex, her heart singing whenever he would look at her with those dark-ringed eyes. He looked exhausted, as did her sister, who fared better on the rocks and was scouting for a way up the cliffs. Hidden behind a jumble of rock, soiled rope and driftwood, they found a tight path to the top. It twisted around long thin grasses, and the remains of dead trees. At the top Gold found farmland and livestock. Wind snapped around them, orange zephyrs addled the sky as they all looked up at a fading sun.

'Storm,' Hazel whispered. A heavy atmosphere fell on them. It hushed life and stilled breath. Among bruised clouds on the horizon there was a black smoke, it danced and flitted like a flock of starlings.

'I've seen this before. Take cover before they're upon us!' Gold shouted above the wind.

Hazel scrambled for somewhere to hide. She dove under a fallen log white as bone, its petrified roots clawing the air. Hazel looked around, unable to see Gold or Alex. Her hood caught on a brittle branch as she peered up over the log. The others had hidden themselves under a shelf of mottled rock. Their cloaks tugging about them. She could see her sister hold up a finger to her lips, motioning Hazel to be quiet. The dark chattering morass held aloft by rods and sticks passed overhead. Hazel uttered a spell of disguise, the patterns on her shawl shifting into white bark. As careful as she dared, she looked at them. They were odd things, with pallid skin and screeching vile litanies.

They were wizened also: with hag's teeth and malevolent eyes set in crow's feet. As Hazel focussed on them, they seemed to change before her. Age fell off them, and underneath they were young. Evil eyes turned to bright ones, their cackling voices became soft and melodic. Some swung low, low enough for her to take a better view. Some of the witches had coloured pennants tied tight to their arms. When they waved all the other witches behind them followed in formation. She followed a set who bore flags of red fish, its bones exposed. Another of a tower painted on grey, crumbling to ruin. The pennants flew and twisted about the witches. A display Hazel wished would linger further. She peeked under her hood at Alex and Gold, who watched the skies with pale complexions. She waved at them to come over as the witches passed, their glamour returning to them.

'They're moving away. God, Hazel, are you alright?' Gold embraced her.

'I'm at a loss. You've seen that before?' said Alex.

'Survived them too. Those hags attacked London.' She cradled Hazel's head in her arms, the wind stinging her eyes. 'You are alright, aren't you?'

Hazel turned to her sister. 'There's something sinister happening. I recognised one of them.'

'From where?'

'From Houndbarrow, from home.'

Charlotte's eyes swam with tears from the wind as she braved the topsail. 'Nearly there, don't forget your balance,' shouted Cyrus. *Foolish bet*, he thought, as he watched her, drunk, waddle her way to the tip of the mast. A crowd of sailors gathered at the mast threw jeers and heckles at her. Cyrus remembered the drink from last night, wine from the Lowlands, red and cheerful. In the ship's mess, it had taken him most of the morning to clean up the vomit. The rags, and his hands, were pink with the effort. He shoved a drunk out of the way, his gaze on Charlotte's balance as she lifted herself up and onto the crown of the mast. She stopped unsure, one hand warding off the sun, before raising herself onto both legs. There was a pause, then shouting and cheer burst from the sailors. Cyrus let go of the breath he was holding.

'Storm's coming,' shouted Charlotte above the racket. She repeated herself and the captain waved away the rabble who were still cheering her on.

Cyrus helped her down from the last rung on the mast. She shot him a dirty look; Charlotte held out her hand to a sorrowful-looking man who parted with a purse. 'You think that was clever last night?' he asked.

'I think this is clever,' she jangled the purse in front of him. 'I think you lost out.' Cyrus stopped before he could respond. He drew his eyes onto the horizon. 'What lost your bottle? Come on Southerner give me a show!'

Cyrus hesitated, meeting her gaze as she jutted her chin out. She flinched, as if he was about to strike her, but he pointed to the sky. 'Here, look, that's not a storm.'

He turned her around. In the sky gathered a series of women with sticks placed under their thighs. They shouted and screamed, cackled and spat.

'Devils!' shouted one sailor, another bent at the knee to pray.

'Hard to port!' Cyrus shouted. He could feel sweat build on his palms.

The captain, a barrel-chested man, pulled hard on the tiller. The *Rancor* swung to port, the wind squeezing the sails. Cyrus could see the fear in the man's eyes-he looked twice as old from yesterday. Everyone moved to hold onto rigging, the more experienced binding rope around one leg. The sea swelled up, throwing spray across the deck. He saw Charlotte shout something over a crash of wave. The witches had now swarmed, hovering above, heckling and spitting. One of them dove down, throwing a metal ball that erupted in a hiss of sparks and flame.

Some of the crew took up arms, whether to fight or regain their courage. He cast a concerned look at Charlotte, hoping not to show his own fear. Two of the witches jumped onto the topsail, with carved sticks in their hands. They uttered curses and chanted. Several sailors threw themselves overboard, braving the sea.

Cyrus grasped his dagger, freeing it from the sheath. Only a handful of men remained, their courage holding fast. The Captain and Charlotte did not move, but their legs shook. She drew a dagger. A look of determination was on her face, fire in her green eyes. The witches stopped their assault and paused, looking at them in turn. One of them flew onto the deck proper. She had a pennant wrapped around her arm; a half-eaten fish painted rough on the fabric. Cyrus grimaced when she spoke. Her brown teeth oozed saliva; her twisted nose rattled with warts as she spoke in a ruined voice.

'Leave now and we'll spare your souls.'

Before Cyrus could drop his weapon in surrender, Charlotte leapt forward. Her blade caught the witch by surprise across the shoulder. It bit deep, spraying blood. The blood changed colour, from fleshy purple to blue to bright scarlet. The witches' skin turned youthful, her warts disappeared, leaving only a white complexion. Soft brown eyes met his own. She was around Hazel's age, with flakes of blonde hair spread across a perspiring brow.

'What is this sorcery?' he gasped.

Charlotte had stopped with her swings as she fell back to Cyrus, unsure, the fight ebbed out of her. The witches surrounded their fallen sister and carried her up. They were normal women. The type a man would court and marry, or see made as happy house-wives with a cluster of children at their feet. They gave him intense glances, looks that could sour milk. Above, an arrow loosed at Charlotte; it struck her in the meat of her side, causing her to ball up in agony. Cyrus could see the shadow behind him before he could react to it. It clubbed him square in the head. His last vision was the Captain, bow-legged and praying, a sword slicing his throat.

☆

Cyrus kicked against the bed sheets. Still cold. He could not feel any sheets or a soft pillow in his bed anymore. There was a cry, of a woman, or girl. She cried out again and again and again. Cyrus pushed with both his arms, his chest creaking. His mouth was hollow and spent, his teeth dry. He tried to groan, but only a whimper came out. A pair of beady eyes, ending in a cruel beak and looked down at him. It cried like a woman, and then flew away. A seagull. He was not anywhere he recognised. The *Rancor* had buckled at the prow. Her planks still floating between rocks, trapped as flies against glass. He felt his throat, it was cut, like the Captain, but the wound had not killed him. He felt the back of his head; blood had matted with his hair, forming a lattice over a goose-egg of a bruise. A trail of his blood carried by the morning drizzle had seeped into his clothes. It ran down below his body, a stain of rust that flowed onto the broken prow.

His arms were spread either side of him; a garland of kelp tangled under his chin. *A noose. You need to move,* a voice whispered in his head. He flopped onto one side, his mouth touching the sodden deck. *Come on old man,* he pushed himself up, the neck wound screaming. Cyrus grasped a flag pole, and wrenched it from its sconce. He steadied himself, moving down to the rocky shore over smashed timber. Above, cliffs loomed, casting dark glances at him. Across the beach, there was a passage up the cliffside. He clutched his neck, almost crying out in pain. *Almost. Come on.*

The last stretch of the climb saw Cyrus on his knees in dirt, his breath ragged, and his mind numb. A silence crowded on him, cloying his hearing. Hidden in his waist-coat was a neckerchief, wet through, but still useful. He tied the cloth around his neck as a bandage. He pushed himself onto his knees, and onto his legs, shaking with effort.

In the pink sky he could not see any witches, and no evidence of Alex, Gold, Hazel or Charlotte on the ground. Tracks once visible had almost washed away. Partly formed

shapes suggested that people may have come through here. Over
the hill Cyrus came across a shack sheltered in a copse. The roof
looked sturdy for the night, and bushes with fruit lay nearby.
Inside it was warmer. Sheets were clean and dust free, the floor
filled with fresh rushes. He dropped everything, gathered a
handful of berries, and ate them one–by–one. He settled onto a
makeshift cot and slept with one eye open. It was not until a
slice of moonlight slipped through a hole between the logs of the
ceiling that Cyrus woke. He was weak still. His body resisting his
urges to move. As looked around the room, candles had been lit.
Cyrus shot upright, groping for the flag pole that carried him up
the cliff in defence. A small face had been watching him from a
corner of the shack. It looked friendly at least. It spoke to him, but
he shook his head, the words had not translated.

    'You're lucky.' It said.

    'Charlotte?' he replied. 'Where are the others?'

    'Gone to town. They're asking around for Elena, but
asking carefully,' she added.

He grumbled. Then there wasn't much else to do. His explored his wound; it had been bandaged over. He looked at Charlotte, who stood, expectant, by the door.

'If it was you who helped me Charlotte, I owe you a debt.'

She said nothing but stared at him, her eyes flickered.

'There's a cave nearby.'

'And? If they're in town, that's where we should meet.'

She slinked closer with a coy smile. Cyrus shifted to the other side of the bed.

'The cave is where we need to go. That's where we are camped. Out of the way, away from the locals,' she smiled again.

'If you lead, I'll follow girl,' he stood, the pole holding his weight.

They walked outside with Charlotte skipping ahead. Cyrus peered at her. Her hair seemed to change in the moonlight. *You're tired old man. Just follow, you owe her that much.* Cyrus was limping so slow he feared that he would lose sight of her, or fall behind. They fought through thickets until they reached the cliff that overlooked the wreck. In the night, he could not see the full coast stretch out in front of him. Only licks of platinum where the waves peaked and caught the moon. Torches paraded an entrance to a short tunnel. They lined inside too, warming a rough–hewn interior. He hesitated while Charlotte crept up behind him.

'Just in there, go on.'

Cyrus stumbled on, the cave ahead stifling and cramped. One by one the torch flames flickered and petered, swallowing him in dark. He turned; not knowing which way was out.

'Charlotte? Damn it girl, where are you?' He heard a laugh. Someone was close by. He poked with his pole hitting nothing. Panic had started to grip. Cyrus spun around, he felt air rush at him, something heavy and solid striking him across the temple. In fleeting consciousness, he wonders whether his eyes are closed or open.

☆

Hazel fidgeted with her eyes closed as had her hair

knotted. 'Keep still child,' Gold scolded. Her little sister huffed,

but finally sat still enough for her to finish. She looked about their

camp, which was just on the outskirts of town. They had

not planned for an extended stay in the Cape of Strangers any

longer than they had to. Alex and herself both agreed that lodging

in the town would raise suspicion. In a draughty little tavern,

locals gave them hints of witches spotted in the area. Ships raided,

farmers seduced to their deaths, the local Council disinterested to

help. There were whispers of a Sabbath between womenfolk and

a coven hidden on the coast. Gold knew it sounded like several

spun rumours, and that no one knew the complete truth. She

decided to walk down to the beach for ablutions.

It was a luxury she rarely had the chance to do in

London. She breathed the clean air, drank the sea, tasted the fruit

of buckthorns and prayed. She had sinned and killed a man. She

knew it was a guilt born from nothing, dogma made from

coincidence and imagination. She wanted to protect Cyrus and her sister, was that wrong to shed blood in doing so? Forgiveness felt as high as the peak of a mountain. In sight but not in reach. She began to ask God for a sign, or guidance or hope.

As gulls screamed overhead, they led her eye to smoke on a distant outcrop, which popped out the prow of a ship. She saw the *Tail* emerge before she had a chance to blink. It sat there, like a phantom, challenging her vision. It struck all its sails, skating away from her and disappearing on the horizon. She ran back to camp excited and fretful at the same time; each emotion fought to be on top. Hazel looked at her with worry written on her face. She scattered her tarot cards and held her by her shoulders.

'Gold? What's wrong?'

Gold shook her head in disbelief. 'A ship–a ship on the horizon!'

'But we haven't seen any for days.'

'I don't care. I'm finding where it came from.'

'Well, where did you see it come from?'

'A cave nearby, it just,' Gold stumbled over her words, 'it just slipped out of the rocks.'

Her hands shook as she packed her satchel. She set a grim look on her face, and marched into town, with Hazel in tow. She took to that Inn where Alex was gathering rumours as to where the coven likely was. She barged past the door, ignoring perturbed looks of fishermen and farmhands. 'Where is he?' she asked. They pointed around back. She peeped through a crack between two heavy curtains, spying Alex enjoying a game of cards. Gold snorted, bade Hazel to stay put, and marched through. The game had only begun when Alex' smile dissolved. He stood, his cards falling to the floor to the dismay of the other players.

'Gold. Have anything?' he asked.

Gold nodded, picturing her father. She sobbed once, and hugged Alex tight. The Innkeeper tugged her on her shoulder.

'No women, wait outside,' he thumbed at Hazel. 'And her with the silver, whores aren't allowed in here.'

Gold paused before planting her fist into the man's nose, much to the joy of other patrons who rolled about, laughing. They escaped from the Inn, retreating back to their camp. Gold could sense Alex was brimming with questions, but he gave her time to think. After the all the equipment was packed, and out of ear-shot of Hazel, she took a deep breath.

'It's the *Tail*.'

'What?' said Alex.

'My father's ship.'

Alex gave her an incredulous look. There was a distance on his face, a need that answered his question before he said it.

'Yes, I know. If we find my father... we could, I don't know, sail back to London. I don't know Alex,' Gold continued.

'Where?'

'Maybe a morning's walk. Not far. What's wrong?'

'That game in the tavern, I was asking about ships due.'

Gold sighed. 'The *Rancor*, she hasn't made it?'

'Worse, it was attacked and wrecked. That swarm of witches we saw.'

'Those witches have taken over the *Tail* perhaps,' said Hazel.

'Too much we don't know. We still need to find where Elena is.'

Gold nodded. 'Everything points to this cave or inlet.'

'Then we need to find Cyrus and Charlotte first, Elena second, your father third. If he is still the captain of the *Tail*, could you persuade him to go back?'

'I do not know. He could be a completely different person by now. He's spent years without me Alex, and I without him,' she bit her lip. 'I need a chance, that's all. Please don't breathe a word of this to Hazel.'

'Do you think she suspects?'

'Yes–and I want to be the one who is honest with her.'

'Then we've no time to waste.'

Well–forged paths through reeds and scattered dunes led them to the wreck of the *Rancor*. The group took a break from the walk as they inspected it, each hoping it was still seaworthy. Each hoping it could take them back to London.

Getting closer, it was obvious the ship had been smashed. No souls or bodies had washed up. An invisible sun shied behind a plume of fog that rolled in across the beach. Tides had crawled back, creating pools among the feet of rocks. The sand beneath was caramel speckled with ochre. Rings of jet stones spiralled out from solitary boulders. Past rushes and tough sea–hedge scattered a flock of birds, each smaller than Gold's hands. She held her breath as the fog dissolved, revealing a vista painted cream and eggshell blue. Heavy clouds were twisting into churches and cathedrals. They towered above, dizzying Gold when she flattened her hand to shade her eyes. The *Tail* eluded them until the end of the day, when the sun bowed low and the nimbi crumbled into thin wisps.

'There, lights,' Gold pointed, 'see them?'

'I see them,' said Alex.

'Looks like they're coming back from London, with supplies.'

'Why would they help witches?'

Gold shrugged, 'perhaps they're bewitched, or being coerced to do so.'

The *Tail* neared them as they huddled overlooking a natural alcove. Gold put away a spyglass, nodding in satisfaction.

'He's still alive,' she whispered to Alex.

Gold saw him look at her as if she had gone mad.

'Look, there. The aft is lit up in a certain way. Only my father would do that,' she explained.

Gold watched the *Tail* sail towards them. She frowned, expecting the sails to drop, or the ship to turn. It stayed on course for the cliffside.

'What are they doing?' said Alex.

'They're going to crash her!'

The carrack sailed on, oblivious. Gold squealed in horror as her father's ship neared them. Alex held her down, out of sight. Hazel was wide-eyed. She approached as close to the edge of the cliff as she dared, pulling her hood tight.

The *Tail* finally slowed; its sails furled in turn. As soon as the ship touched the rocks it became immaterial. It shifted from vision, dancing between opaque and invisible. The rocks enveloped it like sap over an insect, and just as quick, it vanished.

'Magic?' asked Alex, his brow folded.

Hazel nodded, her face fighting between fear and wonder. In the night they banded torches together and set off to find a way down. What paths there were down to the that magic cove, either were sealed with stone, or too treacherous in the night. Luck saved them from abandoning the search when Hazel spotted a lantern keeping the dark away. It swung from an old yew, glowing with an absence of fire.

'More witchcraft,' said Alex, under his breath.

Hazel took the lantern down; she inspected it, turning it over. Every time she did so a *thok* would rattle the panes. There was a ball inside, made of entwined fur and hair. It shone brighter when Hazel squeezed it.

'A witch–ball. I've read of them. Folk–magic.' Hazel tore the ball open. A sliver of quartz nestled inside. It was bright for a few seconds longer, and then died in her palm. 'I can use this.'

By the tree Hazel wrapped string at one end of the quartz crystal. She rubbed her finger at the tip, chanting a rhyme as she did so. It glowed, just bright enough. Alex and Gold crowded over her, sheltering the worst of the wind. The quartz sprang upwards, hovering in one direction. It pointed over a hill crest, then back towards town, between a copse and the Plum. Alex beamed at her, marvelled.

'You needed a guide,' smiled Hazel. 'And a guide you shall have.'

'We should be off; the less time we spend here, the more we have of getting to that ship.' Gold said.

Gold took lead, with Alex watching over Hazel. After consulting the quartz compass twice for direction, they found a hall built up on a mound of earth. Hearth—fires highlighting gaps in the timber. A grand oak erupted from the centre, smoke ringing its branches. They waited for guards to appear, but none came.

'This is it,' whispered Hazel. 'Couldn't we wait 'til morning?'

'We could,' said Alex, 'but there's a chance we might see Elena tonight.'

'This will be difficult; the longer we linger the more likely we'll be caught by her kidnappers. If the town is at the source of the river, then what is this? An old village?' said Gold, wringing her hands to stay off a chill. 'Doesn't seem likely.'

'What are you suggesting?' Asked Alex.

'This could be the coven that we're looking for.'

'The witch-ball suggests it.' Hazel's teeth chattered, her shawl and hood wrapped snug around her.

The hall opened, and people walked out, their jackets and cloaks held around the neck. Alex recognised a few. 'Fishermen from that card game,' he said.

'Something's wrong. Why would they bother walking that distance to here? To trade?'

The answer struck Gold clear in her mind. 'Worship. It's a cult. Look at what they're holding.'

Alex and Hazel saw what Gold mentioned. The townsfolk carried hymns and books, some handled golden idols of men with spears. They prayed as they walked back home, the dirge sombre and slow.

'So, a coven and a cult.' Alex sighed.

Gold looked over at him; he was long-faced, with bags under his eyes. 'Maybe we should rest tonight, for everyone's sake. We need to figure a plan.'

Alex nodded, stifling a yawn. 'And where do you suggest, that no one will find us?'

'There,' Hazel pointed. 'Under that thicket, out of sight.'

Wheel of Fortune

— Plum Village, The Storm Coast —

A hot morning sun had brought an early mass below, in the

village. Sarah rose naked from her bed, her sheets falling to the

floor. The nightmare she had was still alive in her mind. It was of

a tempest had brushed away her efforts, leaving her vulnerable to

Turner. The Lord himself assumed the role of a demon. His

blackened skin flaked off into her mouth, choking and poisoning

her. Rivulets of fire flooded out of his eyes and soon the village

was ablaze. It spread to the sea, turning it into sickly oil.

The Tail sailed straight for it. Sarah wrestled with the air as she tried to divert the ship, but it was too late. It erupted, sending

sparks towards her; a great crucifix of fire burned in her dream.

She had chastised herself as soon as she woke, but the

nightmare had born a seed in the back of her mind. A crippling

doubt of who she was, what she was aiming to do, and how to

finish her goal. She needed her anchor. She crept downstairs. Her

home, built behind the main hall, opened into a veranda in which

sat John. His black hair was rough-cut, his once fearsome beard

trimmed and smoothed with wax. He looked at her with his

cobalt eyes; he drained fresh tea from a cup, a smile forming.

'Good morning,' he said.

'Good morning.'

She sat in front of a cup of tea for herself. Her

nightgown loose.

'It reeks in there,' he said, pointing to the bedroom.

Sarah curled an eyebrow and smiled at him. She reached

over and smoothed his beard some more, twisting it in her

fingertips. She purred, nuzzling his cheek. John did not move.

'What's wrong?'

John replaced his tea, and fixed her with that look he rarely used. She braced herself for an argument. Her mind checked through conversations from the last month.

'We got this here, how?'

'What, got what?' Sarah sputtered.

'The bohea, it comes from London?'

'It does, yes, *but—*'

John held up one hand.

'And who brings it over?'

'Your ship,' she said. 'Your crew.'

'Sarah, I'm not happy being a glorified merchant. The Sisterhood can provide for its own. This is just luxury.'

'What you provide keeps us together, keeps what we've built, together.'

'What we've built? This was all for you.'

'Then,' Sarah drew her breath, 'what do you want?'

John folded his hair back and smoothed his beard, his expression unchanged.

'To be free again, to do what I've always done, to do what my father had taught me, to do what runs in these veins.'

Anger rattled inside her. *I want you to be happy. Why aren't you?* 'To be free? You nearly got killed last time my love. It was only through the Sisterhood you were saved.'

'My father taught me how to live. I don't want to abandon what you've built.' He cradled her, 'I want more freedom, not to just courier goods.'

'Your father only cared for his ship, his way of life. Sad to see you've become a poor example yourself,' Sarah choked on her words as they left.

John was silent as he stared down at the tea set. He smashed it with a sweep of his arm and left her be. As the pieces of china settled on the floor, Sarah sat, her mind numb. Regret came, pricking its way through her. She pulled her hands away from her face, her palms were wet. She turned. Selene was there, waiting against the wall, her face expressionless.

'He's a man of the sea my Cwen. You knew it when you were betrothed to him.'

Sarah did not reply, she smoothed her hair out, and placed both hands on the table. She rubbed them across the nicks and marks, feeling the bumps and scratches the old dining table had. Finally, she buried her head in her arms.

'He's a man who's tasted the freedom of the waves. The Sisterhood has shunned menfolk for a reason.' Selene scratched at her stump, 'he belongs to Neptune now.'

'Selene, I need to be alone. Will you go through ablutions and prayers with the Sisterhood in my stead?'

'And the girl we captured from the *Rancor?*'

'I'll see to her in due course. Make sure she's fed and watered, her wound treated. I need to meditate on events.'

'Of course, my Cwen,' Selene said. She twisted on one heel and left.

Sarah looked around for dustpan and brush. She began cleaning, her mind distracted. After the accident had been disposed of, she dressed for the day. A long white gown, which covered her arms and legs. The cloth patched where her knees would rest as she prayed, the fabric loose and discoloured.

Her hand traced a bookshelf, until she found the catch. She pulled it; a mechanical click came from behind the case. Hesitant, a thin door opened to her left. She designed it to be near seamless, a trick entrance built into the brick that ran on coasters.

She stepped through a white—washed passage, bending low enough not to smart her head. Inside was a small sanctuary. Gold leaf shone against a cramped cupola that shed light over a desk and stool. In the opposite corner was a statue of Mars, a near copy of the one she saw on the expedition, where they had found him. She knelt, prostrating as she did so. Mars had given her two daughters, an immaculate conception, a miracle. Her research about the Roman god described him as a warrior. A being who stitched war and peace, and granted gifts. Her prayers, as pious as she could muster, fell silent. Rituals and communion were one in the same. They both required patience, skill and determination. Sarah could not sense anything. Her voice ignored. She stopped in frustration, giving the statue a glare. Was it in his nature to not answer? Was he bound in duty as a warrior would be? Forever at battle, unable to reciprocate questions and wishes? Sarah sighed and sat in the centre of the sanctuary; her legs crossed. She closed her eyes, her fingertips manipulating the strings in flicks. Her spirit walked out of her mortal shell. It began to see the stacks of books on the nature of gods and magic, the golden cupola, and finally herself. Head bowed in a deep trance. Her body could rest. Her mind needed to take recess from this place.

Sarah's spirit floated, a foot off the ground. It twirled in the air, and sprang up through the ceiling, jumping higher into the clouds in short bursts. Here, she could meditate. Stacks and columns of clouds lay ahead; the pale sun shed slow warmth. Her spirit stayed there, enjoying the view. She turned and looked down at the village they had created. At sea, the *Tail* was leaving, it buffeted against choppy waves and disappeared from her sight. She sighed. Want bubbled inside her; she wanted John to be here and to be happy with her. She floated for a while, enjoying the nothingness that being insubstantial can bring. Her mother had warned against using such a trick too often. *"You go mad, you lose yourself and never want to return to the strife of being Human.*

You'll never want to live ever again. You'll turn into a half-thing Sarah, a Ghost that never died."

A snap made her look down. Three strangers crept around the bush and bracken at the back of her house. She felt a tug on her body and reversed herself back through the sky and back into her sanctuary. In the stillness she gathered her breath and organised her thoughts. Could she scare them off? She doubted it. She could give them a sense of unease; put up a wall of mist and frighten them a little, as if they were robbing a grave. She pulled back on the strings, folded them out into a sheet, and then unravelled. On the veranda thick mist cloyed the air outside Sarah's home, she could not see the intruders. *But they cannot see me.* She took a spell book off a shelf, a tome that dealt with form and textures. She tweaked the strings of her own face. Her hands slipped and pressed the flesh until she was a monster with golden eyes and a crystal red mouth. *Suitably grim.* Outside, the mist shrouded her. She could see the interlopers creep to the front of the hall. As they kept watch around themselves, the man of the group stalked inside, through one of the side doors. She looked at the younger girl from behind an outcrop. Her wan hair jutted out of her hood, silver locks resting on a plain shawl. The older woman was different, with long sable hair and well—travelled clothes. Sarah blinked indifferent as the older woman turned and stared at her. They locked eyes for a minute, both furrowing their brows. The woman squealed at the younger girl, and the man came half—running back to them. Sarah's heart squeezed inside. She had not figured on this outcome. The man unsheathed a dagger, the older woman drew a pistol and cocked it. She said something, the accent Southerner. Memories tumbled back to that day when she lost her children. Her god—promised daughters. Sarah shook the spell off her face, touching it to see if it had returned to normal. She smoothed her dress as best as she could and stepped out in front of them, her arms raised in peace. They stared back, unsure of what to do. Their game was over and a sense of relief had struck the man's face. The woman folded herself over the younger girl, shielding her. The younger girl was muttering something under her breath.

'Gold. Alex. Do you not recognise me?' Sarah asked.

A beat passed. Alex shifted his weight and looked up and down at Sarah. 'You haven't aged a single day, if this is real.'

Sarah smiled warm at him. She also knew John's daughter was alive through all these years. That Cyrus had not failed to protect her. The wind blustered around them; droplets discoloured bare earth where they fell.

'All of you come inside, rain has started. We've got plenty to converse,' she said.

Inside her house, they settled until comfortable, although she could see Alex preferred to keep standing. Sarah lit the hearth, the tang of driftwood smoke drifting through the study. On two rickety chairs sat the younger girl and Gold. The young girl almost hugged Gold's side. She was nervous; her legs shook, whether from cold or lack of nourishment Sarah couldn't tell. Her hair was a strange metal–white; silver–spun locks far above her age rested on a spotless complexion. She began to ask of her when Alex puffed his chest and broke the silence.

'What is this place?' he asked.

'A haven of sorts, we teach girls and women of certain... disposition, whereas they would be ostracised from London.'

'You teach witchcraft? Here?' said the young girl, unable to hide her surprise.

'We do. There are the villagers, you've no doubt seen, and there's the school beneath us.'

'The Church allows this?' said Gold.

'It has a dim view on the black arts, hence why the students disguise themselves as witches. Ironic their normal identity is their disguise also.'

'We saw,' said Alex. 'Why play to people's fears?'

'Why pretend to be innocent when the world believes you to be evil? An innocent monster is still hunted down and destroyed. Better to live up to the rumours, better to share in the power of superstition.'

'But you attacked London. People have died. You cannot justify that,' said Gold.

'Forgive me, but we were attacked first. After Turner's men were beaten off the *Tail*, they gave chase and sent more privateers into the coast. We lost several lives in his pursuit for me. Retaliation came soon after. An eye for an eye,' Sarah rose and poured tea for each of them, the atmosphere in the room had changed.

'Why, may I ask, what happened for Turner to take such a set against you?' Alex said.

'That's a sad story,' Sarah cleared her throat and began. 'It started on an expedition to find a treasure. On the basis of an earlier expedition my father took me on when I was but a child...'

They conversed into the night, each asking questions and Sarah answering in turn. Each question answered in truth. Soon they all knew of her story. Of how fate had twisted her life into what it was today. How Sarah became separated from her miraculous daughters. How she had married again (but not who she had married, sensing that Gold believed her father dead). Alex was civil and taciturn. She knew the reason they had come; to take Elena back, back to that rancid city. She had expected as much. Sarah invited them to dine with herself; taking time to put Gold's feelings ahead of her own. She did not know how John would react to seeing his daughter again for over two decades. She needed time to plan their reunion. Supper was peasant food prepared from yesterday, and kept chill. Thick blackbird pie and vegetables, followed with the last of her cider. Before long, their shoulders had slumped, eyes were listless, and limbs weary. She called for bed sheets and cots for the hall, with embers poured into a small pit. Sarah left Alex and the young girl to slumber after their journey, and took Gold, alone, back to her house. She asked Gold to wait for her husband (as it would be a person of interest), and talked until sleep got the better of them.

'He's late,' said Sarah. 'My dear, I must apologise. Not only had he not shown for supper, but now he's not returning home.'

'Never mind then. That's men for you,' she laughed. Gold wiped sleep away from her eyes.

'Get some sleep. We can talk of this in the morning.'

Gold rubbed her chin, then knotted her fingers, her eyes burning.

'That girl, Hazel. Do you recognise her? Sarah, she's your–'

A loud cry rang out from outside; several Sisters came running into the room.

'A fire's broken out Cwen, you must come quickly!' said one of them.

'Mars! Where's Selene?'

'Out flying, The *Tail* is ablaze.'

She ran outside with Alex (leaving Gold and Hazel to rest), plus the students who warned her, down to the dock. She could see the flames rocket in the in the night sky before seeing the whole of the blaze. A conflagration that heated her cheeks and burned the air.

'Move! Quickly now!'

The ship was steaming at the hull, timbers roaring on deck. Most of the sails had erupted in a blaze, leaving the masts barren. The crew was safe, as soon as it grew out of control they had jumped overboard. They huddled together as the Sisters looked after them. Men worst off had sluggishness from inhaling smoke, others had light burns. Sarah took note of now many heads were missing.

'Where's the Captain?' Sarah shouted at an older sailor.

He looked at her with languid eyes, face dirty with smoke. He shook his head unsure, gaze fixed on the ship. She rolled back her eyes, summoning her spirit. Sarah floated through the smouldering heaps of sail and rope. Pausing to search each smoke-filled cabin. John was in the bilge, lying flat with a wet blanket curled up around him. She retreated back into her body.

'He's still there! Everyone put out that fire.'

With each pail of seawater, the fire simmered away, leaving a charred mockery of the proud carrack. In turn, Alex and Sarah fought down to the lower decks; Alex scooped John up in his arms, and out into fresh air.

'Is he still with us?' Alex asked.

'He's fine,' reflected Sarah. 'The smoke did not reach him. But the exertion has knocked him out.'

She squeezed John, placing a kiss on his brow. 'Old sod, he wanted to be free—I've kept him cooped up here like a pet.'

Alex made sure John's breathing was normal, and heart steady. Sarah asked questions among the recovering sailors. She came across the boy who had been on in the nest before the fire. He propped up another young man, both testifying what happened.

'A great ship came upon us Lady.'

'Aye, like it was a sea monster. Took advantage of the weather, and rushed us—attacked before we knew it.'

'Who?'

'Looked like soldiers. They were using queer shot on us. Cap'n said they were setting the sails alight.'

'The sails they bore—any flags? Banners?'

'No but it was the size of a galleon Lady, hard to see details like that when you're at night.'

Sarah scrunched her face up, passing a hand over her brow. A horn struck out through the underground dock; it sounded long and deep. They waited in silence as the noise drowned, each man, boy, woman and girl looking at her for guidance.

'The village is under attack,' she barked to everyone around her, 'man the palisades!'

As the underground dock emptied in panic Alex used the opportunity to steal away. He wondered where the prodigal daughter was, where Elena could be hiding. Alex weighed that building called the Hollows and Sarah's bitter ambition, were equal in scale. That woman had changed for worse. She had become hard inside, a self—made tyrant, a reflection of what her life had become. Just a single conversation had seen through what hospitality she had attempted to softer her character. She was an antagonist that sought to control every aspect of her life until nothing could pain her. Until nothing could hurt her any longer. He recognised it. Nothing had softened her after all these years. Which, he imagined, with a sigh, all this would have been exactly what he would have done in her situation if he had two children who were lost in an instant.

He stalked deeper into the Hollows, and avoided all contact until he found a modest workshop and library built into the hillside. In the library he noticed Elena's red locks as she cowered behind a shelf that bowed under the weight of tomes. He rounded the door and snuck up on her as she huddled next to a lantern for comfort.

'Elena.'

'Alex!' she squealed and embraced him.

'What are doing here? Are you well?'

'Sarah told me to stay put—she feared I'd be taken again.' There was a bellow that sounded twice. 'Alex what do we do? Should we help?'

He considered her. 'Might be dangerous, is there any way to the clifftop from here?'

'There's a staircase at the back of the store, leads to a hatch.'

'Lead on.' He unholstered a pistol.

They ran up a flight of granite steps, to a spotless storeroom filled with teaching equipment. On the other side were stacks of crates with enough sundries to last the winter. Between two rough pillars, damp steps led further up. Alex could feel wafts of fresh air; Elena gave a whistle of relief as she breathed it in. At the top they opened a locked hatch, smothered with sod to keep it hidden. Alex pushed hard and the rust cracked in the hinges before relenting. Up on the hillside, a fat moon gleamed down on them, bright enough to highlight the village. An orange flash of light on the coast spun them both around.

'That's a cannon—do you see it? That's where the thunder is coming from,' he pointed out to sea.

Elena flinched when cracks from the cannon fire rebounded across the sky, rumbling. The cannons fired again. They put a broadside into the village, smashing homes apart with ease. After another volley the cannons ceased. Several boats were poised, away from the galleon. They reached the shore in minutes, disgorging men with torches and guns. They saw small flicks of fire as the men marched across the dunes and grassland. Their muskets firing at houses that survived the onslaught. Alex heard no screams, no panicked shouts or cries. The witches had managed to hide the villagers. He looked over at the hall; lights shone through the beams, and a mob had assembled in front of palisades. The invaders had not reached them yet.

'Come on—let's get to the hall before we're spotted. Keep low and use your wits.'

Elena nodded. 'I know of a path through the back of here, follow me.'

☆

Through thickets and scrub they kept low. Elena stopping to rub warmth back into arms, her robes pulled as snug as they could be. Alex removed his coat and draped it around her shoulders.

'Thank you. We should hurry.'

'Wait,' he said, unsure.

'We don't have time; I must get back,' Elena bit her lip. 'The Sisterhood will protect us.'

'How much do you know? How much has she let on?'

She moved away shaking her head. 'This is not the time for questions sir.'

'Has she told you about that girl we brought with us? Has she told you that much?'

'I haven't been told anything. What about her?'

'Elena, that girl is your sister. Sarah is your true mother, not Sophia Stone– '

She thrust her hands into the air. 'I know! I know.' Elena placed a hand over her brow, as if steadying her mind. 'I've felt it every day since coming here. Every day, like it's a fever that's taken me–this place feels right, but it doesn't feel like home. Sophia feels like my mother, but I know she isn't. And my sister– I want to meet her dearly, perhaps, perhaps, once this night is over.'

Alex stared. The soldiers were starting to gang up on the hall. They nestled in rocks and bushes, firing at precise intervals. The villagers hunkered down besides the palisades. They took shots of their own, some firing wild, others in formations.

'Might be a night that never does end,' he said, with more spite than intended. 'I hope reuniting you with Hazel will show you what you really want.'

She stayed silent, staring back at him. A twig snapped, which made them both jump. A soldier stood there with flintlock trained. For a split—second Alex wasn't sure if the man had seen them. The man grunted in Southerner, thrusting his gun at them, his eyes focused on Alex's pistol. Alex cursed under his breath. The pistol grip felt heavier in his glove. Was it loaded? Of course it was. Would he have time to lift it up and pull the trigger? Maybe not. He pushed Elena aside and lifted it. The trigger pulled, making a snap and punched a shot through the chest of the soldier. He dropped to ground, shock on his face. Alex expected Elena to convulse, or to scream and shout at the injustice. But she stood there, her eyes searching his.

'I'm not weak,' she panted, a hand to her chest. 'Don't take me for a lightheaded girl.'

She bent over, clutching her stomach, gagging. After a spell she righted her posture, and breathed deep. Alex apologised, his curiosity gripping him. He pulled the corpse by one hand, finding a spot better in the moonlight. The soldier's jacket was new, his boots black and scuffed.

'Not a military man. His boots are filthy,' he said.

'That was Southerner he spoke, was it not?'

'It was.'

'Which begs the question why are they so far from home?' asked Elena.

'Mercenaries. Purses filled with guineas,' he jingled a purse. 'And orders.'

'What does it say?'

He held the note up for her to see. It was Tuner's signature, LPT, and the East Indian Company's seal; he pocketed the note. Alex followed Elena down the hillside, through footpaths and closer to the conflict. He herded her out of sight, asking her to stay put.

'I want to go with you, I want to help.'

'And I want to see you safe, as I have done with your sister.'

'Why?'

He considered her again, shoulders drooped, scratching his stubble. Instead of responding he gave her what he hoped was an anxious look. Gunfire was closer still now, although the villagers had not relented. Alex could see two still bodies from here; both knelt as if in prayer. His stomach dropped when he neared the skirmish. The soldiers had begun to retract themselves. They fell back in groups to the jollyboats still on the shore. He guessed what would come next: further bombardment as the mercenaries reinforced. Undisciplined, but had strength in numbers.

One—by—one a witch flew in, taking the pause in fighting to circle above the hall. Each balanced on their sticks with one leg tucked under the other. One hand folded over the front, the other free. They spun and twisted around each other, chanting. Alex stood, transfixed. The moonlight played among them, giving the bare skin of their free arms a pale glow. As he squinted a spark was forming in the centre of them; it was a dull blue, with snaps of electricity. It grew in size until it became a ball, the blue core turning a hot white and green. Alex covered his eyes when it outshone the moon; it spun there, before shooting up into a cloud. There was stillness, a heartbeat away from chaos. When it came, lightning scorched the earth, illuminating all. It cast sharp shadows on the faces of the witches for a second, then, in unison they attacked. A group swooped down on the jollyboats, another towards the ship. A cannon shot before Alex could hide, it smashed the hall's oak, cleaving the great tree in two. Shards fell on him, jigging their way into his skin. As he wiped them off, a thunderhead broke above him, shattering his ears. He covered them as they played their swansong, and stumbled his way inside.

The walls had not breached. Only branches, twigs and sticks fell about him, most burning up in the fire pit. Sarah had moved the villagers that could not fight and the wounded to the rear of the hall protected surrounded by natural stone. Those witches too young to fight helped the injured and children. Alex found a space in far off corner and started to remove the splinters that had dug deep, wincing as he tugged.

'What's happening out there?' Sarah asked.

'Your students are weaving a storm.'

'Good,' Sarah said, perched on her throne. 'Turner will soon realise he cannot take what is not his.'

Alex twisted around. He had washed off his blood with the help of a witch who was ensuring the feverish had a damp cloth to sooth. He rose, shaking the last of the ringing out of his head.

'They're Southern men—you knew that right? It's the Company you're facing Lady. There's plenty more where that one warship came from. And if it's Isolde or Turner, they've got the money to keep them paid.'

'If it is Turner, he will never have her,' she dismissed him. 'He will never have that city.'

'The obvious is eluding you,' Alex ventured, daring to push her foul mood. 'All this over Elena, all this over one girl?'

Sarah stood and walked over to him. Her white dress was grubby, her hands smeared with blood and soot. She signalled one of the young witches over and washed her hands in the bucket, wiping them dry with a clean cloth.

'There's little you know,' Sarah answered, sibilant. 'My daughters are immaculate. They are divine, that I am sure. To lose them again is to...'

Alex searched her eyes for fiction, some twitch that would give her away. There was nothing. 'Die twice?' he ventured.

She frowned at him dismissing his answer with a wave of her hand. Outside rain erupted, drenching the roof; the sounds of the battle were over. Hesitant, the few able in the hall wandered outside. Alex followed, halting what conversation he was about to start. Sarah took a slow step behind him. First light smouldered in the distance. Parts of the sky were sparking like hot steel under the smith's hammer. A tumult of clouds stirred, cheerful as lead.

The witches had huddled together, under Selene's leadership. They stopped in front of the hall, all facing Sarah.

'We have driven them back my Cwen,' said Selene. 'Are we welcome among the villagers?'

Alex noticed a pause before Sarah spoke; her hand was stuck in a hesitant gesture.

'Of course, of course you are. Come Selene, out of this drizzle. You have all won our thanks.'

She gave Alex a warning look, and he waited for her to finish her speech before slipping away. Relief washed over him as he found Elena still at the back of the house, covered up, sheltered beside a log pile.

'What happened? Is it over?'

He looked at her, weighing his conscience with tugs of his mouth. He feigned exhaustion.

'Sarah has asked me to take you back, back to London, for safety. There's a sloop just beside a jetty–the witches use it from time to time,' Alex lied.

Elena looked disheartened. After a moment she nodded at him, a resolve in her eyes. Her hand shot up, scaring Alex, as if she was about to refuse him, but then it folded, wanting. They set off without a word, past the hall and village, past Sarah's home and down to the dock. Alex seized the tarp off the boat and locked the oars. He pulled his hood tight over his head, shielding the worst of the rain. Elena came aboard, her legs shaking.

'I cannot hear any fighting, have they finished it?'

'The fighting was taken to the hall and far down into the cliffside. You'll be safe with me. Your mother promised that.'

Alex grunted, losing the sails. The waves had calmed around them, but the rain did not relent. It soaked through cracks in the waterproofs they wore. In time they were clear of the dock, Alex keeping a wary eye on the mercenary galleon that was still anchored. It was magnificent to behold; eerie as they went past. Alex muttered a quick prayer that the witches would not follow in pursuit. That he would have a day to get to Greenmarket, and with fair weather, back home.

Strength

She watched events unfold from a corner in the hall where debris

from the fallen oak had not touched. She had not intervened with

any of it and stayed put, absorbing details around her. She noticed

the hesitation in Sarah's voice. Just before the Sisterhood mixed

with the villagers. She also noticed how upset Sarah was with

Alex, but didn't pursue an argument. As Sarah Saville marched

to her throne and sat with one arm poised under her chin, their

eyes locked. Hazel paused before broaching a conversation with

her. There was an intelligent woman sat on that wooden

chair. One with the charisma and guile to persuade people to

follow her. Hazel leaned on manipulative and cruel. But Sarah was careful to hide her true intentions. Hazel could almost see it. An ugly ambition that bobbed just beneath the surface.

'You do look *like* her,' said Sarah.

'Pardon me?'

Sarah shook her head. She smiled, placing her head in her hands as if wanting to reveal a secret. 'There's a girl, Elena, she's about your age. I bet you two would get on famous,' she said. 'She's gifted too.'

'Is she part of your cult?'

'Not yet. She is my daughter however, and the next Cwen perhaps. But, before that happens, I have to secure my legacy. I have to make good of this place. To show tyrants across England that our craft is something to be feared.'

'Your craft is something to be cherished and understood, surely? Not something to frighten and breed hate.'

'Do you think they would understand? That man is capable of being brave in the face of the unknown? They blind themselves to the world so it better suits them. Let them. Let them carry on an act of falsehood and capricious gods that set their lives in a comfortable box, all bound by rules. It is rot. Magic should be as this: feared and respected above all else. Witches, witchcraft—we should have the rule of this land, as we did before.'

Hazel stood still; her arms folded. She repeated the conversation in her mind, over and over; the words turning with a strange connotation that had not yet resolved. In the lapse of her thoughts she had finally settled a debate that had plagued her since she had first met Sarah Saville. She wanted to be as far away from that woman and this place as soon as possible. Not from fear or avarice, but it was the way in which Sarah Saville spoke to her; the way her eyes dulled and shined on certain topics; the way her lips dripped poison and honey without effort. Sarah was the architect of this little world she had built; and whatever control she had lost in a previous life was now spent on ensuring it would never be lost again. Hazel could only guess at the changes that had occurred for this woman to become what she is now.

'My dear, I would ask something of you. Could you find my sweet Elena for me? She seems to have hidden herself well,' said Sarah.

Hazel nodded, 'I can try.'

Hazel left the hall lost in her thoughts. Dawn raced ahead of night; it brought a cool horizon and the first birdsongs that made her yawn deep. Bleary she made her down to the dock, where the *Tail* sat, abandoned. Parts of it still smoked; a wet musk that washed over her, giving her nausea. Sarah's right hand, Selene, was in charge of salvaging the wreck. Her and a few Sisters, with dark—ringed eyes, busied themselves with the task. It seemed futile to Hazel, why salvage an old boat like this? She strolled past, pottering through the corridors until finding the library. It was empty, with a few candles lit. Hazel marvelled at the construction behind the roof. Fluted and panelled gaps between the wood vented warm air to the surface. She could feel a strong draught underneath the stone floor that provided fresh air. It helped keep the books dry, which was the most important state to keep a book in, she had read. Elena was nowhere in the Hollows, despite exhausting every location. Gold soon found Hazel, curled up, back in the hall, a blanket stretched over her.

'Wake up. Here.'

'I am awake—I was listening to the gossip,' Hazel replied.

Gold pressed a bowl of soup and a hunk of bread into Hazel's hands. It was warm gruel but kept her stomach from complaining. She looked up at her sister who was sat next to her; they both smiled at each other. Hazel pressed her body close.

'I have to tell you something important,' said Gold. 'I'm not sure if this is the right time.'

'That Sarah Saville has lost her senses? That we have to escape?'

'No, not those. But I do feel we've outstayed our welcome here.'

'What is it then?' Hazel asked, finishing her soup.

Gold eyed the hall. Certain conversations had dropped, the silence unsettled her. 'Not here, outside—but you do trust me, right?'

'I do. I do trust you.' Hazel fixed her shawl, and followed Gold outside.

The galleon that had attacked was still anchored, still dressed as an East India ship; a Jack on the main mast still flying alone. It was a sad sight to Hazel, who saw the ruin that spells could wreak, again. She had never considered the Sisterhood had wielded that power. Nor had she considered how used to violence they were in their crusade against the world. Gold stopped, just before some scrub, her eyes had glazed. Her mouth turned open, and then shut, as if in communion. Finally, her sister furrowed her brow and grunted, as she would when faced with something that niggled at her conscience.

'Hazel. I'm—I am not your real sister.'

Hazel could feel her heart lurch. She had suspicions. The dreams, her strange upbringing, the way Gold protected her.

'And who is my mother? Who brought me up as a child?'

'Victoria did. She is a beautiful and caring woman. She still loves you as her own. I love you too. That hasn't changed.'

There was an odd shake to her sister's voice; Hazel had never seen her so fraught. She turned from her sister, absorbing the morning sun, watching terns play over the waves. Hazel closed her eyes and enjoyed the tattoo of sea spray on the rocks below.

'You are my sister,' she said.

'No, that's not what I'm saying–'

'Gold you are my sister and I love you as such; no matter what between us. You are from a separate family, and suffered hardships to win me. Am I right?'

Gold looked relieved, and nodded. There was a tug of a smile forming. 'Something I've kept from you for a long time–a long, long time. This is not Cyrus' fault, you understand that? He had no choice. I was there, a young child, but I was there.'

Hazel hugged her sister tight, feeling her chest rise as she drew breath. They both flopped onto the grass. 'Tell me what happened, all of it,' she said, 'please.'

'I was even younger than you are now. We were attacked, again, by privateers. Sarah Saville did everything she could to prevent her daughters being taken. That's you and Elena. She's your sister by blood. Sarah sent me away with the pair of you, placed all her faith in me. Isolde, curse her name, forced Cyrus to give up Elena, or give up everything he had; his house and Victoria. By chance, we held onto you. And so,' Gold shrugged, 'you were everything to me—you, Cyrus and Victoria, a small family. They were happy times growing up together. We made the most of what we had.'

'Now, we're here—trying to rescue my true sister from her own mother,' said Hazel.

'Who just happens to be a queen amongst her own kind. Her hate has gone on too long Hazel—she's no longer the woman I remember. There's a hunger in her eyes, as if only destruction of England itself would sate it. It frightened me.'

'If we had help, we could find Cyrus and try to leave tonight,' Hazel suggested.

Gold thought for a minute. 'I know who can help us,' she finally said.

The Hermit

There was an open hearth that crackled and spat at him. Hot sap

would ignite and pop. Small blue flames licked the blackened

stone and baked earth that surrounded it. Its heat was close

enough to be uncomfortable and inspired him to move. Beneath

Cyrus was a rough-spun cloth; it scratched at his cheek,

scrubbing his skin. An old woman sat in front of the fire.

She watched him on a rickety armchair, enjoying either a cup of

hot broth or tea, he could not be sure. In the air was a pressure of

change. A volume of something unspoken and meaningful, as if the old woman's essence was this place, infused into the earth and wood with time and energy. The home, such as it was, balked at him. He felt like an intruder here, as though his presence was somehow his own fault; his own body a foreign object that had disturbed a delicate harmony.

'Where am I? Who are you?' he demanded.

'You are always exactly where you need to be.'

With that response, Cyrus kept to himself for a moment. The scab from the wound on his neck had fallen off at some point, leaving only tender skin. The bruise he had suffered however, was fresh and sharp.

'Where's the girl? Charlotte?'

'I am that girl.'

Cyrus shivered. He steadied himself up, wincing as he tried to walk.

'You're an old woman—she was a young girl.'

'Do you always trust your eyes then? Men seem to have complete faith in what they see and hear.'

'How else would I view the world?'

She turned to him, showing the two milky orbs where her eyes were once. Cyrus swallowed; he could feel his stomach creep, bile climbing his throat.

'There's more than looking to know the world.'

'Who are you to keep me prisoner?'

He stumbled to the entrance, only to find the door stuck fast. The crone coughed; there was another chair by the fireplace. She flicked at single, daggered finger at it. Cyrus rubbed his bruise, submitting. He sat, gazing at the pokey hovel. The mantelpiece above the fire was bare soil, a wooden board squeezed into hardened mud. The floor was smoothed stone, while black beams supported the low ceiling. He could spy two more rooms from where he sat, and guessed they were the pantry and bedroom. On the stone floor was a woven rug he had rested on, edges frayed, the colours bleached. If he focused, Cyrus could make out figures and animals in a grand segmented story.

'It was a gift from my husband,' said the crone.

'Pardon me?'

'It was an age ago—I was still full of whimsy. He was young back then too.'

'And where is he, your husband?'

She let out a cackle that disturbed him; tea trickled from her lip. With a shaking hand she wiped her chin and composed herself.

'Died in his sleep years ago,' she gave him a sly smile. Cyrus swore under his breath. *She can see me fine even with her eyes lost.* 'I can see his successor as of now. Desperate; consumed by the past.'

'Your husband's successor? Do you mean Lord Turner?'

'Lord Turner indeed.' The old woman sat up, armed with a poker, and stabbed at the fire.

Cyrus stirred in his seat. 'Your husband was William Saville?'

She nodded. After a strange whimper left her lips, Cyrus refilled her cup with fresh tea from the stove.

'I still feel sorrow you know—even with my eyes ruined so. I cannot cry, but I still feel the pain.'

Cyrus nodded. He was afraid of asking the questions that darted around in his mind. He sat back, enjoying the warmth of the fire. The old woman threw another log on top, where it hissed before settling.

'My name is Cyrus. We were asked to take Elena Saville from here.'

She nodded. 'You did yes.'

'Then you know about her? Where she is?'

'I do.'

'How?'

'I did tell you there are more things than looking to know the world. By your knife you're a man who can fight?'

Cyrus held onto his sheath. 'I've seen fights.'

'But what do you feel during the fight?'

'Ready. Alive.'

She nodded; her lips slim. 'Then to explain it to you is pointless. Clairvoyance is the opposite. Men and women are different in the ways they knit the strings together.'

'Strings? What do strings have to do with finding Elena?'

'I did say there were more ways than looking,' she smiled. 'But, Elena, she's far from here now.'

'*Alex.* Must be.'

'Yes, the other one, the rogue.'

He breathed a sigh of relief. 'What of Charlotte? The girl I journeyed with?'

'You fancy me as some kind of oracle? That I have the truth tucked away for your convenience?'

'She's important.'

'She is your little sister, of course she is important.'

Cyrus crumpled his lips. His gaze cast down. 'She is the only family I have left. Although she does not know it.'

'*Charlotte* will journey soon, with others, and her family.'

'Hazel and Gold? Where will they go? Home?'

'You've answered your own question.'

Cyrus stood. He wiped away fatigue from his eyes and stretched. He checked his dagger. He looked at the woman, shrivelled and delicate. She huddled in her black furs and magenta dress, her face expectant.

'You don't have to linger here,' he said, 'come with us.'

'You are all unwanted folk. You cast of villains. You all have a bloody future ahead of you. Leave me be. There's little in London worth for me to go back to. There's more to do here.'

'How so?'

'Cwens come and go—some more quickly than others.'

Cyrus had never heard that word before, and wondered on its meaning. He opened what he hoped was the front door; it skidded wide, shedding grime and flakes of paint. Outside, Cyrus could see the cottage hid below a copse perched close to a cliff. The shrikes of crows and the stench of mulch drowned the silence in the small house. He took one last glance at her.

'You never mentioned your name Madam.'

'Eleanor.'

'Eleanor,' he added a flourish, 'may you find peace here.'

'Be swift Cyrus. Keep the daughters safe. They'll be heralds of all our fate.'

Before Cyrus could shut the door, it closed on its own, sealing the old woman with her rug, secrets, and a smile. The door was on a threshold, between a bank of rushes and a slide of earth that he saw the village before him. In the distance, he could see the spires of the neighbouring town; the wind pushing him inland. A galleon poised in the bay, smoke ringed its wood and burnt sails. Cyrus could see no life through the miasma, no shouts, no cries of distress. He cocked his head listened. There was a constant clatter at first, as if he was at a cooper. Or, perhaps, watching women wash their clothes on that striated board that bled the filth out. It rattled louder until he had to find shelter, his ears echoing the noise back inside themselves. His head was slick in ruby red pollen and his legs sank into slime below. A black morass flew overhead; cheering and heckling the morning sky. It was the witch–flight from the other day. Powerful drafts of air carried along the outcrop he hugged in vain. Cyrus considered it a miracle he wasn't seen. More and more they came, a vanguard of evil sisters. In the centre of them was a tall witch, her mucky white dress fluttering erratic as others sped past her. She barked some orders, and then shot off just as quick. Her staff balanced between her legs, its tip pointing north. Back to London.

Once all the witches became a single, sullen cloud in the distance, Cyrus raised himself. He shook from the cold; his skin and clothes sodden from the shoes to his shoulders. The walk to the village was stilted. His blood quickened. Noises made him twist around in paranoia, movement made him duck behind trees or bush.

From broken earthworks, formed into a rough ring, he saw a group of villagers emerge. They stumbled and fell, running in the direction of town. There was a commotion from inside a hall that had a bird's eye view of the beach. Cyrus noticed a great oak had split by some titanic force, caving the roof in. It was Charlotte who emerged from the hall, flailing her fists, followed by Hazel and Gold. They were in the process of being thrown out, pushed and prodded by young witches behind them. Dumped in front of the villagers who themselves were unsure of what to do. He moved out to greet them, not believing that Charlotte had lived. He pushed an impulsive thought to the back of his mind that he knew she was always alive. A bond that reminded him of her ever so often. Family. That inescapable force. Even if she didn't know it. She bounded to him. Her skin was ashen pale, her clothes steeped in muck. He looked her over for any signs of mistreatment, but found none. Questions poured through him, fighting and spilling to become the first to pass his lips. She shook her head and slapped him on the arm, clasping one of her wiry arms over his neck.

'We should be dead,' he said, after a time had passed. Gold and Hazel kept distance, smiling at the scene.

'Yes, you're right,' she mumbled.

'What happened to you?'

'They thought me a spy sent by Turner. Kept me locked up in a wine cellar they did,' she swirled her tongue around her mouth and spat. 'When the fighting finished, I was let free. Those Sisters, they're led by Elena's mother. Do you know what that means?' Cyrus nodded, but waved her to continue. 'There's going to be a conflict between them. That Sarah Saville is not going to rest until she has her daughter back. Or perhaps die trying.'

'What about Alex? What happened?'

'I didn't see them. But he's disappeared, along with that girl.'

Cyrus doubted Alex had evil intentions. He wondered how much Isolde was willing to pay for his effort alone. If Alex even planned on selling Elena. He looked over at the galleon, still there, ready to sail.

'It takes a large crew, but we've got enough for a skeleton,' said Gold.

'That galleon is not exactly conspicuous. There are two problems. First, whoever attacked, I would guess at Turner, will send more ships. The second is avoiding the Navy coming into London, assuming we can manage the work between us,' said Hazel.

'Yet again, she's right,' said Charlotte.

'Know of any tricks or spells Hazel? Anything that would push us in the right direction?'

'You cannot push a ship, young master. The sea would always fight against you.' There was a booming voice, a voice of a stern father, of authority or command. Cyrus could see a coarse man strapped into a white shirt and brown leather breeches. He rested on a walking stick, his breath in short gulps. There was a reflection of joy in his eyes as he recognised Gold. A shade of sadness circled them as she dropped to her knees in a flurry of emotion. She sobbed, as the man rested one gnarled hand on her shoulder. Her tears streaking past her closed hands that stuck fast in disbelief.

'Ease Goldie, ease,' the man choked. 'Your old man is not dead; he has been well enough.'

Gold managed a hug, squeezing hard enough. Words had not come to her mouth yet. They remained frozen behind shivering lips, her wet eyes scanning him as if he was still a figment.

'Her father?' Hazel turned with a strange pout on her
face.

'He died in her story. The one she's been telling for years.
How he was a hero, how he saved many at the risk of his own life.
Does he look like a hero to you?'

Cyrus' question caught Hazel unawares. She stayed
quiet, and observed the reunion. When she looked back at
Cyrus, Hazel flushed red.

'Now that's a heart–wrenching sight–' said
Charlotte. Her attention was on the group of sailors who had
stood behind the man. Their arms folded, eyes heavy and stances
firm. '–and there's your crew,' she added.

'It is that,' Cyrus looked among the men lined
up. Several had begun to board whatever boats were at the
dockside. They made for the galleon. He walked over to Gold,
who was composing herself. Her puffy–raw cheeks belied the
love in her eyes and the smile that was curling upwards.

'My father. Captain John Frost. A hero if there ever was one. He has saved more lives that day than was killed. This is Cyrus.'

Cyrus stood before the Captain. In his prime he would have been a bear of a man. Now, he could tell age had mellowed him. Perhaps what once was a mind and soul filled with adventure and the sea, now wisdom and guile had taken root. Cyrus shook the man's hand, and had to grip it with both of his own.

'If anyone can save more lives than that tyrant puts down, is a friend of mine.'

'Tyrants,' mused John. 'Turner and Isolde are in league with the Devil, the faster they're taken out of power, the better the world will fare.'

'There was a coven of witches, out there beyond the cliffs,' Cyrus pointed. 'We should be cautious.'

'We should, but they won't attack if we fly our colours.'

Cyrus' brow thickened. 'Why? They've attacked me, and others.'

'My wife is leading them, that's why Mr Cyrus. And, that's *why* I must chase after her afore she gets herself killed on this crusade.'

'Crusade?'

'She believes one of her daughters has been kidnapped. Kidnapped after being reunited all these years, how can one man be cruel enough to do that to a mother?'

Cyrus exercised his mouth, but nothing of merit came forward.

'You have something to say?' said the old captain.

'That kidnapper is my colleague. I know exactly what he is planning to do with Elena, and where he will take her. He's a straightforward man, straightforward motives.'

John gave him a measured look, scratching his beard with hooked fingers. He turned and looked at his crew. The oldest and most senior of which were waiting for his command with a knowing look on their faces.

'Well lads? What do you say? Shall we put down this monger of misery Lord Turner and rescue my wife afore she gets killed?' They roared, rattling their swords and batons with one hand. The others thumped their chests. From the rear of the crowd came shouts of returning to London, to the sea, and back to the life they had left behind. 'Then back we go!' Another roar of appreciation came at once. Cyrus moved among the seamen admiring their spirit and energy, ready to cast his lot in with them. He helped Gold and Hazel in a boat of their own, and manned the oars. As he rowed towards the ship, looking back one last time at the cliffs, he could see a speck of black. A woman shrivelled by age but no less potent in her twilight.

She smiled at him, one hand in a wave farewell.

The Tower

It had grown more intense. This feeling of trepidation repeated

in Elena's mind: this is not the answer; this is not the right way.

Alex tacked a gale that sped them into the waters of London.

Despite their sloop battered by the worst the sea could throw at it,

it had managed to cut through the water without disaster. Elena

checked herself. She had changed. A year ago, she would not

recognise who she had become. Now, she was daughter to a

Witch Queen; her father a captain of pirates. It had the makings

of a fantasy. She hugged her knees close on the swaying vessel.

The sea was plate–grey as it danced to the rhythm of whatever

drums the deeps beneath beat. Her hood had lost stitching around the nape, rubbing her skin there. She scratched at it. She wondered in cautious thoughts how fortunate someone with a loving family was. How lucky she would be, to be safe and happy once again? How happy she could have been. Dots of tears slid down her cheeks. She mistook it for rain at first, convincing a part of herself that she was not upset. Relief that when the pressure finally did relent it came as a broken cry, one that Elena stifled. *I am a witch then.* Only daughters born of witches become witches themselves. What could she do? No magic for sure. No curses to cast upon anyone, no daggers raised in sacrifice, no spirits or animals had spoken to her. She was useless in her usefulness; an unwanted necessity. *That's not true. You are wanted, you are needed. Soon you'll be home, warm fire in front, a belly of hot food. Your mother planting a kiss upon your cheek. But you know who your true mother is, don't you?*

'Lies,' Elena broke the silence.

Alex slumped over the tiller; sight fixed ahead. 'What lies?'

'Nothing.'

Alex shook his head. 'Get some rest, London is close by.'

'Think there's passage? Do you have money?'

'Just this,' Alex held up one arm, showing her a mark of a tower faded in spots. 'And I can palm this old boat off to someone.'

Elena closed her eyes. Whatever that tattoo was, she trusted Alex to make the right choice for her. A rumble followed by a groan of her stomach broke the silence. When she reopened her eyes, Alex was dividing a morsel of tack and berries. Salted meat and fish turned her stomach as she gathered a scrap between her teeth and swallowed.

'Hot food in London I promise that much. There's a tavern that serves dumplings in gravy year-round. Nothing better after traveling by sea.'

'I believe you,' she gave him a thin smile.

Mother, father, I'm finally homeward. Would they recognise me? Has it been too long? What am I worth to them? It was a sick feeling, a sick idea that jolted her upright, her mind bitter, her heart aching. I'm just value, a figure for men. A tidy sum paid in coins and remittance; nothing more than marks on a paper and a nod of agreement. They were free, weren't they? Those women, flying on sticks and making witchcraft, they were happy enough, weren't they? I am stupid, stupid.

'How much?' The words came from her own mouth surprising herself and Alex. He looked at her with that glance meant to silence; her anger flashed. 'How much am I worth?'

Alex stayed silent.

'Enough then, is that it?'

No answer.

Elena stared at him with disbelief unchecked. It was true then. Greed. After all this, after all they had been through; all a false pretence.

'I thought it was more than this,' she sobbed.

'It is. You're overthinking the situation.'

I am a fool to believe anything he says.

A feeling of trepidation repeated in her mind. As her heart caved, Elena shrank within her cloak, mind numb. Indigo swells shook the boat as London came into view. The city spread flat in a wide oval, bell towers upon bell towers mashed with churches and steeples. Chimney stacks assaulted the air with acrid smoke. Elena had dreamed of houses of cinnabar brick, towers of shining metal and grandeur. Not a purgatory of soot and pale figures struggling amongst themselves. Everywhere there was man, doing what he did best. Progress and discrimination in equal measure. The old and young passed invisible amongst the rich and poor. Each pitted face had a story, and each story was alive in front of her. Singsong street merchants pitched everything to do with the sea and terrestrial pursuits.

'Almost there. We're going up the Darkwater, past Boxwood and into Greenmarket.'

Elena nodded, sullen. She gave the closing embankments a sandy-eye. Escape was slowing turning in her mind. A mooring was free beside a stinking dock, its smooth stone rubbed bare from the river. Clumps of filth had left their mark in dried lines, showing where the water had risen or fell. Alex paid the dock master for the birth, venturing the sloop in exchange.

'Ready?' he said.

She expected him to scream and rage at her when she did not move. Alex stood, hands by his sides, his face a mask of pity. The new owner of the sloop had turned up with his fellow, and had started to match Alex in his distain. Elena cursed as loud as she dared, and staggered up from her warm spot. She braced a rusted ladder set into the stone, and stood onto the dock proper, her legs shook with the effort. The merchant and his fellow both cast a grimy look at them as they set off down Darkwater and out to open water. Elena would have sunk to her knees from fatigue if it wasn't for the hate that rolled in her gut.

'Come on. We're both tired and hungry.'

He led her to a tavern that was once a goods house. She saw it was the only clean example of hospitality on the dockside stretch. Everywhere looked as though it was reaching the end of its natural life. Elena hoped she had set her eyes to the worst and brooding look she could summon as they walked in. The smell of food was rich and inviting. That sour punch of ale seemed to lift from the floorboards and starched drapes trapped in time. The only motion was that of a rowdy set of musicians and the staff, preoccupied with service.

'Stay there. Don't move or touch anything.'

She almost hissed like a cat at him; wishing one of her legs would lash out as he walked past. One oil painting in the tavern stood out from the rest. Two candelabras lit a dark tower surrounded by bright copper rooftops. At its base was a group of one woman and two men, scarred in spots on their faces. Both men wore finery of the past; the woman wore a blood-red dress, laced with gold. An enormous ruby highlighted her cleavage. She looked out of the picture with a sneer. Alex conversed with the owner. He was gesturing at his arm, showing off his tattoo of a tower. The same tower that's in the painting. Elena looked around, waiting for nothing to arrive. She pulled open the door and walked outside, leaving Alex to argue. She was alone. London was alien to her as the Storm Coast, the two interchangeable. Her stomach complained. She rubbed it to calm the pangs. Now was a perfect chance to run. With what reserves of energy left in her legs Elena sprinted down the dockside, through a collapsed building that had sank back into the earth, across a rickety bridge that spanned sewage and finally into a marketplace, which was a maze of carts and stalls. People bumped into her; they shoved and poked her into crowds enjoying the rare weather. Her hood was up as Elena scanned faces behind her. Nobody had followed. Alex was either as lost as she was, or he had not bothered to check she had left him. She relaxed a modicum. There was an alcove, a small oasis in the throng of people. She sat down beside a heavy grey statue, the plaque long since worn, her mind swimming from hunger. Around the market she found a coin there, a coin here. To look for them was easy enough if she avoided feet; a shine or sparkle in the dirt gave them away. Several coins more she guessed to have enough to eat from a stall. She haggled for quarter of a meat pie with foul beer to wash it down. After eating, curiosity forced Elena back onto her feet. She walked within earshot of a single man was spreading news to any who would listen. He spoke of the evils of the French monarchy, how a civil schism was overdue. She waited until his congregation had finished listening to his anecdote. They had left him to recount his thoughts from a battered journal.

'Excuse me, sir?'

'Hm? Yes? How can I help one of such beauty?' the man doffed his hat, slicked his pencil thin moustache with one slim finger. The fingers reminded her of dry twigs, and the moustache of hairy caterpillars.

'You've arrived on a ship from France sir?'

'You're in luck, it's still here.'

'May you tell me where? It's important to me you see.'

'A trifle, there, you can plain see it, the one with the tall masts. The bright yellow canvas. She's called the Cambion.'

'My thanks.'

'Well, pretty girls like yourself should not be all alone in this city,' he licked his lips. 'In fact, pretty girls can be quite safe with me.'

'Thank you, but I must leave.'

He rushed at her, to make a snatch for her arm, but Elena whipped away quicker; her legs jumping through clearings in the ever-busier market. It wound down and through London; stalls and vendors never ending. Greenmarket proper. There was a brief sliver of the Darkwater before Elena skittered around a corner. She caught her breath as the names of each ship came to her: *Merry, Warrior, St. George.* Ahead loomed one with tall masts, sails as bright as mustard: *Cambion.* Up and down the dockside Elena looked, no sign of Alex hunting her, no sign of anyone running or seeking. Surly seamen gave her curious looks, commenting on her clothes. I need to act. How would it be best to stow on-board? Which one would head back home? A gust shook her hood; a chill fell onto the wind, raising her hairs on her back. There was a pall over the dockside. Workers paused as they worked, silencing their conversations. Sailors pointed at the crumpled air, muttering and shaking their heads. It was rain, of no doubt, but it carried a warning. The first shakes of raindrops burned themselves on her cheeks. A flash of yellow stained the world; the rain grew colder still, forming into hail and sleet. Elena watched as the city fled from the downpour with disbelief on the faces of many. It was unnatural. Lightning slashed at wounded clouds; the sun retreated with every spark. As hail

skidded across stone and wood, Elena saw the swarm. A witch-

flight that sped across the London skies. Her heart jumped,

squeezing hard in her chest. She was there at the centre of it all,

leading the clan, her mother. It was a sour dream; a nightmare

unravelled. Sarah swallowed and bowed her head, hiding herself

beneath her cloak. She saw Alex across the way, shielding the

worst of the storm with one arm hooked over his soaked head.

She locked eyes with him. They were glassed with regret. She ran

towards him, her arms hugging his chest. She could feel a huff of

surprise followed with a sigh. One rough palm smoothed her

head, tickling the hair behind her ears. Her ennui melted with

each stroke. She looked up at him.

'Alex, thought I was nothing to you.'

'That's not true, you know that.'

'Then why have you lied? Why deceive me?'

'How could I court you, a daughter of a witch and a

Lady? I'm just a thief—a pick-pocket at best. People like me, we

can never be anything more. Unlike you.'

'You are *something* to me,' Elena said.

She didn't want her words to wound or hurt; she wanted the truth. She wanted him as a whole, not divided by greed or pride, or ostracised by the world, hesitant by whatever feelings were inside him. He grunted *sorry*, as close to a form of apology she was likely to get. Elena could feel herself smile and shook her head.

'Come–this storm is not natural; you've noticed the witch–flight too I see.'

Elena nodded, taking his arm. She looked down at it, strings spun and danced along his skin, forming a lattice. They sparked wherever she held on tight. She led Alex on until he saw what she had: an old clock tower, standing tall above the dock. The air inside it shivered with energy. Timbers had suffered time, stone that was set long before she was born. Elena imagined mechanisms, a constant *tick tock* inside, but there was none. It was a cessation from the hail, a dry roof above their heads. They took in the empty black–and–white house around them. Abandoned long ago, with its single bedroom and meagre

pantry. The rest was a workshop, fitted with iron tools and rank
grease. In a draw of an oak worktop she disturbed a tinderbox
which helped illuminate the room around. Their sodden capes
were cast to one corner, boots stuck to dry in front of a tiny
fireplace. The storm drew too much attention to ignore. It rose in
crescendos of violence, rattled the sashes and pawed at the glass.
Elena sat waiting.

'Scared?' Alex asked.

'I am.'

Strings that formed around him now were cloying. Too
many here, too little there; they danced over him, passing through
him with ease. She had never seen so many, never seen so many of
her secret around a man. She had never spoken of it. How could
she? Anyone would think her mad; sprouting nonsense of strings
connecting everything. My father would not understand my
affinity, nor Lady Stone. To explain it to one who cannot see is
difficult. Strings that are transparent when viewed, and disappear
in a prismatic blink. They defy description. She focused on Alex,
her eyes falling back onto themselves in round submission. A

large cluster of strings tugged around his side, just below his

chest. She raised an arm, feeling, searching. It was akin to

touching dry paper, or brittle kelp. Insubstantial, delicate. Strong

when pulled, weak when torn. She imagined a blessing of fire, of

warmth and love. A nook or nest, filled with desire and dreams, a

sanctum of wishes. The weave bloomed with her touch. It

surprised her to how much effort it took, as if she were on a

precipice with danger of falling, the fall below unwelcoming in its

vastness. To run on and plunge forward would be her goal.

Pricks of pain tingled behind her skin and eyes as she kept

kindling the spell, kept willing it to fruition.

'You have that same look as your sister. What are you

doing?'

There was no need to talk. The spell was cast with a twist

of her wrist. An arrow loosed beyond her control and

responsibility. The room grew warmer; flecks of gold dusted the

scrappy air from nothing. The fireplace burned softer. It

shed more light than heat, until all the dirt was gone.

It cleaned the floorboards to the ceiling, cheered in a fresh indifference. The old place spoke to Elena of thanks, but she smiled and shook her head. No need for thanks. As the spell grew larger her skin tingled, sending waves of succour forth, each cleaning what had remained, straightening crooked iron, fixing dented wood. As the fugue around them cleared, she sighed in a climax of energy. It lifted her, lifted her soul up, but not enough to separate from the body. Slow, slow, her spirit sank back down into her, her magic opened as petals of a flower, exposed to all.

'My first,' Elena gasped.

'Your what? What happened? Everything looks new.'

'I don't know.'

'It's warmer.'

'Do you think we're safe? Will you let them take me?'

Elena expected a hesitation, a thought before answering, but Alex didn't.

'No, I won't. You are important to me. You know this,' he said again.

She stood up from the floor, a neat patch of silver dust left in a neat circle where the spell had missed. A kiss was simple compared to a spell; a kiss was a giddy prospect. Her lips fumbled

on his stubble. She backed off, looking at him. They kissed again,

wanting each other. He brushed her shoulder, raked his fingers

down the small of her neck. His grasp became firmer as they

explored. They were warmer than the room around them, his

skin smoother than she had thought it would be. The small

make—shift bunk looked inviting as desire filled her. They both

sank into it, stripping themselves of garments, easing themselves

under the cloth. Heckles sang along her pale skin as she cupped

him fierce in an embrace. They were both wet and wrung, both

needing company after long travel, both wanting an end to the

tension.

Evening crept in. As they listened to the cries and shouts

of the witches above them, Elena waited, nestled close to him. She felt the heat, the fleeting excitement that she had lost her

innocence. *No longer a girl in waiting.* He was asleep when she

crept close, tired lines sketched his face, drawing her to touch

them. She traced a map across little nicks and scars from whatever

black history his past had been. They both had a glow about them,

synchronous in joy; both young, both with hope still left in their

hearts. Little had the storm relented when Elena tried the door

outside. It still poured down, her candlelight denting nothing of

the night. With a push the old door clumped shut. The pantry

had rot. She separated some edible cheese and bread from the ripe

meat that stank out the small space. Elena considered

whether she could transform the inedible edible, but she was

content.

'Hey, eat,' she said, nudging him.

Alex woke, his eyes fluttered open, and a coy smile rolled

itself out for her. She smiled back, fighting the urge to wrench

him off his pillow. He groaned and complained but ate. *It is a*

small pleasure, she thought, *to watch another enjoy something simple as eating.* She felt a belonging rise in her chest, it bubbled up to her cheeks which pitched in union.

'Well,' Elena spoke, choosing bread over the hard cheddar, 'are we waiting till morning? Or are we here forever?'

'Waiting for what?'

'Escape of course. What else?'

Alex gave her a plain look. 'We can't.'

'We can, just straight through that door– '

'No, they'll be ready, sure as day. The moment we walked through they have us.'

'In a city as large as this? Then what about now? In the dark?'

'If you want to take the risk, I'll be right beside you. But I suggest that we wait. The witches out there cannot keep that storm going forever. As soon as it goes, so do we, straight the nearest ship. Besides, nobody will sail in this.'

He was right. He didn't have to quash her mood, but he raised a point. Elena pursed her lips. She sauntered back to the single window where a sliver of dawn was heaving back the night.

'Do you suppose they'll be merciful?'

'Who?' said Alex, dressing for the new day.

'My parents. They would understand?'

'Are they kind?'

'They're... More so than Sarah Saville. But Sophia, she has a cruel streak. A bitter mood that rises up every now and then.'

'Your father? Not the real one.'

'He's kinder in his way.'

'Then appeal to him. Seek your blessing from your father, and Sophia will have to follow suit.'

She nodded resolute. She knew the course of action to take. A second opinion with his voice seemed to solidify the plan all the more so. It gave it weight she couldn't summon on thoughts alone. By a moored barge that had survived the night, a figure was pointing at her in the gloom. Its miserable form matched by another, and another, until a gang stalked towards them. Elena squealed. Her breath caught between her teeth.

'What is it? What's wrong?' Alex surmised her expression and bent low, ready, 'how many? Are you sure they spotted you?' She nodded, frightened. Her limbs shook, her eyes grasping at anything familiar.

'Come, we have to go.' They dressed and he led her up and along a wooden box staircase that twisted into the clockworks proper. Holes and disrepair. She sensed finality in the air as they ascended, further upwards to a creaking trapdoor. They heard a crash below as the front door shuddered on its hinges.

'Alex, please don't let them take me.'

Alex growled. The rest of the tower was detritus, the attic dominated by a tang of cold metal which hit the back of the tongue. He went first up a ladder to the roof, lifting her up after. The summit was spectacular, causing them to wheel around for danger hidden in the fog. London crooned. It woke once more as the storm passed. Dock workers headed to their stations, sailors and strumpets parted, bakers pitched morning wares. Fresh downpour stopped any sense of a bright day; thick rain came down as sludge. The air curdled to a bone-yellow that stole

Elena's courage. The witches came not from the sky at first, but from the hatch that emptied out onto roof. At first, only two came out, arrows notched ready on grim bows, scowls set under wet hoods. She could feel Lady Saville through the clocktower as queer as the sense of someone watching her from behind. The Lady herself emerged; she stamped her boots on the old flagstones, her face enraged. Alex moved forward, his pistol out, ready to defend. Elena took his arm, and lowered it.

'Don't take me back—set me free. Let the past end, it cannot pain you further,' Elena appealed.

'You cannot be free to whore yourself to whoever you please, you are my daughter. Under my care and my responsibility,' she spat. 'Do not go back to Turner either. He is mine to destroy, and anyone who interferers—such as this man,' her finger stabbed at Alex.

Elena saw the bows taut and ready, her mother's hand ready to command. Her legs buckled as they twisted in front of the arrow's path. There was no thought to the pain, no feeling as the arrowhead snaked into her thigh. She gasped as another hit Alex across his shoulder. He stumbled back, winded.

'No! Please–' Elena saw the world fade around Alex, his wound slick. She summoned a tumult of breath, ragged and rasping, searching for any more strings she could pull on. Her eyes glossed as her head lolled back. A bolt of light flashed from the heavens. It pierced the miasma the witches were now struggling to control. She felt it, it was so far, so distant, but she grabbed at it, scrabbled her will towards it, hope filling her. Light filled around them, a corona stretching wide. Before the witches could arrest her, before her mother could bark orders, the sky split. It became a crimson kaleidoscope that broke everything in two. It pulled at cloth, sliced skin, blurred vision. It popped sharp shadows and vented violence. Elena willed it to be, it was her want: *more, more, send them to Hell*. It obeyed, delighted. An orb of fire cleaved witches that had arrived by flight, the sticks and rods they rode on, turned to cinders. Those with bows bent in half as they clutched their eyes in pain. Her mother tried to move towards her, she attempted to take her, arms outstretched.

No, no, you died the day you lost me Mother.

Sarah Saville's hands trembled and then froze. She brought them to her face to cast away stress, her eyes set in the distance. Elena had never seen a change of mood so mercurial. Rage boiled in Sarah, replaced by quick thought. A memory danced between her eyes, where it ran down her to cheeks and twitched. A lance of sun rippled in front of the Cwen; her face compounded in puzzlement as she started to melt. Her clothes became ash; her skin bubbled and sizzled in great blisters. She didn't scream or cry, but sank to her knees, her hair the last to ignite. Serenity gathered in her eyes. After an age she became still. Her legs ceased to kick; her hands had stopped twitching. Elena freaked on the horror of the corpse in front of her, at the havoc about them. But her spell did not stop; it drank more energy, the air growing thick with a heatwave hotter than any that had preceded it. Elena covered herself over Alex, part shield and comfort.

As the temperature grew so did the chaos below in the streets of London. Bells rang, and voices became hoarse as fire broke on rooftops. Sails of ships had caught alight, and dry stores

engulfed. Under her cloak the inferno dimmed. Elena gathered

her thoughts. The echo of pain she now felt was like a chasm that

had opened in her, one that still craved. She turned her neck.

There was a charred skeleton glassed to the stone; the skeleton of

a Witch Queen. It was still, the bones blushed jet, hands held in

atonement. Tears fell as she let the shock overwhelm her. As she

drew in the hot air, her head nuzzled his chest.

    Alex stirred, cradled her with one arm, and confessed his

love for her.

Temperance

– London, Post–Calamity –

Her voyage had ended. Hazel arrived at a London in panic. Its

stoic enthusiasm stolen by some cataclysm; its atmosphere

pacified. Their galleon slinked its way up Greenmarket dock.

Theirs was a ghost–ship that moved in reverence amongst

skeleton boats and sullen men. After docking Hazel followed

Cyrus into town. They listened to the district crier to the point

where he ventured into fantasy. She asked him to repeat

himself. Even as he explained again that the sun had torched

a circle into Greenmarket and beyond (an act of God Almighty), even as she saw the burnt wreckage that marked the area where the sun itself had razed the earth, her mind refused it. That was not the magic of the witches; it was not any magic at all she had read of. The scale was in the realm of the impossible. As Cyrus and Charlotte followed their pragmatism, Hazel followed her instinct towards the esoteric. She allowed herself to fall deep into the strings.

To weave a ritual that would need concentration and peace. She sat in amongst the livestock of the galleon; to suffer nature was not to. It was the way of things to her. An animal's soul was life expressed at its most modest; Man was the only creature who believed the world is wrong. The sheep she was amongst were docile, the chickens clucked until she fed them. They each drifted into a sated slumber. Every so often a beady avian eye would pop open to observe the circle she had made from candles. A glass of water sat in the middle, the medium between here and the next world.

The men on board, she had suggested to the night before, should avoid the area with utmost severity. She added they might be transformed into swine or worse still. That did the trick. The bilge was hers for as long as she needed. She waited until midnight, when the strings were malleable enough to glide through the ship's hull and gather into bundles. The thickest she stuffed into iridescent balls that dotted the circle. With a moon above her fat with light, she cast the spell. There were no fireworks, no immediate sorcery other than a glimpse of where Elena had gone. She had fled, across and south, following the coast down. The trail finished; its magic hollowed out, leaving nothing but more questions.

The following morning gave Hazel a chance to walk through Greenmarket with Gold. Cyrus had uncovered clues, and some grisly details; but nothing that she had already deduced. Rumours held that the infamous witches of the Storm Coast had flown again over London. A short while since they had attacked. The sun had burned them from the sky turning them into ash. Hazel wondered if they had all perished in this cataclysm.

'Why did Alex and Elena go south? Why?' asked Hazel.

'Hmm. Somewhere hot and sunny for the lovebirds. Somewhere distant and unlawful, away from prying eyes. Eyes like yours,' said Gold.

Hazel stomped her feet and huffed, the puzzle was left unresolved. They swept along shops that still remained open. Gold became enthralled by a necklace of opals and blue glass. The jeweller summed Hazel's mood, and unfolded his arms in an open gesture.

'Fake you know,' said Hazel.

Gold gave her a disheartened look. She paid the craftsman for the necklace and shook it in her hand, where it jingled for attention.

'Now, here's a lesson for you,' said Gold, placing the necklace over Hazel's head. 'What's fake to you, is real to me. The difference is attitude, and what a difference that makes in life.'

Hazel stuck out her tongue. She closed her eyes after, and smiled somewhat, lost in a daydream.

'You did lie with him then,' Gold said.

'What?'

'Alex. I can tell. That morning there was a sparkle in those buttons of yours. How was he? Rusty I'd imagine. Ah! I was right–blood has rushed to your face.' Gold laughed.

Hazel felt her cheeks heat. That she had even attempted to sleep with that man embarrassed her. But, that night, under the stars with him would remain ever personal for her. Locked away, it was a good memory that satiated an itch when she required it. All she had to do was close her eyes and drift a little. The stars shone from that night as those opals on her necklace did now: a tulip's pink, a navy–opaque, a titanium white. She touched Gold on her shoulder, face taut.

'Would your father sail south? Would he chase after them? Escape London? Isolde will still hunt me you know.'

'She will. But John wont sail with the hostilities. You know that. Besides I wouldn't let him.'

'Would you do it?' Hazel asked.

'Would I? Yes, maybe, for a price. The bill would be big. Lots of mouths to feed, lots to buy: sundries, gunpowder, good men, and the most important, trust.'

'Is it possible, with that galleon? Even without your father as captain?'

Gold paused with one of her silences. Pros and cons jumbled up and down inside; her hands shook as if she divided invisible totals.

'Yes–but it's money you or I haven't got.'

'But, the only remaining heiress to the Saville estate perhaps does,' Hazel tapped her chest ever so lightly.

Appreciation dawned between them. Gold spread the largest smile Hazel had ever seen her make in her life.

'When do we set sail my Lady?' Gold curtseyed, spreading her arms out wide.

'When we are ready to find Elena and Alex, and the truth of why London was set ablaze.'

The Lovers

– Deep South –

On the day of her mother's death, Elena Saville fled London

with Alex, a thief, just as foretold by the songs Sarah Saville had

heard from her mother, and just as foretold by the songs Eleanor

Saville had heard from hers, and so on.

Odd tidings as magpies swooped in front of them. One,

two, three, four, five, six, *seven*. They raced through the streets,

burnt, singed, rank with smoke. Elena felt relief; Alex felt

emboldened. She grasped his hand, and squeezed three times. He

squeezed hers three times in return. They looked into each other's eyes again. It was a covenant made there and then without the use of speech. *We are together.*

They boarded a ship bound south. Deep South; further than either was comfortable with. The distance matched the passion in their hearts, the quickening of their blood: lust, meaning, adventure, the unknown, and otherwise; both within themselves, and without.

Alex paid for passage in toil, and Elena in the galley. Every night he would whisper secrets to her in one ear, and truth in the other. He would sometimes be sad, sometimes happy. As the sun swelled in heat, the lovers would share in delights aboard the ship, dancing, singing, and making merry for all the crew, much to their joy, if not for seeing a couple in throes of love, but as a distraction from the monotony.

The ship kept going. It kept sailing. The sun unrelenting in increase. Hotter, hotter still. Elena was worried. Her once pale skin tanned over, her red hair, free and soft, became lank and straight. She felt a beat louder and stronger than any she had heard of before. It grew, quick and intense, a calamity of noise, a constant reverberation each and every mile they journeyed. Elena lay in her bunk, her hands covered over her ears. Alex shook her to force a response, and yet she couldn't hear him over the noise, the booming of the drums that roiled her heart, and quaked her soul.

One day, it stopped. Elena rose from a dreamless sleep, and grabbed Alex from his slumber. She shoved him out of their bunk and onto the top deck, half-naked and waiting.

Before them was a blazing sun, a halo of glory above the sinful earth. Its gaze destroying shadow, and burning heresy without compassion. As this baleful god broke above the waves, and the mirage of land bubbled ever higher in the horizon, a golden city grew before them; it spread its wings, vast and uncaring.

It spoke to Elena only. *Welcome to Providence. You will find your destiny in me.*

☆

The House Series will continue in the next instalment

The House of Gold

♀

Acknowledgements

Massive thank you to all those at the Amazon KDP team for making this book a reality. Thank you to my friends, family, and work colleagues for their patience and seeing the potential in my early work. It sounds silly to say that everything helped, but everything really did. Every comment and every criticism, especially in those early days where I was naïve enough to believe that three drafts were enough to finish a fiction novel for publication. Encouragement to keep writing because people see potential, is the best motivation a writer can hear.

Thank you to my secret early readers and editors (you know who you are), and people who maintained a never-ending interest in seeing this novel published, again, thank you.

And an enormous thank you to Illustrators Djinn Black, and Mirella Santana, who created the map of alternate London, and the cover respectively. I feel blessed that such talent has helped bring the world of The First House to life.

Now, to write the next one. Ad infinitum.

About the Author

Robert Allwood studied art & design at the Isle of Man College, followed by a degree in Illustration at the University College of Falmouth. Robert switched to fiction writing after several years in both private & public job sectors, eventually agreeing that it suited him best.

The original ideas for this novel were conceptualised in his twenties, when his interest in writing short stories and characters was more diversion than work. In writing several short pieces that interlinked with each other, he was excited by the concept of mixing mythology and astrology with them: the result, The First House was born.

Robert currently lives in Peel, a seaside town on the Isle of Man, surrounded by maps, books, & notes.

He can be reached at: robertallwood87@hotmail.com

46187544R00254

Printed in Poland
by Amazon Fulfillment
Poland Sp. z o.o., Wrocław